THE SECRET DOCTRINE OF V. H. RAND

DAVID BRIZER

Fomite
Burlington, VT

ISBN-13: 978-1-959984-36-8
Library of Congress Control Number: 2023947926

Fomite
58 Peru Street
Burlington, VT 05401
www.fomitepress.com
01-05-2024

*For Franz Bardon; for my parents,
Manny and Stella, who came back
to life for me during the writing of
this book; and for Marc and Donna.*

CONTENTS

Editor's note: For ease of reading, Rand's journal entries have been formatted as discrete episodes — as one might sort chapters in a book. Newspaper clippings found among the Master's effects have also been included.

How does it come about that magic cannot resist the Inquisition?
"Because [the monks] have a greater number of devils at their disposal than we have."

—Casanova, *Memoirs*

I see history as an unfolding farce of self-aggrandizement, occasionally interrupted by acts of kindness and good works.

—Father Freddie Figueroa, interviewed at
rest stop on Pulaski Skyway (undated)

Victor Hippolyte Rand mounted the Catherine wheel of life — and found himself wanting.

—Victor Rand, journal entry

Le Figaro...[16 MARS 1939]:

Victor Hippolyte Rand, purveyor of stage magic, legerdemain, and the latest Vanishing Lady act, treated Paris today to a gory spectacle crowned by the mass hysteria of a frenzied crowd.

This was Rand's first public act of magic.

The resemblance of the opponents (phoenix, dragon) to statuary was remarkable. The bird's beak, a hook-like promontory extending a full two meters beyond the body, snapped at the air. The creature seemed to *savor the moment*. Its opponent casually lumbered up beside it, unclenching its reptilian jaws, threatening — at first only threatening — a scalding breath of flame.

The griffin (part lion, part eagle; all quadruped) beat a wing, acknowledging the presence of the other. For the moment it did little else. The dragon uncoiled a serpentine neck (actually, there were three), pulled back, snapped at the bird, who, enraged by the temerity of the attack, fanned its wings in protest, toppling the dragon...who lay for the moment akimbo, belly up, exposed. The griffin dived, making for the lizard's soft parts. The griffin lunged and pecked.

A brown torrent of reptilian liver oozed forth.

Sir Dragon was incensed.

Gendarmes cordoned off the church. Only firemen

and ambulances could get through the barricades. Women and children were quickly led away. The authorities did what they could to contain the scene. The dragon showed his true colors (ambergris green, toad brown) breathing fire, the nostrils twin Hellesponts of flame.

An apocalyptic roar filled the district, outdistancing the sirens of *pompiers* and police. Rising on the currents, the dragon suddenly ensnared the eagle in the coils of its second neck. Wings slammed up and down, fluttering in insane counterpoint to this primeval *pas de deux.*

Payback time! The mighty dragon hurled its winged prey against the stones of Sulpice; in the process, several were dislodged. Without pause, the phoenix regrouped, hurling itself, a veritable missile from Hell, straight at the dragon's flank. Said body part instantly whipped back, avoiding another painful jab.

The dragon reared on its massive hindlegs, bracing for another assault. Wisps of smoke then actual flame arced through the sky — slightly toasting the bird, but not bringing it down. A calculated wing beat (dragon's, not bird's) grazed the errant griffin, tumbling it ever closer to its destiny, its enemy, still waiting for it there in the public square. A sudden clawing action raked down the griffin's flesh, three rivers of bright orange *ichor* flowing forth.

Maddened, the griffin flew to the height of the tallest building. Taking the measure of its opponent, it brooked no further delay and dived, catching the dragon completely unawares. The griffin's beak sank to the hilt, deep in the dragon's eye. The dragon, now stunned, swiped like a dazed gladiator at the empty air.

Another precious moment forfeited to the game. The griffin, who seemed to beat a hasty retreat, in fact did the opposite. It idled for a moment, then swooped, once again catching the larger creature completely off guard. The yellow beak, plunged down in full throttle, transfixing the dragon where it really hurts — its bursting liver. The dragon screamed in protest, its mammoth bulk finally collapsing upon the spindly forelegs beneath.

Raw Youth.

Father's *boucherie* sits in the lap of luxury, in the 16ième Arrondissement of Paris, a stone's throw from St. Sulpice and the Jardin du Luxembourg. The 16th, with its shops and restaurants — and *Pere Rand & Fils* — is a truly historic district. A *bijou* in the tiara of the City of Lights.

The hacking, sawing, grinding...they are constant, a merciless assault upon the ears. Six days a week my father cracks and chops, packs and wheedles, making a name for himself and his family. When I am of age, he hopes I will 'join on.' Try as I might, I really don't understand...why my father Romain Rand works so hard, his life ground down, chopped meat I suppose, in the service of family and some exaggerated if not oneiric sense of duty.

'Père' Rand — Romain Rand, my father — must be an artist at heart. Heart of Romain: not heart of lettuce. His strivings, Parnassian and otherwise, express themselves in eccentric and, I might add, flagrant, ways.

Père Rand — that's my father — knows everyone. Everyone, that is, who matters. Porters, superintendents, and handymen, good friends all, who catch him up on every death, desertion and abandoned apartment in that celebrated quarter.

Father's chief joy is victimless plunder. Romain 'liberates' gewgaws, knick-knacks and *objets d'art.* The leather bound first editions and gilt-framed portraits line up at the butcher shop, taking their proud place alongside cornichons, *choucroute*, and jars of beastie body parts.

A different man in a different time would have handled his artistic leanings more discretely. But Romain's eccentricities cannot flower at home. Mother objects — hideously, forcefully, to the utmost extent of her spleen — to the books and prints and paintings he would storehouse *chez nous*.

Chalk it off to *choler*, to fury, to domestic excess: she will dump his stuff often, and without warning, and irrevocably.

Mostly she is otherwise engaged. I am, you see, the only boy in a platoon of girls. Somewhere between Amalie, Emily, Victorine, Daphne, Isabelle, Camille, Celine, Marie, Oceane, Brigitte, Madeline, Delphine, and Odette, I arrive.

Such is family life. *Chacun à son gout...*

I love Romain. I fear him. I hope to follow in his footsteps: not with racks of lamb and veal chops, but with the life of the mind!

Father: surly, dismissive, judgmental — yes. Rapacious in his way. His frustrated inner artist, exhumed, is a rotting carcass that offends.

Home economics is even more problematic: thirteen girls do not a healthy dowry make! Father is forever pulling strings, wheedling, crafting deals to make our frayed ends meet.

Sometimes he will cut me to the quick. A casual remark, a comment upsetting the apple cart of my otherwise fine day.

So I get to him the only way I know how — through books. His books. I pore through the purloined collections with the morbid fascination of an archaeologist: the heartfelt avidity of an archaeologist whose heart is a child's; whose survival depends on the museum-readiness of the treasures he finds.

I find a great deal. My efforts are amply (or modestly, or on 'off' days poorly) rewarded. Books, books, books... Books that I paw, dog-ear, devour, with the frenetic curiosity of untamed innocent youth.

Grab a chair, then it's up and over, Romain's closet kingdom of books mine for the taking. What I find there: novels; histories of the Great War; dime-store *feuilletons* with lurid titles and illustrations (these are my favorite)...and deadly serious departures from common sense.

These 'departures' are broadsides, tracts, expositions...lunatic theoretical discourses, even, on the paranormal. Father, given to superstitious lamentations at home and abroad, is obsessed with finitude, limitation, death.

Consider, for example, Romain's book *You Don't Have to Die.* This volume immediately catches my eye. An exposé of the crack-brained practices condoned by the medical profession — which immediately sets my pulse racing. And inspires me with my first real intimation of mortality — a terrible foreboding I can never quite shake. Or, *The Laity and the Illuminati:* a treatise on the 'mystical Kabbalah, documenting the lives and times of the rabbinical champions of that intellectual franchise' – another of my father's very obscure titles...

Romain has dozens like these. Knowing my father, studying him, is serious business: not to complain, but trust me, it is serious work, requiring for starters a deep knowledge of philosophy: Rosicrucianism, Theosophy, Free Love, even Satanism itself.

A tough row to hoe. But I am determined. I will hoe. I will know the man, I will move heaven and earth, no matter what it takes.

My father, Romain, is sometimes vacant, barren as a standing stone — a pebble in the quarry of deep feeling. Romain tramples down my fascinations with glib disdain. Nothing I serve up — neither Victor Hugo, nor the legend of Charlemagne, nor the abstractions of Zeno — seems to impress. Nothing seems to suit. He is niggardly with the praise. Is he aware of this? Is his disinterest casual, perhaps the consequence of ignorance or benign neglect? I could tolerate that. But the possibility of malfeasance — actual enmity, lived, breathed, and acted out by the man, is another thing all together. Father considers my inquisitiveness *symptomatic*; he wants a practical son. He wants me clinging to him, if only by a tendon, like some rendered retail joint.

He wants me by his side in that damned *boucherie*.

School and lessons permitting, I put my time in. I watch Papa Rand upending sides of beef; 50 kg. boxes of chicken; spinning out yards of sausage, ground and seasoned and stuffed right there before my eyes, before the eyes of the world.

The books are one thing: the meat is quite another! The meat quivers, red, bloody: for all intents and purposes, still very much alive. Rand's cuts are premium, elegant, *marbled*. Over the years Father has acquired a fawning — let's be honest, servile — clientele. They depend on him, breathlessly awaiting his specials, sales, and choice cuts. They will go nowhere else.

I aim for a kind of quasi-scientific fatuity. *The thigh bone connects to the knee bone...*(something like that). I watch him working, heaving, wiping his brow...knowing I will never follow in his footsteps. But my curiosity, enough for a lifetime's worth, is very real.

I want to know how living things — chickens, pigs, people — how life itself — works.

One day an opportunity presents itself. A chum of mine, Guillaume he is called, has been traipsing after me. At *collège,* on the street, on the way home. Guillaume is meager, *mince,* a puppy dog of a fellow, afflicted with punishingly thick glasses and a weird febrile glow.

I welcome the attention.

My ears prick up as he talks about his dad.

His father is a doctor, a doctor who makes house calls.

That's all I need to know.

House Calls.

Guillaume leans into the wind (the boy is featherweight; my first thought is to somehow anchor him to the ground) as he describes his dad's appointed rounds.

Doctor Dupin — Guillaume's dad — ministers to the sick. You know the type: a hero of the quotidian, a prince of expertise and poise. (I gather as much before ever meeting the man.) On occasion Dr. Dupin will gather him up and take him along.

Afternoons when it rains, Guillaume is often parked at a desk in his father's clinic. I am drawn to this sickly companion of my youth — especially to his morbid stories. Some I assume are exaggerated; some are not.

I am interested in the latter.

I ask if I can come with.

We skip stones by a brook, walk, share a smoke. The afternoon sun beats down on our unprotected heads. A crow, all wings and violence, flutters once, twice, jarring the peaceful day.

Guillaume flinches. I ask again.

"Can I come?"

"Why not?" he says, picking up his hobbled stride.

—*m*—

In a *boucherie* you can buy legs of lamb, breasts of chicken, other savory viands and fare. You will find pâté, *saucisson*, rillettes and my personal least favorite, pig's ears, at the *charcuterie. Père et fils* is not a charcuterie.

Doctor Dupin works from a different menu, serving up different fare: an unending banquet of the sick and suffering, their complaints ranging from costive stasis, to lumbago, to the dread *phthisis* (still very much afoot in the land.) The occasional birth, the resulting afterbirth, and the fortunately less common still birth make for a dramatic counterpoint to routine. More serious cases Dupin refers on.

Dupin's work means long and frequent absence from the home — his, certainly, and sometimes from mine. Dupin's nostrums, potions and moxibustions (recall: this is the era before penicillin) are still in high demand.

Guillaume soaks up the drama — and I am an eager witness in tow. Under cover of night, Père (Dr.) Dupin terminates pregnancies, lances buboes, sews up wounds. (I believe he has an ongoing arrangement with the local funeral director as well.) I admire Dupin's iron will, his indomitable disposition. I become adept at preparing poultices, setting bones, applying bandages.

Many times the doctor and I go out alone. It occurs to me that Dupin might actually prefer me to his twig of a son.

I audit the bedside consultations with fervor; the late hours inevitably take their toll. One moment I'm handing over calipers, sutures, gloves...the very next, I'm drifting off, literally sleeping on my feet...at the bedside of the afflicted! The acute abdomens, the 'hot' gallbladders, the riotously painful gouts and stones, each a potential portal for infection, possible death...debridement and amputation sometimes the only recourse...extreme but necessary measures that stave off the otherwise implacable footsteps of the priest...Terminal cases, fulminating crises...

Dupin usually sends these on — to the hospital and to *le prêtre* and the undertaker...When all earthly ministrations prove futile, doctor and patient must needs surrender to holy water and last rites.

The doctor is terse — to the point of rudeness. He is driven to extremities — understandably so — as there is no end to the late-night consultations and desperate calls.

Dupin's house calls are a rough and tumble prelude to (what can loosely be considered) my 'greater calling' (more on this to follow.)

This goes on for several months. My sleepless thrall to medical work becomes tinged, then eventually suffuses, with doubt. I tally the hits and misses of Dr. Dupin's 'cures'.

I find his method grievously wanting.

Daylight routine — good God, even school! even homework! — becomes a welcome respite from these morbid sallies at night. *What is all this pain about, anyway? Why must we suffer? Do we have to die?*

'Modern' medicine, an improvement over the grotesque improvisations of mountebanks, charlatans, from centuries past, still does not serve. Sorry: *do we really have to die?*

I mention my misgivings. Dupin listens, welcomes my doubt.

"Look here," he says one night. "Consider the following actual case. Mme. Frangipane has already consulted the brightest and the best. The brightest and the best have passed judgment: I might as well tell you, they consider her daughter incurable. *I suggest that she is not.*"

Guillaume works at his sandwich, studiously avoiding the conversation. He also avoids my gaze.

The doctor continues.

"The so-called 'experts' have treated her nervous symptoms — her neurasthenia — tirelessly. With everything but imagination."

He arches an eyebrow, then winks.

"What did they leave out?"

I am speechless: I am fourteen years old. I have no idea.

"They left out her mind. Her *mind,* young man. Can you imagine that!"

Visions of brains, diced and sliced, left to rot in trash bins in the open air, dance before me.

Dupin suggests a method. He draws me close, sweeping the air before us in great pedantic arcs.

"Here's what we're going to do..."

———

The scene changes.

Later that night, loading up the landau, Dr. Dupin takes me aside.

"Do exactly as rehearsed," he says, applying thick coats of pancake makeup to my cheeks. The makeup and the night air give me an unearthly pallor. Now I look more like Guillaume — Guillaume who has once again called in sick, complaining of migraine and a severe turn of 'the vapors.'

We enter the building, a tenement tucked between the loftier more grandiose stalwarts on Boulevard Raspail. My briefing continues up until the moment Dupin rings the bell.

"Now remember: look off into the distance. Be ethereal, other-worldly. Say her name three times. Then faint."

Strange procedure, granted...but who am I to object?

M. and Mme. Frangipane greet us at the door. They usher us in, the suspicion in their eyes nailing me to the spot. Right away the doctor makes nice.

"Meet my assistant, Victor Hippolyte...Don't be put off by his apparent youth. Looks sometimes deceive you know. He is not wayward. Consider young Victor Hippolyte here an envoy from the spirit realm. A precious envoy, I might add. A most talented envoy. In a word, Victor is your daughter's only chance."

The woman of the house wants to rush off, boil water, soak towels, do something, anything...Dupin stops her in her tracks.

"That won't be necessary, Madame... There are no ablutions for the Other Side."

No one least of all Dupin knows what that means.

We approach the patient. The girl, hollow-eyed, staring, is no older than twenty; but her face is care worn, creased and lined beyond her years.

The mother throws a grievous look at Dupin: *Please, doctor. Reassure us. Will anything help?*

Well, perhaps nothing on earth...how about beyond the stars? Dupin reaches for the girl's limp wrist.

"Just as I thought," he says. "The pulse is threadbare, weak — I fear impending vasomotor collapse."

He makes a practiced pass, mumbles something about *animal magnetism,* and *Saint Germain.*

"Hippolyte, here — touch her forehead."

Wordlessly, I place the palm of my hand on her brow. The girl's forehead is cold. And disagreeably moist. We wait. The girl's eyes flutter. She stirs beneath the covers.

—⁓—

"Please Miss," the doctor says. "The young man is here to contact the spirit realm. Close your eyes at the count of three. Please. That's right... Now breathe deep. Deep breath. To someplace far far away..." His voice modulates to a whisper, then finally trails off.

Dupin calls the shots. The young miss lowers her eyelids, takes a deep breath...holds it and waits. I hover over her, ready to take her in my arms and somersault right off this Plane.

"Abramelin...Xerxes...Imenhotep..." the doctor chants.

Nothing happens. He tries again.

"One...two...three..."

My cue! I hit the floor like a ton of bricks. I gasp and moan. I throw my contorted cantilevered body halfway across the room. The Frangipanes are astonished. Mother runs to daughter and father runs to me. He cradles my head in his capable arms.

I roll my eyes toward the ceiling, then make a good show of finally coming to.

"It works!" Dupin cries. "He has made contact!"

Distracted by the commotion, Mademoiselle Frangipane throws aside the bedclothes and shakes off her cares. She stands before us, practically newborn, in all her newfound miraculously healed glory.

My playacting has accomplished what half a dozen specialists could not.

I brush myself off, helping myself to my feet.

They shower us with compliments.

Dupin collects twice his usual fee.

—*∿*—

A dizzying progression of cases and miracle cures follows. With or without Guillaume, we pick and choose our way through a bumper crop of disease.

One week it is Rue de Varennes, hawking tiny blue phials of 'Lourdes' water among the sick and suffering. St. Germain de Près and streets near St. Sulpice seem to favor dowsing rods: twigs or saplings held above the inert body of the afflicted for intense spellbound moments until the 'crisis' has passed. Dupin promotes his own brand of hypnotism, loosely culled from the anointed diaries of Mesmer, Casanova, Rasputin, and Cagliostro. The patients believe that their deficient *animal magnetism* will be lastingly cured by serial applications of touch (my hand) and Dupin's sidereal exertions.

We will be the very last to disabuse them of these notions.

All is well and good. I come to know the streets of that quarter of Paris like the back of...my hand! My therapeutic touch becomes more confident, ever more bold. Dupin urges me on, assuring me that our ministrations are righteous, ethical, strictly within the limit of the law; according to him, we are doing the work of the Lord. We thread our way through courtyards and alleyways, the doctor explaining (always in guarded terms, *sotto voce*) the theory and practice of *suggestion.*

"An aspect of medicine that has been largely ignored," Dupin explains as we make our way past bums, past bistros, down boulevards.

"Tragically overlooked. The patient usually knows what is wrong, you see. The patient has her own talent for cure. Which as it happens resides wholly within her imagination. But she doesn't know that; so we apply hands, water, magical oaths. And we hope for the best. Suggestion, Victor, is the royal road to health."

One success follows another, Dupin always ready with an explanation

— even when our best efforts fail. He blames the patient, the misalignment of stars, the Congress of Vienna. *Whatever!*

Things might have gone on like this indefinitely. Dupin probably had bigger plans for me. But the best intentions of mice and men — are stand-up comedy material for God! Best intentions are invariably cold-cocked!

Finally the whip — an angry boyfriend, a complicated 'miscarriage', a stool pigeon spilling the beans — comes down. My father, in bloodied shirt sleeves (another killing day at the shop) asks me what is up.

I feign ignorance: but so what? He persists.

Romain glares at me something fierce. He has that glacial look that immediately takes me down, leaving me bereft for days.

"Your mother and I are concerned," he says. "We did not raise you to be the Infant Jesus. Look around the shop, son. See any loaves and fishes? Hippolyte, you are not the Miracle of Lourdes. In point of fact, *you are half Jewish*. Please — stop!"

He is furious. I have disgraced our family. Father's reference to Scripture is never a good sign.

"Do I make myself perfectly clear?"

"Yes sir." (He has.)

Next Romain contacts Dupin. Tells him to cease, desist, lay off: I am strictly off limits.

The meat cleaver has made another broad stroke.

—◦◦◦—

In one fell swoop, Guillaume and his doctor dad are taken from me, gone from my life. Forever. There are hushed conferences, putative negotiations.

During these, my mother Mme. Stella Rand — whom let it be known, stood forever opposed to father's birdbrained plans for me — figures prominently. The baccalaureate is looming. Soon I will graduate — i.e., I will be thrown upon my own paltry resources. Or I will be thrown upon the street. Or worse still, ingloriously indentured to the butcher shop...For several days running, my uncertain future is a matter of debate.

Finally the situation is resolved: they have rescued my future.

My mother, her ample chest heaving (where is the apron and rolling pin, I ask you?) in a jubilee of self-righteousness, announces that I will in fact be continuing my studies. Not from home, mind you, but from the Academy of Sulpice, a Jesuitical haven for advanced studies, for worldly and spiritual success, and for the bac.

A monastery on the outskirts of town, nestled amongst the banlieus...

There is a growing lump. In my throat. Of which I am increasingly aware.

I swallow but it won't go away. I consider the possibilities. *Au fond,* it's my parents' way — or the highway...so I surrender to my fate. Whatever comes next is God's plan, not mine.

I'm not sure I believe in God.

I know what I believe.

I believe in the power of suggestion.

This marks the (first) eclipse of my scientific zeal. I will be sent away, boarded and schooled in the Jesuit tradition.

Hearken.

The bells of St. Sulpice are calling.

The Cloister.

The Jesuits work us hard.

The day begins at 4 a.m.: Matins, Vespers, plus a 'host' [sic] of other liturgical commitments and ordeals. In between are lessons (there are many of these); devotions; and translation (from Latin, to French, then back again.) Many hours spent parsing the lives of saints and Fathers of the Church. Every now and then, bless their costive hearts, the Brothers throw us a bone: mere sprinklings, secular versions of history...grade school mathematics, even more primitive versions of science. The latter imposed, I imagine, as mandated curricula by the state. I put on a good face. I meet these challenges. I have already survived the *boucherie* and the spiritual experiments of Doctor Dupin. These didn't kill me outright. Let's hope they make me stronger.

I endure these indignities with a kind of insouciance, a genteel brand of defiance, gifted to me by nature or nurture or some idiotic conflation of the two.

I experiment — on myself. Physical exhaustion, for example, can be overcome by inner 'work' — i.e., ritual, practiced transcendence of spirit. My young heart takes wing. Wings that beat bravely, heroically, carrying me far beyond animadversion, manumission and adversity.

Hey, I *feel* something. Something is changing, shedding, molting. The acolyte, heretofore living on miserable but equal measures of dashed dreams and bitter doubt, now stands tall... Tall, proud and questing, above the Academy walls. I cement the mosaic of my inner sanctum with the hard shellac of acceptance. Celibacy, rigorous discipline — all in the name of — *what?* Some specious Higher Ground, tenanted by lissome angels bleeding from torn-off wings?

This is clearly a sea change. My letters home outline the contours of my metempsychosis. I describe in flattering terms the largesse of the Brothers, who take (a little bit too much, thank you!) interest in my education and moral growth.

I share a room with two other boys. The Tyrolese lad's linens are untidy, stained, absolutely horrid — unfit for wear. The other fellow, an effeminate Belge (where are all the French?), lords it over us, rewarding our compliance and camaraderie with handouts of tobacco, licorice stick, tiny bottles of bay rum.

Gradually I acquire the habit of 'pretend.' (It is, after all, a matter of survival.) I play the Brothers' game. I pretend: pretend interest, pretend effervescence, pretend acquiescence with every admonition and mortification they can hand us in that cheerless terrible place.

I wear the sea change well. During visits home, I am all deference — deference alloyed with tarnished pride. I ask after friends and relations, listen with ear to the ground for news of Dupin.

No news is good news.

Somehow I am more confident — which seems to show. My parents pick up on this right away; Stella alludes to my 'healthy glow.' Father, tentative at first, asks about weekend work at the shop — mentions how he could use a helping hand. Nothing new there! Mother, bless her heart, kills the suggestion outright.

My words have a new...Catholic...ring. They no longer catch in my throat. What is happening to me? Have I transformed, transmogrified, transubstantiated? Am I a true soldier of Christ? (This seems to be the common perception.)

I know otherwise.

I *am* a soldier. But I march to the beat of a very different drum.

—*∿*—

My mentor, Frater Fréderic Figueroa, is a strange wraith-like figure. Friends back home would consider him a freak.

F.F.F. takes me aside one day, offering to instruct me in the unwritten dogma and ritual of the Church.

His interest in me goes way beyond carnal. He seeks candidates for *true initiation*. He takes me aside and says, 'Call me Max.' Which of course I do.

He offers guided tours of a kinder, more recondite Golgotha.

Figueroa's appearances are brief, phantasmagoric. They are not so much arrivals, or appearances, as *visitations* – he shows up anywhere, anytime, any hour of the day or night. F.F.F. pauses in the refectory, fingers beads in the nave; I see him wandering the sun-starved depths of the catacombs. He seems most comfortable in the ossuary.

His visits coincide with mine. My roommates, who generally avoid reliquaries and catacombs, rarely see him. Figueroa is a specter, a phantom, albeit a quasi-saint who ferries his charges – the chosen, the elite, *me* – from this fallen world, step by step, to the one above.

Figueroa, in threadbare surtout and equally fossilized sandals, carries his head aloft. This anchorite is proud – after all, he presides over otherworldly schools. Sometimes he talks to himself, his portentous utterances ringing hollow on the abbey flags below

But when he is good, he is really good.

I understand: I may be the only heir to his transgressive wisdom. Transgressive, *shmansgressive...* His teachings are profound. I learn – and recoil! – from these with more brio and self-confidence than I ever imagined possible.

Father Figueroa: hurried conversations and hushed confidences, far from the madding monotheistic crowd.

Clandestine confabs in the realm of the miraculous.

Figueroa's knowledge is broad, impressive, universal. It both encompasses and subtends the wisdom of ancient Egypt, Ptolemy, Theophrastus, Pythagoras, Pliny, Hermes, Trismegistus, Solomon, Moses, Dalai lamas, Copernicus, Newton, Galileo, Zanoni, Fludd, Saint-Germain, Anabaptists,

Cagliostro, Blavatski, the lesser known Patriarchs, *and* P.T. Barnum. (This is just the short list.)

I receive the information gratefully, my heart making small leaps of forbidden faith each step of the way.

—*∾*—

My progress as a fledgling adept is slow but sure. Of one thing I am certain. I may be clumsy, awkward even, but I am always poised ahead. I stumble, I fall, my head clatters like a set of broken chimes. I make my way with trepidation, feeling out the walls of my spiritual confinement from cloister to carrel to carnival (see below.)

Something has changed.

I am falling, I am tumbling...and I am rising to ever greater heights.

—*∾*—

One February day — when there is new snow, the shop keepers out on the *trottoirs,* but barely keeping up — I arrive at the *boucherie.* I am armed with certificate, papers, and various letters. I upend the soggy mass of parchment into my father's outstretched hands.

"Father, please take these. Since I won't be needing them."

A smile of deep satisfaction lights up his face. The man positively glows. He wipes gristle from his hand across his bloody smock.

"I see you've finally come to your senses. Welcome to the business!"

Romain Rand takes me around, reaching for an apron, ready to suit me up right then and there. I know the man. He has that *Rand et Fils* gleam in his eye.

Dream on, Papa.

"Father," I say, "I have seen the light. I now know the way."

Uh oh.

In Romain Rand's eyes — Romain Rand the butcher, the burgher, *le propriétaire,* the householder — I am delinquent, defiant, delirious. So what can he make of this, my latest insane proclamation?

My announcement could only mean one thing to Romain: my latest and most inglorious downturn. I understand: he has shown forbearance, he has forsworn every pleasure, earmarked every last centime in order to send me to school.

Discomfiture, frustration, anomie — I see these spreading like a petulant rash across my father's face.

I rise to the occasion.

"Father," I explain. "I mean to practice magic."

Father, contemplating which weapon of persuasion — mallet, red hot tongs, or hack saw — would best suit, winces.

Magic!

This prodigal son was surely no Rand.

Romain leaves the room in a huff.

A moment later I hear them in the pantry: "You tell him! He's your son!"

"Not mine — yours! Not possible..."

The impasse breaks and they both charge out.

"Over my dead body," my father says.

"Magic is no different than medicine," I try to explain, my voice breaking. "Each has its merits. Each complements the other. One must discriminate...compartmentalize...one must pick and choose...wisely."

I cringe at the sound of my voice. I am a glossy magazine ad; I am The Prevaricator, touting the marvels of what may after all not be in the public's best interest: 'Magic' no less!

I bite my lip, my fists clenched bloodless behind my back. I am sorely tempted to tell all, to explain everything. Dr. Dupin's animal magnetism, his cathartic rays, his homespun remedies. A far cry from science, to be sure. But sometimes nothing else will serve. Eye of newt, skin of toad...

"What are they teaching at that *meshuggeh* academy, anyway?"

Pause. Then she answers her own question — with a question.

"Magic?" my mother asks. She is stupefied.

I retrench.

"Well not really *magic*. Nothing quite like that," I say.

"More like — *tricks*," I explain. "I perform tricks, prestidigitations, sleights-of-hand. Town and country — Paris and on the road."

Frater Figueroa would have handled this better. I know that.

But Romain will have his say.

Father stabs at the air with his fingers, a hand puppet *poignard* he would like to sink deep into my chest.

"Romain!" my mother yells.

My father glowers, harrumphs. Actually stamps his feet.

"Fine!" He says. "But know this. I will never attend these...what are they called — *séances?*" The word slides from his lips in a glissando of pure disgust.

"Rest assured Victor, you are a living disappointment to me. Never will I attend such shows."

(1948 — featured article on Maître Rand.)

Papa Rand had other plans for his son.

What began as a series of informal consultations and asides soon mushroomed into a growing concern. Papa Rand was convinced — and he would soon convince Victor — that Victor was a healer.

Life was so fragile, so easily foresworn, in this time of rampant crib death, childbed fevers, and miscellaneous ailments that sent children in droves to the cumulus-besotted ramparts of heaven.

One day, the father caught the son napping. Not actually napping, but slowly turning the pages of a medieval grimoire.

"Ah, up to the usual tricks I see," he said. "Victor, I think we can put your talents to better use."

Victor unhanded the volume, casting a doleful look at his dad. He was surely in for it now.

"We've lost too many of your sisters these past few years," the man continued.

"There is serious work to be done."

The father drew himself up.

"There's always the butcher shop, I suppose. I could use a hand."

Victor thought about it, long and hard — all night, in fact. By the next morning, he was fully resolved. He would do it right: save his sisters, save the world, save *himself.*

Young Victor laid it bare.

"Father, I had a dream. A man in a satin frock called to me. *I am Apollonius of Tyana,* he said. *You are my student. I will teach you to heal.*"

Romain Rand listened to every word. But he played it cool, casual. Feigned disinterest — absentmindedly reached toward the meat rack for a string of *merguez* on a hook..

"Saucissons...we're practically giving them away." The sausage oozed as he stabbed it with the sticker pin.

"Which girl are you most worried about, father?"

"It's the baby, Victor. Your sister Odette is not taking milk. I've half a mind to call Dr. Dupin."

"That won't be necessary, father. I'll consult my dream oracle. *Je m'en occupe*. Trust me: Odette will be fine."

Victor's parents mounted an exuberant sham concern. Hemming and hawing, objecting, accompanying Victor into the child's room, baiting him, besieging him with questions.

"Hush now," he warned, handing them the little girl's bottle.

"I want you to mix up a decoction of rose hips, nettle leaves, and honey vinegar while I minister to the child."

Romain and Stella did just as they were told. Victor made a great fuss of passing his hands over the baby, muttering names and abjuring archangels in a derivative form of Latin known only to him and to select Oxford dons.

"Is that what they teach you at Sulpice?" his father demanded.

Victor lowered his hands — which seemed to have taken on a life of their own.

"Exactly," he said.

"Here, pass me that formula."

Odette drank hungrily, passionately, from him. By week's end, she was in the pink of health.

By week's end, the word was on the street.

Victor Hippolyte Rand was a miracle worker.

Stage Magic.

Le Chat Noir is neither a cat, nor is it black.

It is a seamy nightclub buried deep in the unhallowed district of the city. *Le Chat Noir* is the stomping ground of the drunks and zombies who come out at night, seeking the plaintive warmth of false *bonhomie* and a cheap glass (or five) of wine.

I regret this *Chat*, this tawdry hole-in-the-wall *boîte*...but for the moment I am pleased. All things considered, I have done well. I take pride in this very provisional gig: I found it. I promoted myself. I will be sharing the club's jerry-built 'stage' with an artless succession of losers and fools.

Hey — so what? *From humble beginnings...*

Anäis Nun — an ambiguously gendered *chanteuse* decked out in a tutu — more like a cutaway habit, some crazy person's idea of mortal sin — shows hot legs and obviously contrived cleavage. Anäis opens the show. Her/his/it's song cycle (a tedious off-key rendition of *La Vie En Rose*) leaves the sparse crowd wanting less. Then a legless stuntman, inverted waist down on a unicycle, does circuits of the stage, propelling himself in fits and starts around the room, blowing kisses and accepting drinks from the laughing crowd.

Neither is a particularly tough act to follow.

Then it's my turn.

I am ready for the world: *I am Rollo Rand, Master Magician*. The capitals of Europe will be my platforms, my launch pads, my proving grounds and my intended stage...

Allow me to introduce myself. I am Rollo Rand. Je suis ravi...

What is this? Catcalls?!?

Undeterred, I throw back my scarlet cape. It drapes over me in ersatz satin folds. I adjust the cummerbund and starch-stiff shirtfront, each cinching my respective parts.

Then follows a predictable round of card and memory tricks. The prestidigitation is *pénible;* it does nothing for the crowd, and little else for me.

This crowd is tough. Several among the already drunk and reeling whistle and hoot, express sham pity, followed by more catcalls and outright hostility.

I ignore their taunts but now the fear is upon me — I dread running out of stunts. I pull a limp and lifeless chicken from a soggy lifeless hat. So be it...My sorties at mind-reading are banal, my attempts at clairvoyance insipid: the shill I'd planted earlier stageside breaks down amid gales of [his own] laughter, announcing to one and all — to any who would listen — that his connivance was cheaply bought...He flashes a centime then throws it at the stage.

I draw my cape tight — I'll show this crowd. The orchestra (one man with a bottle, a bugle, and a tambourine) plays a muffled tattoo. I save the best for last. Solange, my assistant — a *salope* if ever I saw one — takes a deep bow, followed by her décolletage. The minuscule crowd cheers her and her breasts on.

Rollo the Great will saw her in half...!

This girl, in the vanguard of several generations of demoralized Alsatian peasantry, was easy to recruit. She was hungry, she was deceitful — and she was unemployed.

Up to my ears in Jesuit-inspired celibacy, I was instantly charmed. At once I swore: Devil take my vows. *This one Satan, right here, right now. I* will love, honor, and obey this trollop — if only she will have me! I am prepared to do anything, be anything, sacrifice anyone! I can remake myself — better yet, I will transfix myself — in the name of love.

For now, I will hold myself back: I will only saw her in half.

She looks straight ahead, hard, polished like a doll. The mascara and triply applied eyeliner ooze under the harsh stage light.

—*◦◦◦*—

I know almost nothing about romance. What little I know I have gleaned from books. Frequent proofs of devotion, most often in the form of gifts, are the keys to a woman's heart. *N'est-ce pas?* To the heart, and hopefully to other anatomic precincts as well! My pockets are far from deep...yet Solange plumbs their depths expertly, every time she has a chance.

Her appetites are whimsical, sudden. They can be tempestuous. She likes passionate avowals, little kisses stolen between acts at Le Chat Noir; she demands champagne... and when the mood is *upon* her, entire jeroboams of *Veuve Cliquot*...And I, stage magician of Place Clichy, am all thumbs! Nothing but thumbs!

—*◦◦◦*—

Can't do anything right — sorry, I have played out my hand. I squander my remaining sous on silk stockings and champagne (for Solange of course) and remain in sore need of distraction. Up to and including stroking until climax. I wander the streets in search of solace. Solange is nowhere to be found. I doubt she knows the unrequited stirrings of an empty belly and a capsized heart like mine.

My spirits and wallet are wearing thin.

—*◦◦◦*—

Catastrophe arrives, this time in the shape of an *en flagrante delicto* sighting. A sighting to beat the band!

With resignation and deep despair, I enter the club. The bouncer, *Pierrot* or some such, looks down his stupid broad nose at me; says he doesn't know me, *Sorry, No exceptions,* some such. Glorious! I move on to the discount cabaret down the street. Or else —

I ignore him and push past.

—*∿*—

Nor do I think to knock. I open the 'stage door' that leads to the closet/dressing room lavatory/erotic abattoir.

Where will it all end? (World War Two, as it turns out.)

I open the backstage door and an obscene *tableau vivant* meets my awestruck gaze: Solange and the Algerian kitchen boy going at it full throttle. Deaf to entreaties, they grovel, lapping at, licking at each other's privates like flayed dogs...groveling, drooling, slurping...where was P.T. Barnum when one needed him?

Solange FINALLY comes up for air. She slides from her lover's embrace, clutching at random stage clothes — a hunter's jerkin, an angel's wings — to shield her still heaving form.

Solange works her dark magic. In the heat of the moment, I too am caught in her spell...She's an expert: suddenly this has become *my* problem.

"Cretin! *Malfaiteur!* Who the devil *are* you?" she cries. "Go back monsieur from where you came!"

Roundly chastised, soundly beaten, I do just that. *Je récule.* Hardly daring to breathe, I slink away.

Somehow I make it to the street.

One question remains: will Solange join me later tonight on stage?

The show must go on.

—*∿*—

Later, much later... Solange sulks and pouts, mouthing haphazard insults, a mess of choice epithets and barbs tossed my way with angry rectitude.

Time for the act. Inimitable Solange rises to the occasion — and damn but she looks good. Her third-hand *Folies Bergère* costume shoots moonbeams, a thousand sequins flashing in the garish light, throwing heart attacks at the guys in the crowd. We seem to be locking horns. She denies me the syrupy confection of her gaze.

So be it: there's still the audience to consider.

Solange, in scanties now, steps into the trick cabinet, a fake-walled box on which is stenciled *Rollo & Solange, Purveyors to the Trade.* Tawdry pink and azure letters, a good meter and a half high. *Purveyors to the Trade*...What are we — wholesale butchers?

I fasten the lid tight, sealing her in. Brandishing my ceremonial scimitar, I steal one last look at the crowd. (Romain, incidentally, has kept his word: he is nowhere to be seen.)

So be it. I am Rollo the Great! I whet the gleaming blade across the heel of my boot, gazing at the steel in the harsh glare of the stage light.

In my mind's eye, there is a shower of sparks.

"*C'est parti...*" I roar.

I gesture at the crowd. To a man, they are in their cups. I require a volunteer. A tipsy gentleman raises his hand. I clamber down, sword brandished. Deftly — I have done this many times before — I pluck a hair from the besotted man's head, holding it up to the light. I examine it, scrutinize it, proclaim that it will serve.

My blade cuts through the air, bisecting the hair, easily slicing it in two. (Another maneuver gleaned from the stage magician's handbook. One simply distracts the audience — palms the plucked hair — then replaces it with a surgically riven one. *Voilà.*)

I return to the stage. Bafflement...wonder...and worry dance about the sweaty faces of the crowd. I bow imperiously, applying the scimitar to the partitioned slot of the box.

Grinding, sawing, hacking...this seems oddly familiar...At last I am done.

No one is prepared for what comes next. At the final touch of the blade, a hideous wail pierces the room. The wail of a cat — the shriek of a feral cat, exactly what one would expect to hear from a *chat noir* trounced by the wheel of a street car.

Bon sang!!!

A din goes up. I tear desperately at the box. Inside the cabinet I find a transected tabby, half alive, mewling in agony to the rafters above.

"That should teach you," Solange announces, tapping her fan on my nose like some grievously insulted coquette. Not long after the gendarmes appear, soon overrunning the place...

She bows to a policeman, pointing straight at me.

"That's him, officer!" she says. "Take him away, *hein?*"

The gendarmes have their man — me.

I would have to look well beyond Paris before plying more tricks.

ELLIPSIS

THERE IS SYMMETRY AND order in nature. But there are also misalignments: brows furrowed by fever; stillbirths, and unexplained crib deaths...babies refusing to rally despite multiple leechings, blood-lettings, and prayer; all those taken by the pandemic croup. Terrible deaths, unassailably innocent victims, deaths unexplained, each engraved forever on my young and still impressionable mind.

Discretionary time — like money, it is hard to come by. Still, I read deeply and widely. The medical books are opaque, unrevealing. I look for omissions, for avenues and interventions that might have escaped Dr. Dupin's notice. I see he has been unsparing in his application of folk, ethnic, gypsy and even (!) modern scientific techniques. He aims to heal. For Dupin, healing is paramount.

One tragedy stands out among the rest.

It is Michaelmas, the season of Shrovetide, a happy time in many homes. Dupin is unable to catch his breath.

"Victor Hippolyte," he begins, calming himself, drawing himself up.

"This has been a dreadful winter. Every night I close the book on another unfinished life."

Dupin talks in metaphors. Other times he gets to the point.

"Your good friend — my son — is dead."

Dupin heaves suddenly, his frame wracked by a single massive sob.

I run from the room. Please, no details. What I'd heard was more than enough: medical magister Dupin, the grand pavilion of healing behind him, could not save the life of his boy.

—⁓—

My father's entrepreneurial zest could have only one outcome: in short order, I became known as the *'L'ange mysterioso du XVIième'* – the mysterious healing angel of the 16th arrondissement. In short order, there were a series of inexplicable recoveries, remissions, and redoubtable returns to life — which meant that Romain Rand's son had the gift, the healing touch, that spark of the divine that could bring life and hope to the denizens of Paris.

We were at loggerheads, however. With each succeeding miracle, my chance of exposure to the authorities got greater and greater. Yet my reputation (and my father's wallet) grew by the day.

One day my father takes me aside and says, "You know Victor, you don't really need them."

"*Them?* Who pray tell is 'Them'?"

"The Jesuits. The Academy. You're doing well enough on your own." Father shoots a look at Stella that plainly says, *Help me out, wife.*

"Romain!" she says. "Hold your tongue."

Which is more than enough rope for me to pay out, lasso some bison, and reel them in.

"I don't want to be the next Edgar Cayce," I say.

"That's all right, darling," Stella says. "You go right on back to that school."

First Love.

Camille: my first encounter with love.

This is a different Camille. The first Camille, my younger sister, was borne away on the wings of influenza...

This Camille, *Camille Saint-Valentin,* is my first heartbreak.

Camille, all heart, big eyes and adolescent bluster, times her appearances at the butcher shop to coincide with mine... She has breasts, she has curves: a woman!

Camille is precise. On point. And her visits coincide with mine.

What can I say? Her insouciance, her welcoming smile: they break my heart. In her eager hands, the most banal transaction (*"A pound of merguez, please..."*) becomes top-heavy with erotic significance. Her hair, mostly untamed, falls in bundles and waves below her shoulders. Her eyes are periwinkle blue. Her bodice is tight. I can imagine her busting out all over.

Camille lives with her family in a cottage squeezed between two palatial buildings not far from mine.

She grows flowers in window boxes in the spring.

I adore her; I am smitten. I give vent to these feelings in volleys of correspondence, suggestive dithyrambs, and wasted metaphor that increase in vehemence every day.

Camille writes back, mentions an upcoming date — a hiatus in the routine at home — when her parents will be away.

> Cher Victor, Fate smiles on our friendship. Angels
> flap their wings in time to the crazy beating of my
> heart. Maman and Papa out of town next week. Can I
> see you? Tuesday, at the stroke of noon? I await your
> word — Breathlessly yours, — C.

My imagination flips, soars, goes on overdrive. Visions of sweet Camille dance in gay abandon about and above my head. I am never alone — she is always in my thoughts. Will she kiss me? Will she have me? I obsess, I cajole, I make bargains with God. And with the Fallen One, too, the Devil...

———

Uncertainty plucks at the bowstrings of my untried heart.

At last I succumb. I reach out to my single source of help.

I ask Dupin for a love charm.

The doctor is not amused. Instantly he is censorious, critical. He reverts to baroque turns of speech. This is bad.

Clearly, he is incensed.

"A love charm? A philtre, a concoction, a potion? What on earth for? To hijack the innocent? Corrupt a minor? Who *is* this girl, anyway?"

I decide to regroup. Cut my losses. Reduce the harm. No way will I disclose C.'s identity to this perfidious geezer.

"No sir, absolutely not. I refer to a *provisional* campaign, that is to say, a *theoretical* sally. If ever I were in love...I suppose an aphrodisiac might be of use."

The apogee of scathing commentary is not yet reached. The doctor's diatribe, ever more strident, picks up steam.

"Wake up, Victor. Follow your heart! Remember your true calling. Think about your studies. The Jesuits demand single-minded devotion. God damn it boy, you were trained there! You were raised there. Single-minded commitment the word of the day, the year, the Millenium! A very simple, very elegant word, Victor: *Abstention*. Abstention plain and simple. Abstention from pleasures of the flesh."

He shoots me a cutting look, tales a deep breath, then goes on.

"You can't be serious, Victor Hippolyte Rand. You want a love charm? Well, don't look at me! All these hours at my side, at these bedsides, presiding, prevaricating, binding the archangels and elements with a theurgic sword of Damocles — and now you would stoop to medieval methods, abandon modern science in favor of witchcraft and humbug?"

—⁓—

The man is a hypocrite. He has coached me in animal magnetism, in the laying on of hands — yet now he disavows these, falling back on the equally dubious claims of scientism, rationality, and worse still — *morality?*

—⁓—

I am chastised, brow beaten...but not yet defeated.

A hag, a disheveled crone who sells powdered animal parts and dried umbilical cords, lives down the lane, in a far less tonier arrondissement.

Some say she is a witch.

Not for nothing! I squirrel away my francs and centimes. I will have my love potion, at any reasonable price.

I arrive at Camille's at the appointed time — a phial of the love philter in one hand, my heart in the other.

—⁓—

Camille is radiant, resplendent, an adolescent boy's dream. Her breasts peek out from the plunging verge of her chemise. She takes my coat and asks me to sit. She has prepared a treat: juniper tea — crêpes slathered in butter and rum — and a smile as inviting as the Seine on a perfect spring day.

She excuses herself — the call of Nature. I empty the phial into her cup. I watch it dissolve.

Suddenly she reappears.

"Oh *mon coeur*," she says, "are you slipping me a mickey? How adorable!"

I scramble for something to say.

"I thought you'd like some ginger...and *cantharides*...in your tea."

She bursts into peals of laughter. Happy peals, sonorous waves of it...

"Silly boy...*Quelle bêtise!* Did you think I needed persuasion? Here I am. Come and take me!"

I stare at her. I am flummoxed. I don't know what to say.

She works at her buttons, moving toward me with open arms and open frock.

Perspiring profusely, my complexion now green, I make for the door. Terrified, I run.

Back To School.

Tail between my legs, abject and abashed, I make it back to the seminary. Camille has rocked my world. I do an immediate about face. My sojourn among the Jesuits has been a precious, blessed thing. The glorification of the banal; the deification of routine; strict attention to minor detail — all necessary conduits to the straight and the narrow. Anything but the quivering reality of warm welcoming flesh...

The contretemps with Camille? An experience I will never forget.

I have escaped with my life — barely. Miraculously, grievously, my innocence is intact, unharmed...very much in hand [sic.]

It's simple: that horrible crisis was nothing more than an encounter with myself.

———~~~———

I am restless, disaffected. Flush with my 'studies,' I am actually bored to tears.

An implacable gnawing tears at my guts, manifesting in a number of annoying nuisance ways.

I show punctually for *Matins* and other stations of the clock. As ever. I bow and scrape. Ever punctilious, self-effacing, I do as I am told.

But my piety wears thin. I give thanks many times a day. Prayers of sham gratitude for the dry crusts of bread, and the excremental slops that pass as nourishment here. From the perspective of righteousness, the alimentary ordeals are a benefice; another turn of the self-mortification wheel.

I recoil from liturgy...and turn to novels instead. Hicham, a French-Algerian lad — a fellow prisoner of the cloister — receives these sinful tracts by post, a recurrent covert gift from one week to the next from his errant folks. (His parents' Catholicism is highly suspect. They are sending forbidden books.) Hicham, thrilled at finding a fellow freethinker, shares these with me. Under cover, by torch — and candlelight, we consume — breathlessly pore over, painstakingly digest — the lurid pages of Pierre Louys, Jules Verne, Wilkie Collins...Huysmans. *Huysmans!*

Once again I'm in love.

—⁓—

Our forays into forbidden books multiply beyond reason, beyond the bounds of available time.

One book stands out among the rest: *Là-bas.* Husyman's anti-hero, Durtal, is a 19th century dilettante, a *flâneur,* a recondite outcast on the fringes of Parisian society. Durtal's higgledy-piggledy adventures — up to and including involvement in a Satanic cult — tantalized me. I was captivated by his ambiguous approach to magic and sex. *Ambiguity* is a recurrent theme in Huysmans. (Poor old Huysmans, grievously confused in his personal life, his 'experiments' gone awry, finally made do with a restive, if not fanatical, embrace of religion...)[1]

---

1   Durtal is not your ordinary anti-hero. Neither a pulp fiction protagonist nor a romantic Johnny-come-lately, Durtal is profoundly ambivalent, a true doubting Thomas. Durtal will keep wandering and wondering — until he falls in love with the wrong woman (at the right time.) The object of his affection? A cocaine-addicted society ingénue covertly hovering on the fringes of a satanic cult — a cult bent on drawing Durtal in...

The pair exchange letters. The promise beckons — brilliant, alluring. At her invitation, Durtal attends a costume ball, increasingly drawn into a web of sin.

Durtal has stumbled upon a nest of vipers—an occult society pledged to pursue other worlds, opium dreams, and the decadent fascinations of the *fin-de-siècle* demi-monde.

The climax and denouement: a roiling scene of flesh, drugs and unbridled lust. Under cover of my horsehair blanket, I savor this anti-hieratic anti-clerical story.

Back to me...and springtime! The cherry blossoms arrive with the usual fanfare — explosions of new color and life. Even the rooftop verdigris seems newly applied.

I feel I am on to something. I subscribe to gazettes, journals, broadsides, white papers and pamphlets — from the continent, and from America as well. These are house organs and bulletins of occult societies. I am already shackled to one cult — the Society of Jesus — so why not choose one I actually *prefer?*

——ww——

I am confined, but not grievously so: I can stray beyond the enforced limits of the cloister, I can push back to learn more about the world outside. Enough with self-flagellation. With or without my roommate's help, I am on the prowl...for further refinements, for far more subtle stuff.

We leave the chapel, the closing syllables of plainchant still on our lips. (The priest who presides is vigilant, continually up to date. He keeps attendance, jotting down tiny crosshatched figures (mini-Christs? cartoons of the students?) in a huge leather bound book. No one dares miss a beat. No oraison or prayer rises heavenward without his approval.

We make our way down the cool flagstones, the sunset melting crimson behind the trees. I steal a glance at my friend.

Hicham is 'French' — but so were Joseph de Maîstre and Robespierre!

"Say there, *mon pote.* Come take a look."

Hicham hands me a garishly colored tabloid. It's a comic book, an old number of *Captain Marvel.* The Captain is a buffoon — a lovable buffoon — in blue tights, an American flag emblazoned across his bulging mesomorph chest. Words float above him in fat little balloons. Hicham chortles happily as he skims and reads aloud.

The ink bleeds downs his fingers from the dog-eared yellowing page.

I notice something else: the inside cover. 'Fly in an Ice Cube', 'Whoopee Cushion' and '3-D Glasses': tricks, gags, party favors, each uniquely vulgar, *A barrel full of Fun.* Fill out the coupon, send in the cash, and the item is yours.

There is more. An apostate, her heart transfixed by a rosy cross, stares out gloomily from the bottom of the page. *The Rosicrucian Society, Los Angeles, California*. I have to tear my eyes away. Who is she — Our Savior's Mother? Some other servant of God?... Or is She a wanton, a wayward, a mistress of the Devil?

I try to hide the violent emotion in my voice.

"Can I keep this?"

I was lost but now, God willing, I am found.

—*m*—

I return to my cell, lingering over the page and its graven Madonna-*maudit*. I can join the Society of the Rosy Cross. I can share visions, annunciations, assumptions. I will out-Durtal Durtal.

For now, I'm done.

I close the comic book, hiding it beneath the hair shirt pillow.

—*m*—

So begins my correspondence with the Society of the Rosy Cross. The True Society of the Blessed Misericordia of the Bleeding Jesus.

Another Society! But this one is different. I can feel it. My third eye winks in sly accord. This Society sends samples — woodcuts — mountains of monographs — all for a price. *How to Succeed in Christian Mysticism Without Really Trying*. Every envelope bears the telling return address 'S.R.C.'

My other-worldly dreams grind to a halt when I realize that it is only a matter of time before my stash is discovered. Before I am upbraided, chastised, humiliated before the assembled downcast eyes of the Academy. My new Society's instructions are fervid, occasionally livid: ignore the dangers of self-abuse (I am an old hand at that) and risk an eternity in the fiery Pit; climb Jacob's ladder without losing one's step; dance soft shoe on the head of a pin. All this and more. I keep the best and trash the rest.

Foreboding becomes reality. Frère Jacques (actually his name!), one of the younger Brothers, catches me perusing one of my ill-gotten 'S.R.C.'s.

He sees I am up to no good.

"That will do," he says, seizing the booklet as he waves a tetchy finger above my head.

———∿∿∿———

He reads it from cover to cover. A dismissive contemptuous scan...The *feuilleton* is transgressive – clearly sacrilegious.

"*Sacred* Heart," he intones, "not *Rosy*...Five hundred Hail Mary's on your hands and knees. And that's just for starters."

Hope beyond hope, I pray: *please God, get me out of here.*

———∿∿∿———

Despite it all, I continue to read: widely, narrowly, anything that transcends. I subscribe to inane bulletins from all over the world. I pray for divine assistance. (Or not so divine assistance – whichever comes first.)

So begin my close encounters of the degenerate kind.

There are many false starts along the way.

One gang of schemers, out of London, call themselves 'The Ordure of the Golden Dog.' They insist they are a renegade wing of that venerable progenitor of occult societies of the West, the Golden Dawn.[2]

I am pleased, practically beside myself with joy: I can audit their lessons through the miracle of postal mail.

Unleash *Golden Dog,* and it might rule the world. They attract a *hoi-polloi* of stumble-bums, losers and *naifs* from every corner of the globe. Admission to the Ordure is on a first come, first served basis – a loose meritocracy based solely on the size and frequency of one's contributions to their soon-to-be swollen coffers.

———∿∿∿———

I have eyes but they are too blind to see.

I correspond with the Ordure through a series of heartfelt missives and *cartes postales*. I never know when their parcels will arrive – which is

2   The Order of the Golden Dawn was for many years the blue ribbon occult society of the Western World. Its membership included such worthies at MacGregor Mathers, Maud Gonne, William Butler Yeats, and Aleister Crowley.

bad, very bad — so I make a point of intercepting the postman...as often as humanly possible. I need to see my mail before the Brothers do.

One morning I depart from routine. I miss the postman and oh how dearly I pay! The Brothers lay it on thick: the scourge, the triple-layered hair vestments (especially egregious in August, at the height of summer), their prophecies for my consignment to lakes of fire, to eternal doom. They threaten, cajole, promise to tell my parents about my grievous moral decline.

In short, I am guaranteed a swift ride to Hell.

THE GOLDEN DOG.

I AM DETERMINED: I must achieve escape velocity. I will persist at this until I succeed.

At last: graduation day arrives. My cup runneth over...

I am twenty years old, and on my own.

I set myself up in a *pension.* How to go on? How will I support myself? How to endure?

Answer: Return to stage magic.

My surroundings are humble, granted, but I have a modicum of privacy. Drawn shades, lights out, goodbye world. No Jesuits going through my mail. No need to ambush a postman at the crack of dawn...

The Ordure's booklets arrive on time, once a week, predictably — on Tuesdays. The *faux*-leather binding leaves a kind of gristle in my hands. I don't really care. What really matters is the content, the soul-stirring spiritual dynamite that lies within. The London-based (they list a toney Oxford Circus address) Lodge welcomes me aboard.

The lessons promise *a review of Ancient Wisdom spanning the centuries, from the Sumerians and Akkadians up until the present day...* Read all about it! Three thousand years of wisdom! There are incantations; meditations on alphabets long dead and gone; heaps of barbaric names waiting to be rehearsed.

I study the material, committing it to memory. With Jesuitical rigor I apply these lessons, study my perceptions, my feelings, my appetites. The Academy lives on within the runnels of my brain.

My pleasures are few and far between. I live on thin soups and celery stalks, sip at gruel, harboring the insane belief that dietary austerity will supercharge my tumble at Initiation.

—∞—

Touching myself — masturbation — is out of the question. Strictly forbidden. 'Physical' appetites — sex included, are interdicted.

Somehow I will survive.

The handouts from home are meager, laughable. Swoon states — aided and abetted by chronic near-starvation — now come easy. I devote entire trances to fact finding. I ask my Inner Chaldean Oracle for help. My Inner Sage nods in assent, reminding me that I am not without resources. Perhaps I can turn stage magic and what healing skills I have to further account.

I resume doing medical 'favors'...up to and including TOPs (that's Termination of Pregnancy)...for pay. Anything to get through.

The odd fellows of the Golden Dog are into me for forty mailed lessons — and several thousand francs. Francs, pounds: it's all the same. *I'm broke.* My thirst for esoteric knowledge must go unslaked. I avidly pursue Golden Dog's course on 'interior redesign'...which borrows heavily from alchemists Lully, Paracelsus, and Avicenna. I convince myself that, like the alchemists' sublimation of 'lead' into 'gold', 'Dog' is a canny metaphor, a spiritual sleight of hand that, properly directed, will lead to self-mastery, Godhead, and — who knows? —maybe even delight.

Nothing can stop me now.

More parcels arrive each week. The Ordure's use of metaphor is further unleashed. Each lesson closes with the admonition 'Rescue a Dog.' I complete questionnaires, inventories, surveys: *Have I ever owned a dog? If so, what kind? What is my 'dream breed'? To what lengths will I go to coddle, spoil, sweeten the life of a pooch? Am I willing to stay up nights boiling chicken, 'in ordure' to please my canine charge?*

The writing is on the wall but, as ever, I'm the last to see it.

Then, like a painful boil, matters come to a head.

I receive an invitation to join my Golden Dog confreres at their annual retreat in Oberammergau. The address of the convocation, *1500 Hundstrasse,* bodes well. I apply myself with renewed fervor to my work. I'm a combination prestidigitator/midwife, raking in the fees and tips, accumulating enough specie until I can afford to go.

My training in cosmic rhythm, in the harmony of the tides and the moon, should have alerted me to what came next. I should have known better: best intentions can (and will!) run afoul. Depend on it: bad weather lies ahead...Bad weather, or what's worse, human error and cupidity.

Suitcase in hand, I stumble my way up to the entrance of 1500 Hundstrasse. What do you think I find? I find a sign, a small but malevolent brass sign: *Goldener Hund Gehorsamsschule.* Golden Dog Obedience School!

I am shocked. I knock at the groundskeeper's window.

"Ja?" An elfin man in filthy jodhpurs and Wellingtons peers through the pane.

I muster my best attempt at Deutsch.

"*Ja,* pardon. I'm here for the training. The Ordure of the Golden Dog."

"*Ja wohl,* sure. You picked the right place."

"Obedience school?" I stammer. "There must be some mistake..."

"Listen sonny. The school has fallen on hard times. Hey, smile. It won't cost you a pfennig more."

He eyes my coat — *faux*-Loden — a little too covetously. I can feel his mental fingers palpating the nap. Fritz (Otto? Helmut?) purses his lips, an insincere imitation of thinking. The tip of his anvil-shaped tongue darts out officiously.

"We pinch pfennigs young fellow. It's not every day one sees a fine coat like yours. Some coats are hair, some are fur. This is one hundred per cent *loden*...Incidentally, they hold obedience classes in the same wing as Kabbalah and Tarot. Like that. *Nicht wahr?* Now let me see your papers."

———

What is it with these people, their obsession with papers, seals, certificates?

I supply the documents, then am duly accompanied, no further questions asked, to lodgings where I will spend the night.

I divert myself with their bulletin of upcoming events.

———

That night my sleep is fitful, interrupted by nightmare. Pit bulls and Pomeranians...nipping and biting at me in my abbreviated dreams. Breakfast — bitter coffee and stale pastry, some infantryman's paltry idea of nourishment — does little to calm my nerves.

We are a rag-tag bunch, hovering over the denuded fare, making polite conversation but not really giving a damn one way or the other.

Finally we are led to the gym.

Sorry — *gymnasium.*

Nothing prepares me for the spectacle that greets my eyes.

"Is this some kind of joke? *Quelle blague!*" I sputter.

I reel in shock — shock, mixed with equal parts amazement, frustration, and despair. I'd scrimped and saved for this trip and now — *now this?*

A lake of mewling mongrels, from cozened Afghans to wily Weimaraners, chokes the room. A discordant chorus of howls and barks makes my flesh crawl. The combined odor is a grievous assault upon the nose and throat. Several among our group turn on their heels and leave.

My further protests are met with hostility. Hostility, outright contempt and disdain.

I depart, beating a hasty retreat to the street.

I am a grown man, not a whelp. Father comes to mind. I imagine him here, standing beside me. I imagine his apoplectic fit. It would not do me any good.

—✳—

Enough with the hellhounds. Merrie Old England calls. The lure, the promise and premise of the world's foremost occult society — the true Order of the Golden Dawn — draws me on. My astral ambitions know no bounds: I want it all. Britain — Stonehenge, Glastonbury, a smorgasbord of Gnostic delight...

My command of the English language grows daily: *Pleased to meet you. Yes, sir. This way, thank you...*

There is little drawing me home.

Next stop: London.

Into the Mystic.

Celibacy and loneliness, man's fate and double curse, draw me down.

I decide to drink myself into a good bonnie stupor. Righteous! I line the shots up on the bar, telling the barman to pour them *just so,* dead to rights, absolutely level. I seek a fatal consistency.

A mustachioed gentleman in tartan plaid notices the drinks. He gives me a high sign.

"You're not actually going to drink that?"

I hem and haw.

"No, not really..."

"But I will!" He roars with merriment, pushing me away. He scarfs down the lot. Then there are none.

Blotches of red and purple erupt on and further corrupt his skin.

"Kiss me," he says, "I'm Irish. And Scottish. And a wee bit Hebrew too!"

He hands me a business card.

"Solomon. Solomon Agamemnon Deutsche, Reality Broker," he says. "*Je suis ravi.* The next time you're ready to throw away your money – give me a call. *Profligate* being one of my middle names."

I take another look at the card.

"I dunno. Says here *Agamemnon.*"

He demurs.

"So it does, so it does. But hey — what's in a name?"

The next question really cuts me.

"Rand, right? The *faux*-Jesuit, the Jewish butcher's son?"

Wha — ?

This surely beats the band. (If there were a band. A band one cared to beat...)

The dog conference, my hasty retreat from Oberammergau — sure signs of defeat. Now this fresh proof. A perfect stranger knows. Knows that I cannot fix my wagon to a star. A perfect stranger — a fairly ridiculous one, at that — who seems to know everything about me.

"How would you know that?"

The question provokes a fresh gale of laughter.

"Simple. I read it on your face. Plain as a Michelin map. Plain as day."

?

Solomon Agamemnon — *Call me Sol,* he says — drinks more. Despite (or because of) this his insights seem to multiply, fester. Poison mushrooms after rain. Rabbits in a hutch. His intrusiveness is wildly asymptotic, ascending, aggressive. The more he drinks, the more he prods. He is especially interested in my recent junket.

Another rachitic wheeze.

"Order of the Golden Dog you say?"...

"Ordure," I say, "not *Order."*

He explains: the German Ordure is a satellite, a laughable imitation of the One True confraternity, the Golden Dawn. The Order of the Golden Dawn of East Anglia, Great Britain.

"How do I get in touch?"

"Get in touch? Ha ha. Patience, my dear — *they* will get in touch with *you.* If you are worthy."

He pauses, tosses back his thirteenth drink.

Sol Deutsche becomes the latest in an already long line of confessors.

"Are you worthy, Victor?"

I am in hot pursuit of the Gift Beyond Giving, the Redemption Stamp Beyond Redeeming, the Grail Beyond Tippling. I fess up. I spill the beans. I lay out the whole bloody story: the *boucherie,* my checkered past as healer, as stage act, my monastic hit or miss at the Society of Jesus.

Deutsche knows my name.

Now he knows my number.

Sol Deutsche (artist's rendering)

Thus begins another love-hate relationship. The true Order of the Golden Dawn is a society dedicated to the pursuit of knowledge: hidden wisdom gleaned from eldritch sources, including alchemy, the ancient Tarot, and the mystical Qabalah. Golden Dawn spans continents, crosses borders, ranges as far as the Third Eye can see. Poets, statesmen, people from all walks of life swell its ranks. And anonymity is sacrosanct, strictly enforced: witch hunts and somewhat lesser indignities are not yet a thing of the past...

Once again I am on the receiving end of 'purple prose': turgid lessons arriving in the mail, expansive (and expensive) to a fault. The lessons are pretentious, wordy, formatted like Chinese take-out menus — but featuring far heavier fare. Golden Dawn missives are smarmy, pedantic, allusive; essays that treat of gods and goddesses, of miracles waiting to be wrought at home...spiritual dynamite, wisdom distilled from apocryphal papyri, vision quests, grievous 'inner work.' The one 'true religion' is universal, a panopticon subsuming all mythologies and religions known to man.

Gnostic symbols are neither glib nor arbitrary. They are the distilled essence of dreams and visions. Like the quests of the Knights Templar and Illuminati, like the search for the Philosopher's Stone, they are glorious revisions and retellings of an age-old abiding tale.

Order of the Golden Dawn (OGD, or better yet, rearranged, 'GOD') serves it up hot and spicy: obscene and outrageous connections between Hebrew mystical tradition, the legend of the Golem, and the Franco-Romanian-Gypsy legacy of the Tarot...all of this I can savor in the privacy of my room.

In the privacy of my doom.

I comfort myself with grand notions, big ideas — nothing new there! I am a latter-day Zanoni — Zanoni, the mysterious hero of an obscure Bulwer-Lytton novel, who casts spells and breaks hearts...Of one thing I am convinced: I am learning heady, important stuff.

The trinity of Zanoni, me and I — and very possibly Sol Deutsche — could be on to something big.

Alchemy has nothing to do with turning lead into gold. *Transmutation*, lead into gold, etc., is strictly metaphorical. Strictly allusive. The unrefined personality, the spiritual 'dross', requires distillation, 'sublimation', in the 'vessels' of the alchemical lab — the flasks, retorts and alembics of the adept's questing spirit.

Nicholas Flamel and Paracelsus — these guys knew what they were about. The codex, the secret language, all the flim-flammery...these were life or death measures put in place to avoid the fatal gaze of the Inquisition...to escape the *auto-da-fé* awarded to witches and sorcerers alike. Men like Flamel, King Lamus[3] and perhaps even Sol Deutsche

---

3 WHO IS KING LAMUS, anyway? We know Lamus from his Beast 666 avatar. Beast chose well: the historic Lamus, a former king of the Laestrygonians, was a cannibalistic giant known to Odysseus.

himself sought the gift beyond giving: 'Parnassus', 'Olympus', 'Heaven', 'Eleuthera...'

My appetite for the mystic arts grows, festering like a sore carbuncle. I'm up at the crack of dawn, celebrating the ascent of Helios' winged chariot (i.e., sunrise.) I take these devotions, the ritual ablutions and morning prayer, in deadly earnest. The progress of Helios' phaeton across the sky is a matter of daily concern for me.

If nothing else, I am a dutiful student. I follow GOD's instructions to the letter. I praise the archangelic guardians of the Four Corners... East, West, South, and North...I invoke (as did the Chaldeans before me) the Four Elements. (*Four* seems to be an important number.) I 'celebrate' the Elements' primacy in the Created World with every waking breath. Then I write letters, generally obsess on things, make journal entries...

I leave no Philosopher's Stone unturned.

—∿—

Deutsche becomes a chronic albeit benign presence in my life. We meet from time to time.

I am a chronic relapsing student, a spiritual mendicant. Which I don't really like. Like most earthly commitments, tutelage comes with shackles that eventually need to be broken.

My afternoons are devoted to more pedestrian concerns — livelihood, trawling for pennies and pounds.

Leaving no Stone unturned, I knock on doors, looking for work. I promote my stage work, *market* my evanescent skills as midwife, doula and purveyor of potions, specifics and nostrums. In the main, I am rebuffed. Could it be my accent — or is it my continental suave?

After a spartan meal (biscuit and butter, gruel, the occasional limpet stew), I study.

And my ambition knows no limit. My grasp of minutiae is encyclopedic — avid — nothing short of remarkable. I study medicine, comparative religion, outmoded philologies...I detect correspondences...the 22 letters of the Hebrew alphabet are resurrected in the symbols of the Kabbalah and Tarot.

———

The Tarot.

These strange cards, debased in the hands of fortune tellers and store window *voyants*, actually carry good news — wisdom, cannily hidden there by rabbis, safe from the incendiary gaze of inquisitors in medieval France. Brilliant, how the ancient Greek and Roman pantheons, the Gnostic and Druidic theurgies, are preserved in these *iconic* playing cards.

The 'morbid' cards — The Hanged Man, Death, The Tower — are anything but. You can't tell a book — let alone a Tarot card — by its cover!

The Hanged Man, *Le Homme Perdu,* has a major advantage. He sees everything right side up! The fellow calmly surveils the world suspended upside down from the bough of a tree. He sees things the way they really are — *not the way they seem.* Not rocket science, perhaps...but sacrilegious enough to warrant the pike, the stake, the gibbet, in days gone by. Hence the encryption in Tarot.

The Tree of Life, the central symbol of the Hebrew mystical system known as the Kabbalah, is a road map of consciousness — a signpost to the innermost kingdom and a gateway to the stars. Or so they say. 'King' Lamus, occult bad boy and knight errant (see below), cites Hermes Trismegistus (another apocryphal figure in the occult world), as he vaingloriously explicates the inner and outer workings of the universe.

According to Hermes, *'As Above, So Below.'* This mantra happens to be the central tenet of occult belief. The macrocosm ('Above') is reflected in the microcosm (man, 'Below.') The Hebrew Star of David (an upward pointing triangle superimposed on a downward pointing one), supposedly reflects this: the microcosm of man mirroring the macrocosm of the stars.

Heady stuff, inspiring deep reflection. Not everyone's cup of tea — but most definitely mine.

Meditation on these symbols, self-discipline and breath control, promote tranquility and sleep. I try it, and soon enough have fast and furious dreams. My dreams during this time are nothing short of remarkable: panoramas of conquest, battles with dragons, mythical villains, dark knights of yore.

Somehow I emerge victorious.

I must be on the right path.

—*m*—

"I am a healer, Sol Deutsche."

One day The Deutsche fails to appear. At first I am simply annoyed.

Soon enough, irritation gives way to concern. I'd gotten used to Deutsche's face, his silly gestures, his comradely rictus.

Where is he? Unaccountably, Deutsche is *disparu.*

—*m*—

Finally I put it all together. He must be *jealous.*

Once again I am drinking alone. As I'm about to leave the barkeep hands me a note.

The note, in Deutsche's manic hand, is terse, brief to the point of madness: *Check your mail!*

Here we go again: once more I am living for the mail.

—*m*—

One letter stands out from the rest. The letterhead, clotted with sealing wax, is histrionic, imperious, slightly ridiculous: it reads, *Beast 666.*

I know that name. Where have I seen it before...? Of course! A new spin on a very old theme: The Book of Revelation, the single book in the Bible I can read without immediately falling asleep.

Dear Seeker (the letter begins), *Dear Aspirant to the Temple.* (There follow half a dozen further florid introductions. We'll skip those for now.) *Let me introduce myself. I am a designated Keeper of the Flame. A devotee of the Goetia of Solomon. A boatswain of the Lost Ark. Demonstrate your readiness with cash (and a telegram) post-haste to the apartments of my Pythoness, executrix* in loco parentis, *GOD: Frau Mädchen Elisabeth Subaltern* (the address, somewhere in the theatre district of Bucharest, is spelled out in tiny letters. Micrographia. Hmm...) *P.S. We need to talk.*

A fine piece of work! He wants to transplant me, upend me from my [albeit and increasingly temporary] digs and set me down in — Romania!

'The Beast' is finally hooking me up: BFD! Everything else about the *lettre de cachet* is presumptuous, specious, foolish.

What does he take me for?

Answer: He takes me for exactly 120 guineas — which I immediately forward by post. I alternately chide and pride myself on this, my 'strategic' move.

I am back in the hermetic game.

—◠◠◠—

Romania — the nightmare part of my *Bildungsroman*, a lifetime of suffering packed into one nasty week abroad.

Transylvania here I come.

At market, at the bank, at the newsstand, I am preoccupied...who is this Frau Elisabeth? Where is she? Could Frau Elisabeth be 'the one?'

Maybe she is. I am convinced that she will somehow appear. But when? Can she use her vaunted powers, displace time and space to meet me right here and now?

Women of any and every description might be Elisabeth. I study them, ferociously eyeing the clothes, the facial expressions, the bounce of their walk. I sense her, feel her moving toward me with feral purpose. Pure delusion, I suppose. What does a 'Pythoness' look like, anyway? Fetching, I suppose...and no doubt very intense. Consumptive circles around the eyes; ostrich feather boa (*faux*-boa constrictor) circling her blue-black locks like some Nefertiti's crown...

Like Louise Brooks.

My patience wears thin. I splurge, treat myself to a high tier seat at the opera (which I can barely afford). Surely this will bring her on, surely she will appear...*Wrong!* My best reasoning lands me in a commoner's stall with four *pédés* -at least two of whom approach me with salacious intent.

The lessons of the Jesuit brothers are burned into my brain; I reject their advances.

I shiver with disappointment. No Elisabeth. No Pythoness in sight. Another cul-de-sac.

—⁓—

An ermine-clad woman (the mink or ermine or whatever it is is very much alive, strewn indecorously about her neck like that) knocks at my pension door...

In my dreams, that is...

In reality, a waif, a gamin, a nine- or ten-year old mere slip of a boy, asks for the 'man of the house': *Might the man of the house be interested in a subscription?*

No, lad, he might not...

Frau Subaltern Elisabeth keeps showing up...in my dreams. In various guises — always duplicitous, always scintillating — she piques my curiosity, rouses my interest, plays the flirt. This Elisabeth is sometimes a heavy-lidded tutor, sometimes a mentor, sometimes a *menteuse*...a Pythoness, a Baltic Jeanne d'Arc...an answer to my strident prayers.

Turns out this is not a season for realization. Or actualization. It is more like a season in hell...The inner mistral blows up fierce and cold, tumbling the spavined leaves down a misty lane called Forever.

I take the cabaret act on the road.

As usual, the public finds it wanting.

No good!

I remind myself, console myself with homilies, affirmations, pathetic statements of resolve. Frau Elisabeth is neither the target nor the goal of what is fast becoming a tedious crusade. I am (or am supposed to be) after far bigger game: King Lamus, and his parent club, GOD...Curlicues of smoke drift skyward from the Bucharest rooftops...I look on in smarmy doe-eyed wonder. (Writers everywhere not excepting yours truly fence themselves in with abject descriptions of time and place. I do my soldier of Christ best to avoid these.)

—⁓—

Sol Deutsche, vacationing (he claims) at a discount resort on the Caspian Sea, is unavailable. More lies, no doubt. I write instead to my provisional mentor, King Lamus, taking fantastical liberties, making bold:

> *Dear Beast, I find myself in desperate straits. My condition is aggravated by the (frustrated) belief that I will soon be enjoying the company of your lovely fellatrix Frau Elisabeth...*

That won't do.

> *...of your lovely (...redacted...) Frau Elisabeth. I deplore placing you in the middle like this but after all the idea* was *yours, no? In any event, let's jettison diplomacy, high flown formality, and cut to the chase. I am willing to quit the continent* if *you are willing to sponsor my further progress in the Great Unknown. At your word I will pick up and fly (actually, take a ferry boat) to England. Sincerely yours, Your humble servant in this world and in whichever comes next, Victor Hippolyte Rand*

King's reply, almost immediate, rouses me from my slough of despond:

> *Dear Sir, Rest assured your patience will be rewarded. (In this world, not the next!) I have been testing your mettle — a 'pataphysical' obstacle course, as it were. Here's the good news: you pass with flying colors! Your ardor for the Infinite is surpassed only by mine & will stand you well in future tests of mettle, devotion, and Akashic aplomb.*
> *Rendez-vous with the Whore of Babylon (otherwise known as 'Pythoness') on the 23rd of October...*

Here 666 cites an address in Cluj-Napoca (Romania.) I have never been to Cluj-Napoca before — but really, who has?

I might get my water wings after all.

I might learn to fly.

PYTHONESS.

CLUJ-NAPOCA, AN OVERLOOKED HAMLET festering in the grip of post-modernity, is entirely landlocked. Surrounded on four sides by smoke-belching factories, slabs of warehouses, boxy little homes.

To its 'undying' credit, the burg has other claims to fame. The unofficial capital of Transylvania, Cluj-N. is the site of the baroque-era Bånffly Palace, and the seat of year-round vampire fests ever thirsty for tourist blood.

—⁊⁊⁊—

I arrive several hours early, hoping to surprise the Pythoness, catch her unawares. In preparation for the visit she sends a half dozen photographs, sepia-tones of Herself at work, in various states of trance and undress; glossy photos of Herself at play.

Iuliu Manius Street, once an 'artery' [sic], is now a narrow lane. The street — now overrun and overbuilt — served as feeder for the mullioned entrance of the now deserted palace. In late October the waning sunlight filters, weak and wan, through the ozone. Pigeons and crows line the avenue in cacophonous witness to a bygone age.

Everything seems vampiric.

I approach the house with a mixture of wariness and joy — a crazy mix of feelings I know all too well from previous 'experiments' and misadventures. Gloom and foreboding are my constant companions; hellhounds dog me at every step.

I tap at the door. Two king-sized rats scurry away. No matter — I knock once more.

The door swings in, by itself and upon itself.

The room, more a vault, is capacious, perfect for echoes and flying bats. It might once have served as beer hall...hunting lodge...or abattoir.

No one meets or greets. The room is way too large for comfort. It is cold. In the grate, dying embers surrender to the greater gloom without. The opposite wall is lined with books, the shelves sagging beneath the weight of familiar titles — *Blavatski, Steiner, Fortune, Papas, Crowley* — dominating the entire wall. Books by and about the American showman P. T. Barnum line several shelves on the adjacent wall.

Curious...strange! My gaze wanders, taking in the aberrant fascinations of the otherwise empty apartment.

"Frau Elizabeth. Frau Subaltern. Frau Elizabeth!"

My cries go unheeded. I press my luck. I step into the further recesses of that unhinged unheated room. I peer into another room, a bed chamber of sorts.

What I see there is gruesome beyond telling.

Nonetheless: a woman's head, decapitated, perching nattily on the duvet. Yes, decapitated. Presumably it is Elisabeth's. Cable-like strands of gristle and vein hang, wet gleaming and gruesome, from the decapitated stalk. The eyelids are at half mast, final witness to the horror that has effaced their owner.

Right beside this abomination is another: the head of a cat (the cat presumably Elisabeth's).

I recoil. I retch. Finally I withdraw...I quit that loathsome chamber, but not before noticing the surgically precise amputations of human limbs and trunk left like small gifts in each corner of the room. Pink and blue guts hang in doleful ribands from the lamp above the bed.

Blood everywhere, blood daubed in slimy trails, rivers of it, leaving little doubt that whoever did this was crazy, a maniac. I lunge for the door, but not before vomiting copiously — twice — on the remains. A third heave lands on the living room floor.

Later, much later, it hits me: She's really gone.

Now I'll never get laid.

—⁓—

Right then and there, though, only one thing seems important: *Get the fuck out!* Otherwise someone/somewhere will end up blaming *me*.

Only Deutsche knows my whereabouts. Deutsche is strange, unpredictable — and perfectly capable of squealing. Deutsche is a phantom, a kabbalistic clown who sidles up to me in bars, in trance states, in dreams.

I can easily imagine him dropping my name to some drinking pal the next time the subject of decapitated felines and pythonesses comes up.

—⁓—

I hit the street, get my bearings, gulp down some much needed lungfuls of clean air. A forlorn lorry trundles past. In my state of mind, everything seems forlorn. The weary street already bears the day's accretion of dust and grime.

I am in a lather — fit, as they say, to be tied. Mixed, as they say, like a metaphor... I flag down a cab, jump in, ask the driver to waste no time.

To my horror, he launches into *'Brother, Can You Spare A Dime?'*

Don't appreciate the joke — so I say, "No — *will Zlotys do?*" I explain I am late for a train — *en retard.*

Now he gets pissed off, glaring at me in the rearview mirror. I must be retarded and there's nothing funny about that.

The day is off to a glorious start. We pass *Regele Ferdinand Avenue*, dutifully washed, renewed, but failing to gleam in the midday sun. Errant beams of light, wildly refracted, puissant, tear at my beleaguered eyes. I try to calm my nerves.

No more invitations to beheadings, thank you.

I am off to London, off to see the Beast.

KING LAMUS.

KING LAMUS — THE Beast — has many names. Some ferocious, some simply asinine: *Perdurabo, Anik-n-Khonsu, the Great 666.* One can speculate endlessly as to the origin of these. Although some are corruptions of recognizable Akkadian, Chaldean and Sumerian glyphics, most were invented by Lamus by and for himself.

Many abhor him — and for good reason. The Beast, born in not-so-humble circumstances at Royal Avebury Spa, England, quickly ascended the Jacob's ladder of European occultism. As a young man and *parvenu* of literary London, his bacchanalian ways turn heads...Sever heads, perhaps? You have to wonder. More often than not, he is refused admission to polite society.

Beast enjoys his rôle as bad boy and poet-*maudit*. His mission, promulgated and publicized through his self-proclaimed religion of *Thelema,* draws upon ancient codex, alchemical texts, and 19th century science fiction. (Jules Verne was approached along similar lines by the then flourishing occult circle in Paris, but regretfully declined. Generations of readers and the world at large applaud Verne's decision.)

In 1912 the Beast is ordinated — consecrated to the Episcopate of England by Carolus Albertus Theodorus Peregrinus. (Those who are troubled by this agglomeration of names are referred to that champion of medieval alchemy, Paracelsus, whose full name was, get this, *Philippus*

Aureolus Theophrastus von Hohenheim.) King Lamus is ordained; the ecumenical validation tightens (in the contrarian sense) his stranglehold on 20th century Satanism. Lamus pledges to guide mankind into the Aeon of Horus.

Beast's subsequent activities — residence on the shore of Loch Ness (the drama of Beast vs. Loch Ness Monster receiving daily coverage in the local papers); mountaineering in Mexico; the study of Hindu and Buddhist practices in India — only exacerbate his manias, further inflaming the public and the press.

—◦◦◦—

In Cairo the Beast is contacted by *Aiwass,* an astral entity who channels *The Book of Jackdaw* to him. *Jackdaw,* a set of teachings and arcane practices, sets the Beast firmly on the throne of Hermetic Philosophy, not only in England but throughout the arcane world.

The Beast maintains an inconsistent pool of interns, slaves and secretaries, located variously at a sacrosanct bier in Egypt; a cenotaph in East Anglia; and in an *ultramondaine* townhouse on the King's Road. His appearances on site are unpredictable, always notable, though few and far between.

He is a cataclysm, a geyser. He is a one-man event.

—◦◦◦—

The Beast arrives early for a meeting of his Council of Adepts. His secretary, (also named Thelema — *Thelma,* for short), nervously tugs at herself — an unclasped garter peeks out from beneath her pleated wool skirt.

He is quick to insult, too.

"Ah, the Star and Garter," he drily observes.

If there were any uncertainty — Lamus is still King! He fixes his ferret eyes on me, trying to place me. Those piercing eyes — two marbles set insanely deep in that highly polished nearly obsidian skull. His physical appearance is important to him, he lavishes inordinate amounts of attention on it, one might consider him obsessed. His costume — whether ritual (for invocations), priestly (for persiflage), or simply homuncular, is flagrant, silky, suggesting a latent transvestism in the man.

—∿—

He asks Thelma to join him inside.

"Across the Threshold," he says. (His words capitalize *Themselves*. That's how he is. He's like that.)

Once seated (the Beast in his absurd purser's chair, Thelma on the edge of the desk, close enough for him to touch), they set to work.

—∿—

Beast starts off with his customary homily, *"Do What You Want, Do What You Like, I Don't Really Care,'* — a louche apology for a streak of white nights and unbridled debauch. (The intent is part administrative, part licentious. Lamus feels fully 'licensed' to do whatever he damn well wants.) For him there is no law, he flies high and mighty above it: *Whatever I want shall be the whole of the fucking Law.*

With that, he tweaks the secretary's knee. Thelma does not react. She is used to this. She is probably accustomed to far more spirited jousts.

"Take a letter."

Thelma hangs on his every word, jots down each syllable, each priceless dithyramb that falls from his mottled lips.

He is good — very good — at lexical games. The Beast's dictation — a lengthy poem in alexandrines, addressed to the dons of Cambridge — is on point, actually seems goal-directed today. There is little trace of the alcohol- and cocaine-induced word salad of the night before.

King turns toward me, his shiny pate a basilica refracting a thousand beams of fright.

Then launches into another prolix ambuscade.

—∿—

"Cher Victor," he says... "The Order appreciates your investment of time and personal resources in the pursuit of

Knowledge. Our previous communications will serve as beach head for your further assaults upon the Mystic. The Order recognizes and deeply appreciates the lengths to which you have gone—and will hopefully still go—to cross the Abyss and join the already swollen ranks of our membership on the Other Side."

In his hands, routine business correspondence reads like an unexpurgated French letter.

Or mixed metaphor. I clear my throat.

"Begging your pardon. Sorry, but look, Sir — *I'm Victor. I'm here.*"

Thelma glances at the Beast's lap. The fabric of his lamb's wool trouser is bunched, accordioned in busy folds, his manroot tangled up somewhere within.

"Please don't pause," he says. "Where was I?"

"*...Swollen ranks...*" she replies.

"*You have navigated the Crossing of the Bar,*" he continues. "*Now comes the time to raise it.*"

He pauses.

"Ahem. Let me restate: *You have seen terrible things. Please burn this after reading...* How does that sound, dear?"

"Excellent, sir," Thelma says. "I'm with you. Keep going."

An ambulance, klaxons roaring, shoots up the King's Road. The Beast probably wonders if the cargo is friend — or foe. In which case it might be a personal victim. Unlikely — King Lamus has not appeared as the evil 'Perdurabo' for several lunar transits at least...

"*This by no means exhausts our bag of tricks. Be aware of the full moon. More trials and tribulations await. Be strong. Only the strong survive.*"

Thelma tightens her grip on the stylus — no doubt Beast has issued proclamations like this before. Silently, she prays for the recipient of this letter. *Even though he's still in the room...*

She only types the letters. She is not morally bound...

"That's a wrap." (The Beast's phraseology has grown increasingly ornate. Now he apes Murnau, good old Fritz, directing antiSemitic vampire films.)

Beast goes on a tangent; he is famous for these. And Thelma knows every move: he will digress, he will divagate; he will explain his wicked traps and games. Poor Thelma winces, wishing that just for once he would spare her the grim and grisly details, the justifications, the ratiocinations... But no, the Beast needs a confederate: she is It.

Beast excuses himself, stepping into the water closet for a 'pause'. Thelma knows what this means: now he will inject morphine or sniff cocaine; maybe both.

———

He soon returns, smiling widely, puffing on a torpedo-sized Havana cigar.

"Much better," he says — all is right with the world.

"I want a three-ringed circus, hear? Three rings of saber-toothed rats. I want a flea circus as well. And a Bearded Lady. And a Strong Man. Plus one order of Siamese twins."

"Sir? Sometimes a twin doesn't make it. One of the heads just hangs there, dead — just kind of hangs there, poor thing. Looking all pitiful and lonesome-like."

"In that case, make it two orders! See what you can do." He is the model of alertness, briskness, efficiency.

His Etonian accent, embellished by his years at Trinity, lends his words an ardor, a snaky urgency that is imperious, undeniable. Phony, haughty, sanctimonious — all at the same time.

"We'll also want a dog — while we're at it. A talking dog. A Hunger Artist. And a Glutton Artist. See what you can do."

She eases herself from her precarious perch.

The Beast pats her ass.

Artificial Paradise.

The new me, sporting a new *prénom* — I now insist that everyone calls me 'Felix' — is not exactly *restored* by these encounters. I am not enlightened. Nor is my wallet replenished.

I install myself in an apartment in Croydon (London): not so much an apartment as a glorified *closet...*closet, or perhaps closer to the truth, a *cell.* (My stint with the Jesuits finally pays off. I am almost comfortable with this 'cell', it is certainly familiar to me; I can ease right in.) The near presence of stranglers, hobos, and other *voyous* provides an odd sense of comfort. I orient to my surroundings. The seedy, the tawdry, has become second nature. There is no lack of street noise. Of course. Or of vengeful creaking lorries...

'Felix': a perspicacious adherent to the paranormal cause. I am ready to sacrifice hard earned cash and precious time to the pursuit of perfection...the pursuit, distillation and refraction of the Inner Light.

Oh. One more thing: I need to get laid.

My patience wears thin. I await word from the Beast. Time weighs heavy on my hands.

Further dips of spirit and integrity are not far off. My spirit rambles on, stumbles hither and yon in ever more crepuscular groves. Within our own mansions — our body and our soul — we must find our way about.

The immediate and most important task is self-knowledge. We must know ourselves. Or so they say.

Except I'm not sure I want to know myself. I'm scared of what I'll find.

—⁓—

I shun alcohol but am increasingly drawn to the apothecary's wares.

The frosted blue and amber bottles exert a morbid fascination. My nerves are frayed, my stamina cold-cocked. I white knuckle it to the end of each day, quaffing the expensive aliquots, the drams and tinctures measured out with ever increasing suspicion by the pharmacist.

Everything in excess, nothing in moderation! (The gospel according to Beast.) The Beast's injunction *Do whatever the fuck you want* (an obvious borrow from Friedrich Nietzsche) soon becomes my motto. Nonetheless, I shudder at the shards of memory: visions of the twin decapitations of woman and cat still dance in my fevered brain.

Powders and potions? Face it: they soothe. I am in good company. Souls nobler and wiser than mine have found respite (and Hints of Truth, and occasional surcease) in the self-administered dram or tincture. William Blake wrote, *'The Road of Excess leads to the Palace of Wisdom.'* He should know: his first publication runs were sometimes in excess of two dozen copies. Brilliant...

One night I toss back not one but two bottles of the good — the unlabeled — stuff. Over the next few minutes, the apothecary's blue bottle comes alive, takes on hellish aspects...actually seems to *jeer* at me! The walls around me contract, weaving in and out, playing me like a squeezebox, a human concertina. I hear something outside — tumbrils? — clattering down the street...bearing cargoes of sufferance and derision.

The collar of my shirt, threadbare, further incites my already chafed neck. Hell...Voices from beyond offer instruction in a thousand unwonted disciplines. Untrammeled by reason, in my mind's eye I find a way out of here, soaring above a highway; then a charnel house; then a mass of limbs and torsos in obscene disarray.

A lorry scuds past.

—◊—

Wandering perception welcomes chaos, persiflage, scenarios of license and *Grand Guignol;* prefers seraglios, scenes of seduction and sin to those of common ways and common sense.

Not the highway to my soul. Not experiences I would ever want to repeat.

Yet there are alternate routes to enlightenment: many ways to skin a cat [sic.] Sailors sang, in a thousand chanties, of certain spices, certain herbs, that dependably gave wing to the soul. Even onboard a lost and lonely ship. Or especially so...

Saffron is one of these. *Nutmeg* is another.

I take heart, gather strength from these isolated reports. I can follow in the steps of those who came before. I can stand on the shoulders of giants. I will trade shillings and pounds of flesh for spices at the greengrocers. The vertiginous heights will be mine.

Saffron, *Crocus sativus,* grows in wisps and tendrils, in bright yellow and orange strands — Darwinian display mode full on. It is packaged, chiefly for culinary use, in little bundles neatly tied for sale. The merchant looks down his nose at me when I hand him the coins.

"Didn't take you fer a chef!"

He winks slyly at me. As though we were complicit in something, partners in crime. I say nothing. I glare.

That's how things are these days, I think. *The simplest transactions are freighted with grief...humiliation and blame rampant on a field of turds.*

Returning to my room — recall, I'm in England, in my mind I'm still rooming with the monks — I examine the twigs of spice in my hand.

But not for long. A strange mix of hostility and ardor, someone else's idea of renewal, follows. I throw my head back, the saffron fibers have made it all the way to the back of my tongue. I swallow. Several strands catch on their way down, seem in fact to have taken root there...but I quash these, drown them with two gulps from the tap. Oh, that pestilential water: murky brown, clotted with the unknown; a harbinger no doubt of contagion and doom... Ah, what I wouldn't have given just then for a glass of cow's milk, straight from a pasture in France...

I dismiss these and all related thoughts; I remind myself that this life I'm living is high octane adventure, the stuff of myth and legend, voyaging deep inside the land inside my mind! I loosen my tie, undo the collar of my shirt, settle back and wait for the chemically prompted fireworks to begin.

With saffron, first there is an aura. Ambient Objects seem to glow from within.

My first thought is, *How cute.* The stack of dishes not just clattering, but carrying a tune — imagine that! The armoire is animated, positively joyous, offering up my shirts, ties and underclothes, in generous burps, belches and guffaws. And get this: the sideboard wants to dance...

'Felix'? ...I am amazed that I have changed my name.

Mnemonic tides, rich with jellyfish, crustacea, sea wrack, flow through the runnels of my brain. I dog paddle, slicing through the air in desperate attempts at buoyancy, telling myself, *It is only saffron, only spice. Victor, Felix: get a hold of yourselves! Hey guys, get a grip!*

The hallucination is soon crowded with symbols — surely to be expected given my pretend evocations, my *history of dreaming out loud.* These symbols — flaming alphabets, Aramaic characters, Zoroastrian cursive, hieroglyphs old and new — flutter and rise, swallows taking wing before a storm.

Wow.

The current sweeps me along, casting me adrift in the saffron-induced *cauchemar.* I could be one of the narcotic-stoked *drug fiends* crowding out King's stories. For a blazing moment I see it all: fierce Apaches in ceremonial garb, ancestral pow-wows, Teutonic Valkyries delivering sermons and happy sermoneers to and from Ultima Thule.

—◦◦◦—

This spume of garbled missense, a *cry-me-a-river* of what will perhaps someday be referred to as 'semiotic' intent, floods me; after all, *je m'ap-pelle* 'Frater Felix.' (In our correspondence, the Beast has grown overly familiar; he now addresses me as 'Frater.' *C'est bizarre, non?* Far as I know, King Lamus has no actual brother in this world.)

I'm a baptismal fount gone awry. Vowels, hieroglyphs and phonemes twist and turn, knock me about, my senses reeling in a hinterland devoid of linear demotic sense. Other kinds of beasts — beasts without a capital 'B' — roam this teleological reserve. I see creatures from paleontological texts...thalassosaurs, pterodactyls, *Archeoptyrix* sporting in mad plenitude across the veldt of my saffron-induced dream.

At worst, the visions are *indelicate.* At best they are intimations on a grand scale of the 'Eternal Feminine' — pornographic obsequies, garish cartoons of breasts, hips, asses and lips.

The visions dance, converge, bleed one into the next. Superimposed, they might be genitalia, female genitalia, ranging across the cirrus-streaked heaven of my interior hell.

I am left with a depressing awareness of moral and spiritual bankruptcy — my own. No doubt others in my place would applaud such shamanism, grandstand their glorious, albeit wafer-thin, cosmogony; but not me!

⁓⁓⁓

One fact remains: all my high-falutin' striving must lead to one place, and one place only. Not Parnassus, not Olympus; more like handfuls of olives gratefully plucked, pillaged or purloined from a mount of Venus.

Oh yes — there was one further episode of vegetable-induced torpor. (When it comes to ill-gotten transports and object lessons, I am the first to admit: I am a very slow learner.)

I read somewhere about *mandrake.* The root is said to resemble a twisted and torn homunculus, a little man who will scream when unrooted from the ground.

The purveyor on the other side of town — not the greengrocer — keeps some on hand. I pare, scalp, then drop the unholy thing into a pot of boiling water.

The damn thing screams.

The root rises from the cauldron, appears to lift itself up over the lid, uttering a single marrow-piercing wail.

The damn thing screams.

Am I losing my mind? Should I lose 'Felix', and go back to 'Victor'? Might that help?

—⁓—

Funny thing, this business of the apothecary, the saffron and the sage. I'm looking for something, that's plain.

But it's none of these.

During this strange time, this epoch of self-exploration, I throw artificial portals aside, wander on eldritch piers, launch strange schooners and course across stranger vistas with the aid of drugs drugs drugs: my newfound chemical companions.

I'd take it further if I could. The Beast — Baudelaire, Poe, and a generation of sensitives before them — created quite a stir with their profligate and unrepentant use of hashish, opium, and cocaine. Their cumulative alcohol intake itself, consumed in prodigious quantities — barrels, jeroboams, magnums — over the course of decades, could cry you a river, if you were of a mind to swim. Other players in other domains — natives of the rain forests, Apaches, *aficionados* of sacred mushrooms and the like — took the task deeper, way beyond alcohol, beyond anything one could smoke. De Quincey made a cottage industry out of opium dreams; the far East, where opium comes from, never got over the stuff. Ask any Opium War-scarred trader out of Rangoon...

The more extreme, socially deviant, and destructive the drug experience becomes, the more predictable, tedious and boring it gets. I leap... (do I mean *'leapfrog?'* Scores of Bactrians are cavorting, sorry to say, springing from one wall of my room to the other) from one disagreeably noetic dimension to the next. I recoil in sheer distaste. I recoil and go to ground. Forward one step, back two, but always in the same direction: *toward women!* Nothing quite so soothing when skirting the stratosphere as the prospect of sex...with the fairer sex. Not with my hand, not with some airbrushed cutie in some version of a culotte catalogue: no, I don't think I'm asking for too much, I want to be touched, loved, appreciated, admired — and that's just for starters.

My forays into the 'unknown', such as they are, are exciting at first, all those tell-tale increments of pulse, blood pressure, *rubor, caldor* and the rest. I pant, I sigh, I heave; the corporeal exertions are in lock step with the pharmacologic and circulatory ones. Drug-taking is a ceremony accompanied by elevated mood, flights of fancy, highs and lows, and apogees of — real distress! And sometimes death! Repeated challenges to the brain and body result in ever faster return to drug-induced plateaus of anxiety and panic. The main consolation being contemplation... and the autistic joys of self-abuse. Women, girls, *jeune filles*, harlots, *salopes, putes,* showgirls, counter girls, barmaids, *infirmières,* trollops — the whole kit and kaboodle, the entire class action suit played out in whatever pastiche and cheap fantasy happens to reassure and happens to be at hand [sic.]

In other words — I 'explore'; explore by taking drugs — I go on a lark... and end by taking myself in hand. Inevitably! A matter of course! The same wretched go-round that bedeviled Huysmans[4] until near the end!

———ᗡᐯᗡ———

At a certain point, this becomes all too familiar. Why not spare the bother and expense? Why not get right down to the task of Onan? Why dress self-abuse up in the raiment of goggle-eyed self-discovery and metaphysics?

———ᗡᐯᗡ———

---

4   Editor's note: Joris-Karl Huysmans' (1848 — 1907) bitter struggle to overcome meaninglessness, whether though licentiousness, profligacy, or devout Catholicism, is portrayed in his epic novels *À Rebours (Against Nature), Là-Bas (Down There),* and others. Conventional literary scholarship emphasizes the Manichean split in Huysmans: darkness and light, Good and Evil, flesh vs. spirit, etc. I believe Huysmans' perspective was ultimately a comic one: the constant juxtaposition of profligacy and piety is after all a surrealist contrast, much like Maldoror's chance encounter of a sewing machine and an umbrella on an operating table.

With each new day, there is renewal. I am still young enough to enjoy a renaissance of hope — however slight, however specious, however tawdry.

～

I fry an egg. A larch sings with the breeze. I watch the bird's exertions through a tiny porthole here that serves as window. The bird continues singing, in unreasoning transport, through the preparation of breakfast.

I write off my immediate instinct — namely, to throttle the life out of the *petit oiseau* — to surliness. Surliness and hangover.

I smack my lips. The single egg is not enough — I am still hungry.

So I read the mail.

In the near distance — at this point, no great surprise — a lorry rumbles past.

What is this? Another Monogrammed Missive from the Beast... Apparently an audience...with Madame Rowena Blavatski...has been arranged, on my behalf, for the following week.

Things are looking up.

Blavatski.

Rowena David-Neel Blavatski: a boxy mongrel-faced slip of a thing, a hirsute monster of intellect hailing from the wind-blasted steppes of Russia. Some consider her an Avatar of the New Age, an unshakeable bellwether from high atop her perch on the Masonic pyramid of European occultism. Her gift of gab, the blue streaks sliding into outright logorrhea, are known far and wide. The telluric rays and Akashic planes are well known to her, they are her calling cards and stomping ground, as it were…Some venture to say she is a militant courtier, a kabbalistic courtesan in fact, wooing the hearts and wallets of the unsuspecting. Money is everything, even on the astral plane!

A meeting is arranged.

I make a grand entrance, fanning the air with a Savile Row cape, purchased at the eleventh hour at a local consignment shop. The Queen of Esoterica looks up from her book, her lorgnette falling among the well-worn folds of her dressing gown. A manservant and lady-in-waiting totter before her, bathed in her purple glow.

Most unusual: weren't ladies-in-waiting things of the Empire, relics of the colonial (or glorious? or Napoleonic? depending on where you stood) past?

I am nonetheless impressed.

Tea is served; we chat, sip and pose, touching upon divers matters, wending our conversational way between polite small talk and grave pronouncements on the state of the world. Madame punctuates her more sensible remarks with snorts, hiccups and wheezing. Her accent is thick but they say she commands seventeen languages, so who am I to complain?

Felix — *moi* — has arrived more or less on time. Madame B. is about to embark on (yet another!) highly publicized journey...My ears prick up at mention of this.

Would young Felix care to hear more?

"Willingly!"

Blavatski

Could one touch this woman? Does she abide within the Realm of the Real? Could one endure it? Would one live to tell the tale?

Teacups clink — tea, and tea chatter, the universal language of genteel intercourse (!)...Madame asks for toast points and *confit*. The event soon blossoms into full high tea: water-cress sandwiches, scones, raspberry jam and clotted cream, 'the works.'

"We have organized an expedition to Kathmandu," she explains. "Costly, I might add, in the extreme. To Kathmandu and points beyond."

Sounds good to me. That could explain the middle name. I jump on it.

"Any relation to Alexandra, Alexandra David-Neel?" I ask. Surely the comment — the mere fact of recognition — will hit Madame where she lives. A spark of recognition that may ignite, may even impress the pants off her...*but is that what I really want?*

Alexandra David-Néel (1868-1969)

Blavatski is so delighted she instantly reverts to French.

"*Je suis ravie!* So you know her, you sweet man? It just so happens that David-Neel is my god-daughter...and my spiritual cousin. 'Goddess-daughter' is what I mean to say...Ah the evenings together, at brake and stile, negotiating the fate of mankind..."

Yecch. Ringard. Keep a level head — bite your tongue, if need be, lad! I am diplomatic, defensive, adroit in the extreme. Madame B. — there she is — my gateway to the stars...not to mention my Royal Road to the Beast. No way I'm burning that bridge...

—⁓—

"Yes," I say. "You people certainly have a thing for names."

"Well! — you certainly don't! For example: have you ever considered changing yours? Sorry, but I find 'Felix' rather pedestrian...I don't know, *cloying* somehow..."

I feel like hoisting her on a petard: *I'm in the frigging room, Madame...* but no.

I keep mum.

She fixes a mischievous grin at me, then signals for more crumpets and gin.

She certainly can put it away. None too sparing with the critical remarks, either.

"Get a new name. Out with the old, in with the new — something more elegant, more autocratic...you know, something more Austrian!"

"Here's what we'll do," Blavatski continues, "We will call you *Fritz*. First things first...We will inscribe your new name in the Akashic Record. Only, that is, if you want to play," she explains.

" 'Fritz.' Hmm...I think I like it!"

I'm politic, flexible, a man for all seasons. A most agreeable sort. This latest adjustment wasn't the end of the world. Hardly. I'd already endured worse: the ministrations of Doctor Dupin; the soporific rituals of the Jesuits; the double decapitation of woman and cat. Flashbacks of that horrific scene still make short work of my sleep. Who knew if — and when — I'd be blamed?

Would the authorities haul me in? On the other hand, the combined suasion of Blavatski and Beast might prevail...might be my last chance at exoneration.

At last we are done. Smacking her fulsome lips, blinking her *Kirghiz eyes*, Madame B. further informs: the expedition awaits. There are many details for us...to ignore. Ach, my dear *Fritz... Franz...Felix...whomever you are.*

God I hate *Fritz!*, but it will have to do. I am after bigger game. This trip to the Himalayas will round out my spiritual itinerary — and rather nicely, at that...

NOT SHANGRI-LA.

THE EXPEDITION, A PARTY of pack animals and porters strung tail to trunk, is a sight to behold. The 14-member crew convenes in Madras (by way of Bangalore, by way of Karachi.) From Karachi a parade of elephants, steamer trunks, porters and sherpas makes its ponderous way to the foothills of Nepal. (Already these are strewn with the leavings of previous expeditions — frozen over tins, refuse, offal and human waste.) An impressive array of sidearms and blunderbuss, strapped on the wagons and bellies of the pachyderms, will hopefully give marauders pause. This ascent will brook no delay. Sidecars freighted with nose flute and lute players provide gay accompaniment, making light of the ever-imminent possibility of foul weather and catastrophe.

Madame and I ride in the vanguard of the train.

Don't overthink it, I silently warn her. *Believe me, my intentions are honorable.*

This head-on assault upon the Roof of the World...might just keep me from prison. There's more: a smiling open-armed Beast waits for me at the end of my *bildungsroman* 'year abroad.'

Funny how a journey that takes years, covers thousands of miles, and costs untold sums can be compassed in the space of a paragraph.

Our arrival at the foothills of Everest is in fact only the beginning. The real trials have not yet begun.

The base camp at Everest: no welcome tent, only thin air and left-over Mongolian barbecue. Starving lungs and empty stomachs will have to wait. It is an airless at best gelid zone, devoid of cheer (nose flutes notwithstanding), hope, and grog...

Following a peremptory invocation to the caesura of the crags (and the faeries of the foothills), Blavatski dismisses half the native guides. Her explanation is perfunctory: exigencies of the pocketbook dictate extreme measures. Expenses must be purged; *less is more.* Henceforth, simplicity of conveyance — modesty and humility — become necessary perquisites to our assault upon Heaven.

Awash in fear, I flip the pages of a recent (Alexandra) David-Neel travel guide...which I see has been translated into 17 languages, including Rhenish, Romish, and Romanian. (The book predates by decades the popular feuilletons of Baedeker, Fodor and Michelin.)

Blavatski's voice rings out, echoing from one otherwise silent canyon to another.

"What's that you've got there?"

I look up, grimacing at my patron.

Fuck her, I think.

No, I think: *that's the last thing I want to do...*

B. takes the book from my hands.

My fingers are frozen. They hurt. They are now a very convincing shade of blue.

I scramble for a reply.

"Oh nothing much," I say. *My Journey to Lhasa.* You know—Your cousin: Alexandra David-Neel."

The remark draws a ferocious look from Madame B. If looks could kill —

"Trash! Pornography! What are you reading *that* for? We'll see about that..."

Suddenly the woman is all business. She doesn't wait for a response.

Finger crooked in mid-air, she motions to the pack-boy, who post-haste lances the offending pamphlet on the point of his stick.

B. nods peremptorily — with three fingers in the air — and the sherpa throws himself...and the guidebook...down, out, and beyond, over the ledge into thin air.

—♦—

So be it. I'm discouraged but not dismayed. With B., such displays are routine. She is exercising her Gaia-given autocratic rights.

—♦—

I need Rowena on my side (we've already established that), in this world and very possibly in the next. A 10,000-foot climb still awaits. Massive peril lays ahead. Hey — *an attitude of gratitude* goes a long way. Especially with monstrous odds like these. Especially in Lhasa, Tibet! I take a covetous look at my backpack, drawing comfort from the fact that a lethal dose of *nightshade* awaits there, should I so require.[5]

Later — hopefully, never — for that.

—♦—

The ox carts, yaks and human masters set off, trundling up the route. 'Vertiginous' would be putting it shall we say mildly?

—♦—

It begins to snow. At first the change is subtle, more rumor than fact, barely discernible...almost welcome. (After all, these are the Himalayas.) Snowfall is the bread and butter — sorry, let's rewind that — snowfall IS the full thickness permafrost of Nepal and Tibet.

No more dalliance...I've sworn off fake names, *noms de guerre,* all the rest. It is high time to look about, plead!!! for luck, and move on.

The expeditionary party has dwindled to a handful of hangers-on.

5 (***Editor's note****: Perspicacious readers will instantly recognize mandragora (mandrake) root as a species of the deadly nightshade family.)*

———ᗯᗯ———

I'm on a wind-blasted tor, not five kilometers from the summit of K-2.

That's right, K-2, not Everest: a different summit altogether. Like everything else recently, I let it go. Everest, Schmeverest: what's in a name? What difference does it make?

Unlikely substitutions of time and place have become routine, a matter of course. Mentors, *menteurs*...basically indistinguishable, one no different from the other.

A fierce gale from the southeast whips up. Meteorological convulsions like these are not a surprise. I inspect my gear...the coat and leggings, I see with icy [sic] detachment, are only worn through with first-generation holes. Meant to protect, to insulate; what they really do, even in their pristine state, is supply the *illusion* of protection. They seem flimsy now, doll's clothes worn to a costume ball many thousands of meters above the sea.

And here it is: the *tramontaine* piercing right through the filament-thin, hole-weary duds, making a cruel joke of my effort to keep warm.

———ᗯᗯ———

Things have definitely devolved, deteriorated, call it what you will: things have come to a dreadful pass (mountain, ontologic, and otherwise.) The lifeless form of our senior guide, still harnessed to the daisy chain of living mountaineers, dangles from its single rope. Eventually it will plummet to the fastness below. From this, my ledge on the edge of the world, I think: *This is no walk in the park.*

Two thirds of the right leg — my right leg — are numb. Ice pellets the size of grapefruit shoot past. The merciless cannonade forces me to close my eyes — just when I most need to see. I see that another member of the party, Dr. Serge Schapirra, a gemologist from Antwerp, is also down. Helpless, he flails from the yardarm of his cable, twisting and turning at the brute whim of the storm. Schapirra spins about, a lifeless puppet, slamming now and again with a horrific thud against the side of the canyon wall.

A wall of ice. I try to gain purchase with the good leg, piercing the frozen fundament with the steely tip of the crampon. Each kick is a calculated risk, capable of hurling me down into the gaping canyon below. Finally I lodge the tip of my snow boot into the frozen rockface. This exposes my butt to the elements which then and then there simultaneously freezes...and hurts like hell. Never let them tell you a frozen death is painless. My ass cheeks adhere, a dildo-sized icicle transfixing my hams. None too pleasant – a precarious overall situation, no?

I take stock: what we have here is one permafrosted leg, one unsteady toehold on the rock face, a rip-roaring ice storm. *Are we having fun yet?*

Poor me: jerk of all trades and master of none! Directly above, the escarpment is worse than sheer. Far worse. The igneous vein runs convex, obtuse, jutting yards out into space. Any attempt to gain a few more feet would be insane. I am no longer thinking clearly – I am far too scared. Shapirra out there dangling like that, I realize one thing: my number might be up.

I might die.

My young foreshortened life parades in sorry tatters before my eyes. I see Victor the child; I see *Rand et fils* that will never be in the *boucherie.* How I cling to that never land, wishing I could have satisfied all the ministers of my growth and education, my father not the least. I see my older self, watching wide-eyed as Dupin randomly ministers (truly, almost randomly) to the sick and the poor. I see my precious books, hidden from the watchful gaze of the monks...More to the point, I see the emptiness in my heart. Worse, I feel an unrequited pressure in my groin.

It's not just ice. Horror of horrors, I will die a virgin, celibate to the very end. Someplace, somewhere, wanders a woman – a better half who will never be mine.

A hailstone – an errant chunk of mountain-top? – ricochets off my brow. The fierce wind interrupts any further attempt at thought. A sudden gust smacks Shapirra against the wall. The Zen sound of one body clapping...

B. now appears, a lone form struggling against the storm. B. is small, clownish, a pathetic snow woman gesticulating from a toehold on the ledge. A hideous bellowing, as of thunder, rends the crevasse.

That's when all hell breaks loose. Bits of ice and snow take on hallucinatory shapes.

The ledge crumbles beneath her feet. Then B. is gone, swallowed up in the mouth of the void below.

The Feejee Mermaid.

Stunned crowds file past a grotesque attraction — a dried-out oddity, some kind of amphibian-like thing, four feet long, on display in a bell jar. The paying public pushes and shoves, fights to get in. Who will be first to see?

Barnum's *Circus of Oddities* is in town — and is the talk of the town. Spectators eager to part with their hard-earned cash (Barnum all too happy to assist) fight with each other for a better place in line.

The chief attraction — never credibly explained — is Barnum's *Feejee Mermaid.* This strange specimen, 'half-woman, half-fish,' was allegedly purchased at stratospheric price from an explorer in the South Pacific. Or so the story goes.

Detractors insist that the upper and lower halves of this 'creature' are stitched together — haphazardly, at that. Close examination is discouraged...in fact, impossible, considering the bell jar in which the Mermaid resides. The jar is air- and water-tight. (Barnum's agent probably attached the head of a woman (or chimp) to the scaly hindquarters of a grandee-size fish.) The entire affair tapers down to an authentic, albeit oversized, fishtail. Easy to imagine the tail making come-hither swoops across the bounding main...luring lust-besotted navvies to their doom...

--- ~ ---

I find out about Barnum's freak show mere months after my Himalayan adventure.

I resume my threadbare existence. The fortunate among us have returned to our quotidian lives. The beat of a different drum still pounds in my head; I am still keen on the spiritual heights. My correspondence with the Beast continues — no mention of the ill-fated Madame B., nor of her retinue.

One morning, taking tea and scones (which I can barely afford, after my expensive swipe at the Himalayan sun) on the Marylebone Road, I spot a curious item in the *Daily Mail.*

BARNUM'S LATEST EFFIGY DEFIES REASON.
(AND DECORUM TOO.)

Beneath the banner headline is a photo. A simian with a shrunken humanoid head and tiny pendulous dugs stares morosely out from the page.

Why is this a headline?

A lorry trundles past, raising the usual clamorous hell.

I study the photograph: *Mirabile dictu!* Is it possible — Madame B. (or what remains of her) salvaged from the icy abyss, staring back at me, looking very much as she had in life?

The Wages of Sin.

My mother, Mme. Stella Rand of the 16th Arrondissement of Paris, is Jewish.

I think about that. I often think about my origins. I ponder the 'Jewish question' of my lineage and conclude that, as a matrilineal Jew, my legacy must surely include the Kabbalah of Rabbi Moses de Leon (a hotly contested attribution I for one am quite comfortable with.)

～～

I am uniquely positioned at the crossroads of occultism. After all, I am Victor Hippolyte Rand. My 'narrative arc' is transected by the Kabbalah of Moses Leon[6] and the Tarot of the Bohemians.

I can overtake Europe. The doors of half a hundred occult societies will graciously admit me. But the lessons of Tarot are clear: *discrimination* must be practiced in all things. *Know* of what and to whom you speak.

For example: there are choices to be made. Across the ocean in

---

6 The origin of the Hebrew mystical system known variously as 'Kabbalah' or 'Qabalah,' is shrouded in mystery. More recent scholarship suggests that medieval French rabbi Moses de Leon, drawing upon his vast knowledge of languages (including Aramaic), wrote the multi-volume Zohar as an extended love letter to his girlfriend. Students of Kabbalah are quick to point out possible correspondences between this mystical system, the letters of the Hebrew alphabet, and the 22 major cards of the Tarot deck.

America, the esoteric is on the rise. Frauds, charlatans and reputed wizards draw flocks of devotees with open arms: *Come one, come all!*

Wrong. Instead: practice discrimination in all things.

I am waiting for the Beast. *I have other fish and other animisms to fry.*

—⁓—

What is occultism, anyway? Occultism is top-heavy with uncontested, smarmy, absurd beliefs. (Not to mention dropsied hacks and outright charlatans.) One Belief Which Sorely Needs to Be Challenged: male seed — the Biblical 'essence' contained in semen and seminal fluid — that loss of male seed, resulting from self-abuse and/or profligacy, somehow drastically reduces 'vital force.' Therefore, masturbation, especially among males, is to be avoided at all cost. I ask you: are vaginal secretions somehow less precious? Descriptions of *chi* force and *chakras* in Eastern philosophy are in basic agreement with the 'don't spend it all in one place' point of view: Balzac's post-coital *tristesse,* the rueful, *There goes another novel* sentiment, (once again) outflanking all considerations of gender parity...Catch my drift?

I recall one sad occasion in particular. Sometime during wasted youth — following a marathon of 'self-abuse' — hey, we all do it — my member was still swollen, turgid, engorged. Clearly something was wrong. In such a situation, the freight of cultural/societal/historical disapprobation — *shame,* in a word — is heavy. In fact, it's enormous! Had I injured myself — as in, *permanently* injured? Untutored in sin, unrivaled (or so I thought) in excess, I considered the many lugubrious possibilities. Would my man-root shrink? Would it *invaginate,* finally quit this realm altogether, wholly and entirely disappear? Or would it continue to swell, overstepping the bounds of tumescence... *until it fell off?*

These and a score of similar possibilities ran riot in my mind. I needed expert advice. Since Dr. Dupin was not available, I asked my dad.

"Father?"

He looked up from the butcher block, a vole, its neck vein severed, still squirming in his hand.

A vole – ? I looked the other way.

"Can't you see I'm busy? As in, otherwise engaged? *Va t'en.* Go play with yourself."

"That's the problem," I said. "I did."

The *eminence grise* of slaughter looked up from his work. Now I had his attention. My plaint gave him pause.

"How so? I certainly hope—" His tone was unmistakable: he was about to launch into a full blown wholesale *condemnation*. A gala of guilt and recrimination. I knew that tone well...something foreboding, something fierce, terrible, and majestic, was in the air.

It was already too late. So I went for broke.

"I...I touched myself."

The gorge rose, visibly, in my father's throat. He flushed, crimson, violet, livid – every possible hue. Veins and arteries sprang up in vermiform profusion on his brow. A pulsatile clot portending future grief...

"What's that you say? You say you touched yourself?" He stared at the ground aghast, suffering the pangs of paternal despair.

"I never did that," he said.

I apologized. I beat [sic] a hasty retreat.

It would be a long (a couple of days, at least a week) while before I beat anything else...

—⁓—

Following that episode of shame, of rampant disavowal, I resumed the habit with renewed fervor. There I was, once again, donning the mantle of disgrace with little or no remorse...

I look back on that time with a mixture of nostalgia, pity, and regret. Prompts for self-stimulation were few and far between: theatre notices; circulars and advertisements in the press; 'marriage manuals' published by certain Viennese factotums; and of course the illustrated broadsheet of ladies' dainties issued quarterly by Claridge's. Which I adored: latter-day Gibson girls and not-so-demure debutantes depicted in varying states of undress. The linens, the pantaloons streaming ribbons; then the first wave of audacious *lingerie...* hey, any port in a storm! I was dreadfully lonely and with those pages, the cheap print smudging my hands, I would have to make do.

I ran the risk of *fetishism.* My nightly (and mid-afternoon and early morning) ministrations probably overrode the bounds of decency. I told myself I was making up for lost time — nothing worse. The years with the Jesuits were difficult ones...there was much catching up to do.

Tossing off might be a bad thing — bad, that is, if one were inclined to guilt (which I definitely was). Down the millenia, the practice had been shunned by men of great spiritual mettle: elders, pharaohs, patriarchs, and a host of pretenders to King Solomon's Akashic throne. And by Romain Rand.

—⁓—

So I put the accumulated belief, the *desiderata* of old wives' tales and alchemical lore, to the test. I ask myself the following: if masturbation is bad, if it vitiates the core person and weakens the resolve — is there any way one could actually *measure* this declension in spiritual, vocational, and biological output?

The proof is in the pudding.

I chart my daily earnings against the frequency of my self-abuse. Here's what I get:

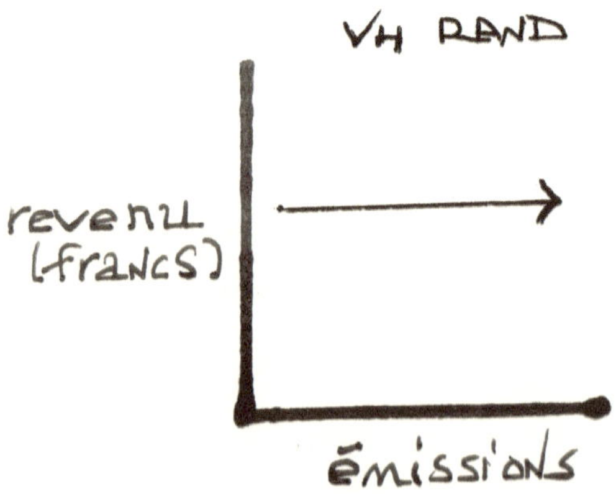

88

This will never do! The resulting wage, it seems, never varies; whether I refrain from self-pollution, or stain my drawers five or six times a day, *the result is always the same.* Pollution versus productivity: does it really make a difference?

What have I overlooked? Is there a better predictor of productive activity? How did Balzac work it out?

What after all is 'productive activity'? Where in the bell curve is 'outcome'? Where in the bell curve is Hell?

I look at my heroes, all these worthies have one thing in common: they are unified by their high level of creative output. I subject these exemplary (in my view) lives to painstaking review. Men like the addle-pated Beast — even Huysmans himself — made their mark *scribbling.* Obviously. But at some later point these men turned to libertinage: EXACTLY THE POINT. EXACTLY WHERE I WANT TO GO.

Suppose I follow their example: *Let's imagine I write.* (And continue to jerk off. There can be little doubt of that.) And with my star on the rise, oh Happy Day, I will conquer the fair sex. In so doing, I will conquer the world.

—*∿*—

The Beast enjoys 'carnal knowledge' everywhere he goes. His florid manifestos — reeking of purple prose and allusions to addle-pated lore — circulate widely. His time as Oxford don finally pays off; the imprimatur 'Beast 666' has become worth its weight in gold. The man is a master wit, he can talk his way through any literary salon or auction house in London, Paris, or Berlin...

—*∿*—

The Beast's diatribes showcase, refract, and amplify the intellectual currents of the time.

His escapades in the boudoir, well known to me at this point, are a matter of public record — and concern. And rampant conjecture. Each day the society page tracks the female plumage, measured in avoirdupois weight, taken down by my hero, 'the King!' His sexual conquests are 'legion.' When I chart King's profligacy versus his literary output, it looks something like this:

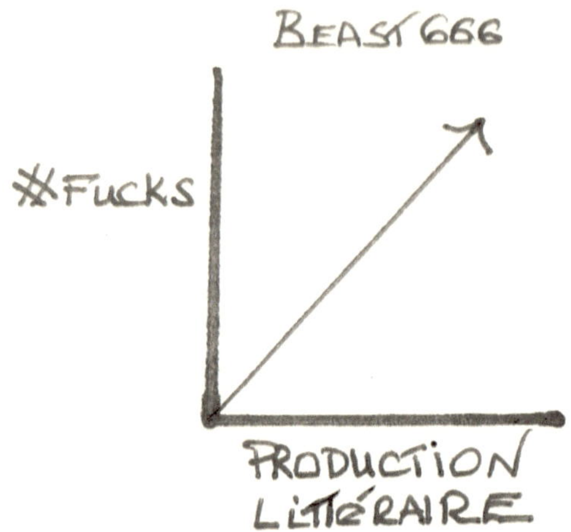

Of course, there is a dropping-off point, at the very zenith of promiscuity...But the graph says it all: obviously I must follow the same course! Huysmans did it; Giacomo Casanova, who wrote 20 volumes, did it; Madame de Stael did it; the Beast does it; and so can I.

I will record my impressions. My life matters. Posterity will be my witness.

First Scribblings.

WHAT IS A WRITER but a rumor-monger, a scribbler, a scrivener?

My first article, published under the pen name 'Gustav Bardon', was a short piece in the *Chelsea Cheat* of 14 September, 1939, titled *Count Cagliostro: Spiritual Monarch or Charlatan-Maudit?*

> Paris. The Revolution of 1789. Danton, Robespierre...ah those rascals! A jeweled crown worth its weight in lusters—or a guillotine? You didn't know what you'd get. Loose talk meant heads would roll.
>
> Madame Lafarge held court. Wet herself each time she watched the blade fall. Or Madame Gavroche: fluttering, stomping, squawking, barely able to contain herself? The epithets and tongue-wagging of the age inciting her...how she loved watching that parade of poor souls, loved it when they took the blade.
>
> A colorful epoch. A good time was most definitely not had by all.
>
> The Arch-Quack (he went by a hundred different names: "Le Menteur," "King of Lies," "Giuseppe Balsamo," etc.) arrives. A crowd, a bristling human hedge, lines both banks of the Seine to catch a glimpse. Would their hero wave to them? Or waggishly toss his Phrygian cap to the adoring crowd? Would he burst upon the scene, borne aloft by his besotted regiment

of familiars...this tatterdemalion Pride of humanity, this babbling, bubbling insect, this knave who twisted their ears with promises—every last one specious—of benediction, healing, transfiguration?

Difficult to imagine how Cagliostro could top his last time around... The freethinker, that satin-bound cockswain, had arrived so triumphantly—straddling the imagination, as well as two giant swans. This time it would be different. A clatter of hooves, the groan and rumble of wheels, the sharp crack of whip on horsehide. Cagliostro and "wife" ensconced in their regal coach and four, the noble steeds conveying them effortlessly to the head of the triumphal procession.

Balsamo (that had been his common name) had been a difficult child. A fractious child. His pranks wore heavily on his nanny's nerves.

The austere regimen of the monks could not deter the youth. Young Balsamo's penchant for mischief went unchecked. (During mealtime readings of the lives of the saints, Balsamo would substitute the names of the most notorious courtesans of Palermo for those of the Blessed.) The Bonfratelli of Cartegerone threw up their hands in despair, letting loose this untutored Apache upon an unsuspecting, benighted world. Giuseppe Balsamo was gone to the world. The sorcerer Cagliostro had risen to take his place.

Cagliostro's accomplice Marano pleads. "My head aches, my temples pound when I think of Cagliostro—that insolent weasel, that reprobate, that satanist—pledging me to secrecy, wheedling me, working me with his confidences."

"*Marano,*" he would say, "*there is a cave,*" and "*Marano, there is a great treasure buried there,*" and "*Marano, the treasure is guarded by demons, by a three-headed dog.*" His requirements were few. Get him a priest for the exorcism and a few ounces of gold, and the box of ancient lusters would be mine...

Cagliostro and Lorenza thus set out from Milan, mumbling paternosters along the way. Their progress from alms- to counting house was infernal, regal, inexorable. Cagliostro, couching his pimpish solicitations in

the language of the Mass, offers the female pilgrim's
favors to any passersby who can pay the price.

Lorenza: a wan Rosamunde barely lit by the dwin-
dling light of the transept. Holy Mother of God, but she
was a looker! A mysterious figure in black baize stoops
at her side. This is the historical Casanova.

Cagliostro and Lorenza overtake him. The votive
offerings flicker in protest. No matter. Lorenza moves
closer, pouring forth the scheme of the New Age into
the aspirant's ear....

Sometime later, the shaken *colombe* pulls on his
trousers, rises to his feet. It was good. Very good. He
is a new believer in Cagliostro.

The response to the piece is immediate. Thunderous! *Chelsea Cheat*
readers rise up vociferously, both for and against. One camp demands more
from the pen of this "strange hitherto unpublished author." A second
camp wants blood, demanding expiation for what is termed "wholesale
libel, black-hearted and mean."

Who are these voices in the wilderness?

I ponder the outcry. I'm greatly amused. And frankly I am amazed.

Did Cagliostro have a following in England? Unlikely. But I test the
waters anyway.

They publish my columns; scribbling soon becomes a welcome break
from the incessant pounding of my hormone-stoked heart.

—◦◦◦—

I'm woken from troubled sleep by a brisk knocking at the door. An
incensed reader? I stumble to my feet, clutching at a grimy robe. I haven't
shaved for days.

In my haste, I throw open the door. My visitor, first of a long line of
supplicants, is a man with an unwaveringly alert, fervid expression. The
eyes look out from deeply hollowed recesses; his unvarying gaze alerts me
to the fact that he may in fact be insane.

"*Monsieur Victor, j'espère? Je m'appelle* Éliphas Lévi."

The tatterdemalion swell hands me a card: *Please welcome this fellow into your heart. Best — 666, The Beast."* The card must suffice. Apologizing for my appearance, I invite my guest in. I offer tea, which Lévi seems to appreciate: at once he becomes effusive and starts to talk with his hands.

Perhaps he's had no nourishment in days. Perhaps his blood sugar is low. He mops his brow with a dropsical *mouchoir,* then states his business: he is here from France. "I gathered as much," I say. "So you know Lamus? *'Le Roi'?"*

"That I do. Believe me, I have much to tell."

Over broth, tea, and stout — many bottles later — Lévi describes his life, his studies, his rapture of the deep. I'm enthralled, a captive audience for his tales of astral skylarking and excess.

Lévi gets that certain prophetic gleam in his eye.

"I can tell you this," he says. "Paintings — bad paintings, actually — will figure very heavily in your later life."

Weeks later, together, we embark for home.

FAKIR-FÊTE.

I've studied the work of pseudo-Agrippa. But Papus?
Faux-Lévi? Further research, I say, more light...!
        —from the journal of Victor Hippolyte Rand

I RETURN TO MY City of Lights. Paris opens its arms to the world in an outpouring of haute couture, culture, and beautiful women. The world responds with a humorless invasion by Huns — Huns drunk on Richard Wagner, on a cultural inferiority/superiority complex of psychotic proportions, drunk on mass murder. And here I am the prodigal son, lately returned. The tail end of dada art and the birth pangs of surrealism cast twin nets of allure. It feels like the very first time, like I've never seen painting or sculpture before...The culture is exploding, with André Bréton's gunsels, who are *au service de la revolution*...and I'm all for that, one hundred per cent. I'm grown now, mature and appreciative, afloat over Parnassus...atop Montparnasse too...

I am sorely challenged by a lack of funds and by my timid (non-) approach to women. So I will subject Paris to all the pomp and circumstance of a demonic calling-forth...

Make no mistake. Despite *or because of* war, occultism, hermetics, and alchemy are flourishing here. In the churches, even in the *banlieus,* a revival, a tidal wave of otherworldly pursuits, would like to wash the world clean. A succession of dizzying encounters with initiate peers and reputed masters alike hastens my progress down the rabbit hole of magic. 'Papus' aka Gérard Anaclet Vincent Encausse (also, aka 'Tau Vincent'), is second in notoriety only to Lévi. Born in the Catalan hills, nourished by the Spanish sun, he blazes through successive careers as physician then hypnotist; Papus then launches the Martinist Order. His dissertation on Philosophical Anatomy cuts the cord — his career as credible physician is done.

Gérard Encausse ('Papus', 'Tau Vincent')

Encausse, a regular at the carrels of the Bibliothèque Nationale, devours everything he can find on Tarot, on Kabbalah, on Lévi. My efforts are no less strident. I lean on doorways, peer into cafes, bars — anything, anywhere, to meet Papus, now leader of the Kabbalistic Order of the Rose-Croix. (A sister organization, the Ordure of the Golden Bull Dog, has already achieved prominence in Paris. Having little interest in French breeds, I defer.) Nightly, I rub elbows with surly lieutenants of the Rose-Croix. ParaMasonic organizations are blooming like wildflowers, among the many seeds of disaffection sown by the First World War. Artistic and mystagogue temperaments sizzle at flash point.

Papus refuses to see me at home. He prefers a different meeting place altogether.

Papus: a wily *hombre,* an able deceiver. Stroking his ridiculous beard, aiming his ferret eyes at me, Papus wins the day. (Papus disavows personal involvement in the overthrow of the Russian Tsar. He visited that strife-torn land on at least three occasions, serving as court physician and occult consultant to Nicholas II and Alexandra.) He insists that his mediumistic forays are limited — too much has been made of nothing. His royal intervention *à la Russe* was a stern warning: definitely shun, adjure, and reject Rasputin!

Papus cossets me in a starry garment of story and allusion. He draws me in, describing familiars, angels and daimons he will 'properly introduce' me to. With loving care, he traces a magic circle on the floor. He mentions five hundred-year old volumes with barbarous names from ancient Solomonic texts.

I'm a good listener.

I soak it up, every last bit, no matter how untenable, bizarre or dreary. As I say, I'm a good listener.

I offer my services as spiritual interlocuter, magical assistant, or Paraclete (any or all of the above, whichever comes first...) Papus, managing a smile from that canopy of beard, accepts.

He smiles then gifts: a battered copy of Lévi's *Dogme et Ritual de la Haute Magie.* I'm overwhelmed. Through my tears, I accept the volume... and hope for the best.

—⁓—

Papus however conforms to the way of the world. In a word, he disappoints.

He arrives at one rendezvous in high dudgeon. He seems distracted, shorn of authority — his outer garment bereft of buttons, his cheeks flushed, his gaze averted. More to the point, he leads a lobster on a ribbon leash! (This is highly eccentric — and unoriginal. Gérard de Nerval, a hallucinatory poet of the late 19th century, got there first.)

—*w*—

A hush among onlookers of Papus' mad parade...crustacean and magister rambling down the Boulevard of Broken Dreams...I find myself pitying the man...and feeling sorry for myself.

At our next meeting (an afterparty at the *Folies*), Papus waxes eloquent, apologizing for the shellfish sideshow.

"Not just shellfish, but transparently *selfish* too. You are an *ēgoist*."

"Listen up, *mon vieux*," Papus says. (I have mixed feelings about 'mon vieux.' I like the idea that I might somehow *belong* ('Mon') to Papus and the larger occult realm. On the other hand, I feel patronized, positively incinerated, at 'vieux.' Early twenties is not old.)

"I'm extending myself here, Victor. I want you to meet a very important person. Henri Vicomte de Laage—" Papus draws out the diphthong of the worthy's title as though savoring a fine wine -"who is the pre-eminent authority and unchallenged head of l'Ordre des Supérieurs Inconnus."

Wow wow wow. My heart skips a beat, the heaviness in my chest premonitory, perhaps presaging further ordeals, greater physical trials to come... A lorry freighted with unnamable parts, junk or high grade explosives (or both), shambles down the street.

I feel as though I have arrived.

Sensing this, Papus reels me in. He runs a tobacco-stained finger through his beard, mentions a time and place, then takes his leave.

—*w*—

At the appointed time — no one shows. I am bitterly disappointed. I console myself, *Hey guy, lighten up. This won't be the last time...*The steeper the path, the harder the climb. Right? Papus is in for it — a piece of my mind.

I phone.

A man, bristling with animus (and likely reeking of garlic), picks up. *No,* Le Professeur *is not in. No, he hasn't left word. No, there is little point in calling back...*

The height of effrontery!

I make not one but several visits to his known haunts. At last I find him, stripped to the waist in the public baths on the Avenue de l'Hôpital. Attendants running to and fro; Papus covered head to toe in a glistening mantle of sweat.

"Well, my boy," Papus finally says, "I can see you're upset. *Je suis desolé!* What can I say?"

Disconsolate, aggrieved, I mention the no-show: what happened? Papus snickers. A distinctly dismissive laugh.

"What did you expect? You are dealing with *l'Ordre des Supérieures Inconnus, n'est-ce pas? Inconnu — c'est à dire 'invisible'!* Or don't you speak French?"

An olive complexioned youth hands a *pastis* to Papus.

I groan.

I bid Papus *adieu.*

—◦◦◦—

The next stop is an atelier, where I find Lévi indulging his painterly passion. As with everything else in his life, Lévi has hand over fist completely immersed himself in his art.

Lévi, draped in the generous folds of a blouse, also wears a smock and beret. The beret is set at a particularly jaunty angle on his balding head, perfectly complemented by the moldering cigar and half empty glass of *vin rouge* before him.

He looks like a blithering idiot.

I mention my less than robust audience with Encausse.

Then I peek at the work in progress. "So the rooster has come home... to roost? The worm has turned? *Je vous en prie...*" Eliphas Lévi gestures: he wants me to step closer.

"A character study," he explains. "Take a look. Note the veterinary slope of the nose."

The canvas is dominated by a face — the face of a young woman. Her resemblance to a sheep is uncanny.

Lévi laughs.

"Rest easy. I'm not trafficking in mutton. A study of physiognomy alerts one to the essential animal nature of all human forms. Especially the head."

Lévi jams the brush into the thumbhole of his palette. Gobbets of ochre, rouge and cerulean run down the wood.

Lévi helps himself to a handful of my hair, sizing me up with a fisheye stare.

Eliphas Lévi

"Which beast of field or stream are you, sir? Fish, bird, or reptile? I'm sure we can find out."

I remove his hand and move away. He is testing me, testing the limits of diplomacy. Quickly I change the subject. I mention the recent humiliation with Encausse.

Lévi roars with laughter."Again with the lobster on a string? *Quel connard.* The man doesn't have an original bone in his body. And then setting you up for a non-meeting like that. Unacceptable."

An expression of resignation, resignation and hopelessness, wilts my face. (Resignation a regular feature of my life these days.)

I hear another lorry but dismiss it: just my imagination.

—⁓—

"All the same, *Maître Lévi*...Papus *does* seem well informed. One must make certain allowances for genius."

"Papus: a *genius*? What's come over you, man? For Christ's sake, get a grip! Here, distract yourself with these."

Lévi pulls out a sketchbook, flipping through the pages: there are snakes, toads, elephants, each the likeness of a man, woman or child.

"He claims to understand *everything*," I counter. "Papus' command of the kabbalistic vernacular is sheer...trumpery. Is he Jewish by any chance?"

"Jewish!" The question launches another salvo of belly laughs from the mystic.

"Next you'll want to know if my family fortune is in *denim*? Denim! Papus — Jewish? Hardly. Papus is a Papist. Devout as the day is long.. He's no more Jewish than you or I."

I ponder this for several moments at least, letting the news steep in the ferment of my mind. Lévi assures: the matter of Papus (né Encausse) is more trouble than it is worth.

"Truth to tell, Victor — you do seem addled," Lévi says. "Too many Beasts spoil the broth, you know."

Lévi lets out a consolatory chuckle, then slaps me on the back.

"I suppose you think Steiner is a Jew?"

He pronounces the name *Shteyner.*

"Or what's worse — a gypsy? My boy, such thinking will get you nowhere. The leopard doesn't need spots to devour you whole."

"I see," I reply. The conversation is sinking fast; I'm treading water off some uncharted shore.

*Okay Victor, sink or swim...*I rally, mentioning my latest scheme: to become an Initiate (celebrated writer, *parvenu,* etc., etc...) and win the hearts of the most beautiful women in France.

—⁓—

"Try again," Lévi says.

"I've already done that," he says. "As your self-appointed tutor and grandee to the stars, I must point out...I fear I'm losing you. Take courage, young man. The Cabbala College convenes soon enough. There are still introductions to be made."

—⁓—

Steiner was the strangest one of all. His piercing eyes and tousled hair set pulses — both male and female — racing (mine included.) This man, still in the bloom of youth, could have been anything: a bomb-throwing anarchist, a seer, a *poet-maudit.* In some sense he is a combination of all of these. Crowds flock to his door, seeking an audience, a momentary glimpse, a minute of the great man's time.

Steiner is Viennese. (Frankly, who isn't, these days?) The number of spurned lovers and abandoned liaisons is apocryphal, rising to ever greater heights. Writers and journalists from every corner of the continent seek him out — yet this intensely private man wants none of it. When Steiner doubts your authenticity, or questions the merit of your proposal, he will toss you out on your ear.

Rudolf Steiner

To prepare for the meeting — a séance with a star — I make several trips to the library, each more grievous than the last. The Paris winter, the extra helpings of wind, rain, and snow, promote attacks of ague and runaway self-pity in those disposed to afflictions such as these.

—*∿*—

My persistence is rewarded. (What I lack in talent I make up for with sheer grit!) The dashing young man with the insouciant shock of hair — *Dr.* Steiner, thank you — has subjected himself to every imaginable academic rigor, returning from those groves a turgid professor flush with history, religion, literature, philology, and medicine. He is fluent in seven languages. And not much older than me.

Steiner has navigated the wasteland of outmoded usages, applying the deadly accurate lens of his mind, unraveling and exposing a half dozen widely accepted "occult" traditions and schools.

—*∿*—

No good deed goes unpunished. Steiner, a vocal enemy of anti-Semitic elements in his native Austria, has been censured for his *pro-Zionist tendencies.*

This does nothing for Steiner, whose books and lectures are attacked by the brown shirts of the nascent National Socialist Party of Germany and the Sudetenland.

Steiner's catalog of studies on Goethe are massive. His historiographies of that great man leave no stone unturned. On their merit alone Steiner will earn a lasting place in the groves of academe.

The press and publicity on Steiner is fulminant — classic purple prose. He is about to incorporate. About to christen a string of loosely related hermetic societies. Or, will soon be receiving the Nobel Prize from the Swedish king. The man's popularity, forever on the ascendant, never seems to wane; and newspapermen, especially the yellow journalists, are hot on his trail...

—⚬—

A trail that leads to my door.

Steiner, about to embark upon his semiannual lecture circuit of Britain, is available for an ever-dwindling window of opportunity during a stopover in Paris.

Thrilled at the prospect, I roll up to Steiner's hotel...without calling ahead.

I weave and I bob, making it past the human watchdogs flanking the hotel lobby. I'm lighter than air, a will-o-the-the-wisp transported on the wings of hope. Good things may come from this meeting. I grease the palm of a mealy-mouthed bell boy. Ten francs change hands and Steiner's room number is mine.

—⚬—

Unnoticed, I approach the service wing. Even here the carpeting is plush. Quietly, one step at a time, I head up the stairs. And here it is: the third floor. I tiptoe down the elegant *couloir.*

Then I see him: it is Steiner! I am prepared. I launch into a well-rehearsed *spiel,* pleading with Steiner for admission to his flagship, the Anthroposophical Society. (The *Society* being the latest incarnation of Occidental wisdom — wisdom dragged kicking and screaming through the tepid backwaters of Theosophy, Transcendentalism, and other argot-freighted Schools.)

The assertive approach seems to work.

"Sir!"

Steiner looks at me, peering from behind his door. He is peering, a little too closely I think, coveting the discarded remains of his neighbor's breakfast. Toast, jam, and tea, each sliding into each other on a tray on the floor.

"And who might you be?" Steiner asks, acting nonplussed.

"Not *who*," I answer, "not who so much as *what.* I am an aspirant...a seeker, a mendicant, a grappler after the highest rung of truth...ready and willing to be torched by the dancing flame of wisdom. I believe I might find that here."

"How did you come by that odd notion?" Steiner asks. And rather coldly: "I see no dancing flame."

"Are you not Reinhold Gunther Steiner, learned adjudicator of etheric ethics? Are you not the author of *Tractatus Solomonus Philosophicus?*

He is quick to reply.

"That's behind me now," he says. "Now if you're quite done, I must be —"

I interrupt, wedging a foot into the door.

"No — hear me out! The *papparazzi* is beating down your door — I know this. I feel your pain. But — and I say this with the utmost humility — I hardly consider myself *rabble.* I may be many things, but I am not a journalist. Here, look."

I show him the remains of my Jesuitical diploma.

"My college degree. I understand you rather fancy colleges."

"Metaphysical colleges," he says. Undeterred, I stay the course, and persist to the bitter end.

"I tell you..."

"No, I tell you!" he objects. "This is stuff and nonsense. Who are you, anyway? Your entreaties are useless. The fact is, I am about to launch a new career."

My jaw drops.

"New career? No, you can't be serious."

"Oh but I am. I am now *patron* — patron, boss, and chief factotum — of Vienna's finest *boucherie.* I sell *merguez!* You know — sausage. *Saucisson...* Retail."

Steiner helps himself to a toast point, then retreats into his room.

With a punctilious nod, he slams the door.

Djuna.

The great Viennese sage (Freud, not Steiner) defined sanity as the ability to work, and to *love*.

I am woefully deficient on both accounts.

I keep my hand in the till with stage magic, making infrequent appearances at supper clubs — but it is a far cry from dignified work and is at an even further remove from love. (No more house calls — fatal fevers, breech births, agonized loved ones — for me, no thank you...I don't envy that other Victor — Victor Frankenstein — the angry, torch-bearing mob scene.) Stage magic is a source of pocket change — and little else. The desultory crowd, blind drunk more often than not, is also impervious to stagecraft; the only talent my audiences notice are of the fleshpot or Grand Guignol variety...

My love life is non-existent.

Am I trying too hard?

...Or not hard enough?

I renew contact with Deutsche — Sol, Solomon, a furtive paterfamilias by any other name — by post. Along with the usual cryptic leavings, the eccentric allusions to intrigue, from time to time he actually *commiserates*...and wants to know, have I dropped lobster pots among the burgeoning demi-monde of Paris yet?

Excellent question Sol. No, I have not trawled Paris...but I most definitely should. There is a flourishing expatriate scene, a chi-chi circle of writers and artists...but one must *know someone* to get in at *Deux Magots*...

—✕—

Hey, no more social lubricants for me. Alcohol, whether *pastis* or absinthe or wormwood, dilutes the kundalini — that I know for sure. I also know that the men and women of the literary circle can drink you, me — just about *anyone* — under the table...and they will. Depend on it.

Why? Because alcohol, like Kilimanjaro, is always there...Meanwhile, they can afford it... and I can't. Which might be a blessing in disguise. My inner inebriate is perched on talons, waiting to pounce — to liberate the nascent drug fiend in me, the homeless *clochard,* the wretch, the *voyou* — anything that takes me out of, beyond, and over myself. Better to make the rounds of local adepts, learn what I can from them, than to open the spigot of chemically induced dream...

These and a thousand similar thoughts sizzle in my overheated brain. Not that my reflections were ever calm, tightly ordered, or civilized: far from it. My lack of progress — in all spheres, mind you — is dead weight, cosmically bothersome, grievous, detestable, tumbling me down headfirst toward the hideous abyss called ME...

Sobering, to say the least. One late afternoon, undeterred by common sense or any sense of purpose, I read the notices posted at Montparnasse. Hundreds of cards and bits of paper stapled to a telegraph pole, rustling in the wind.

One in particular catches my eye.

I take a closer look.

Writing Partner, it says, *Wanted for the End of the World. For a good time, call Djuna.* A number is listed.

Bizrre. *Chelou.* What I'm looking for.

—✕—

No one can see, no one is looking. I tear off the paper and walk on. *Call Djuna.* Hmm. I ask you: why not?

—*∿*—

Then it hits me: a 'writing partner' could be a bed partner too.

I phone her (a local exchange) right away and I'm glad I did. This seems to be working out...may be a good thing. The voice on the other end is by turns husky, sultry, teasing. Everything — the call included, especially the call— becomes a game. We are *dragueurs* in a bagatelle for two. Which I like...so we finally arrange to meet...*chez elle,* at her place.

The neighborhood is sketchy, barely residential: a district of used button shops, costume jewelry, and other dubious gew-gaws.

Let the exertions begin! She rings me in and I climb, climb, climb to the penultimate landing, stopping for breath at what comes to seem like every point along the way.

Her door is identical to the others, save for the card taped beneath the peep hole: *Djuna of Delphi.*

I don't know what to make of this. Just as I'm about to call it quits, the door opens a crack and a young woman peers out.

'Victor?'

Too late. She's got me. I nod politely, beret in hand. Her eyes have that faraway look —is it opium? — a look that deeply appeals. Her kaftan — linen, beaded, quaint — hugs her body.

Oud music drifts in from the other room. Her makeup, sparing, tastefully applied, accentuates the dreaminess of her stare, the opalescence of her skin. She is *mince,* fawn-like. She's got me, hook, line and sinker — I'm a goner and I pray she'll reel me in...

Welcome to Djuna's world...a helter-skelter planet, a planet of haphazard things, an asteroid given to bouts of languor, poetry, and they tell me, delight. Inside, I see cones of incense, ranks of aromatic candles: benzoin, patchouli, signposts of a life given over to reverie and suggestion. Two or three sleek cats approach then disengage, backing off — like their mistress, only interested in the fleeting, the ephemeral...

There are piles of clothing, undergarments, books, papers, every-where you look, in severe and royal disarray...Djuna dismisses these, as if to say *Doesn't everyone have clutter? Isn't it normal?* Stockings and brassieres and shoes — many, many shoes — I don't mind them, don't mind them at all. They only add to the charm...

I forget why I'm there. Djuna reminds me.

"You write?" she asks.

Think fast, Victor.

"I do. Yes — write. Yes indeed I do."

"Really." I love the way she takes it all in — the way she seems to be inhaling me.

"Do tell," she says.

I mention my passing interest in hermetics. My passing acquaintance with occult masters past and present. She is fascinated. I tell her about my Cagliostro piece. A piece which, I say, "made the critics sit up and think."

———

"But enough about me," I say. Here I pause, then " — Do you really think it's the end of the world?"

———

She blushes, she defers. Djuna explains how she's new to the writing game. That she has been granted squatting rights at a *soirée*, a literary club of sorts; the price of admission being a story, one per member per month. This group means the world to her — and that's where I come in. She desperately needs inspiration...and a hand-copied manuscript, one story a month.

"Interested?"

She flutters her long dark lashes, *moues*, then turns away.

I'm at a complete loss. My nether parts are screaming, *What are you wait-ing for? Of course you're interested!* But the upper regions (including the little that remains of my working brain) beg to differ. We — my brain and I — know better. We must object. The will may be there...but the stories are not.

"You will be fully compensated, rest assured of that," she says.

I stare.

"I'm not without my resources, you see..."

What follows is an *Aha!*...you know, one of those moments where the goddess comes down and anoints the hero's brow. Suddenly I am radiant, glowing with rectitude and the last inspiration of youth....

I move closer, managing my best look into her eyes.

"You can assure me of that?"

—⁓—

The oud music, a nuisance phrase of it, keeps repeating. She moves to the turntable and advances the needle.

"That's a Victrola," she says, licking her lips.

"And I'm Vic," I say.

"I know," she says.

She takes my hand and leads me to the bed.

—⁓—

Winter tumbles down and so does our newfound love. I barely notice, they are upon us so soon, these exorbitant rhythms...Djuna's apartment is small and poorly lit; but I am happy, nestled; I feel appreciated, fully arrived. The snow muffles street sounds, the sound of footsteps. For once there are no passing lorries.

Day turns into night, night into day — but who's keeping track? We mark the passage of time with kisses, too many cigarettes, too many bottles of wine.

Djuna comes to me with open arms, at all hours of day and night. Either she lets down her hair, or she pins it up; the sheer mass, its sheer exuberance, is a godsend, the sheer dark bounty of the thing. I love the way it feels on my face, in my mouth. I swoop down and take her once more.

I take her, she takes me: many times over. Djuna is my mentor-come-lately: my first and my last real lover and perhaps she will be my only, my forever, my last. In our school for scandal, she teaches everything and I audit everything, one crazy course after another. She stretches, elongates, elucidates beneath me, traps me in her baobab of silky limbs. One upon the other we dance, a skein of body fluids, haste, and etheric glue. I prod, I caress, the excursions of my tongue are languorous, experimental...I dally and delay at the aperture of her sex, ply her folds. Clearly she loves it. Her juices come down in a torrent, rewarding each stab with a tiny fount, a gush of plangent joy. Everything is permitted, everything is sacred. There are moments when we utterly coalesce. The room vibrates in time — then time stands suddenly still — we climax at once.

We break from sex every now and then, just for sleep. Sleep is another blessing, cradled in a total embrace like that. Out of modesty or signaling release, Djuna forecloses nakedness, wrapping herself in muslin. I hold her close. We listen and watch each other breath.

Then we sleep.

⁕

Bed is not the only thing we tumble into: we also fall into a routine.

I rediscover myself. I find (once again) that I am a creature of habit; I adore waking before her, throwing together a sweet breakfast (croissants and confitures) which I serve in bed.

As she shakes off the last vestiges of sleep (which takes a great long while), I move to kiss her but she pouts: she must have her *cafe au lait.* I scramble back and forth, ever the dutiful boyfriend; in my imagination we are husband and wife. When her guard is down, I pin her against the pillows and renew the campaign. Which she pretends to fend off — barely. Mostly we wind up where we started — now well past noon — and the day is barely on.

I wouldn't have it any other way.

⁕

The world does not end. Far from it. There is every indication that renewal and fresh life are afoot. Pink buds appear on the trees and the sidewalks gleam. Life is good.

Coming up for air, I dimly recall Djuna's mission: writing. She laughs, remarking that she too hasn't forgotten about that, but given recent *entanglements...*

I laugh. She elaborates further, describing her weekly 'seances' with a group of would-be writers and artists. *It's not much*, she says, *but it's a foot in the door.* Like her, these fellow travelers are starting out in creative life. She brings them her stories. They welcome her in.

What little free time I have, I devote to scribbling. I record my impressions of the city in bloom, my memories, my fantasies, setting them down in word portraits and pastiche. I trade my magician's hat in for a pose at prose.

I do all this behind Djuna's back. My secret hope is to surprise her with my work. Maybe even tag along and join her at her next working/drinking confab. I luxuriate in sweet visions — the two of us sipping absinthe, toasting our lives, celebrating our joined flesh and spirits, on the boulevards of Paris.

—*m*—

It strikes me that, beyond the call of nature (to copulate, that is), there may be something else astir. At least for me. The tropism toward Djuna, and toward all compelling creatures of the fairer sex, has more than mere hormones behind it.

This is borne out by recent experiences with my mistress. Twice now, once on top, the other below, I find myself face to face with the Eternal Feminine. Djuna's face, adorable to begin with, takes on new aspects and meaning as I churn, as I pump and stab. Her eyes, her cheekbones, her lines and curves as she struggles in my arms — are somehow *generalized, genericized* if you will, so that I see all women, females of all tribes, in the depth of her rigor and in the depth of her smile. Anthropology and archetype burst forth; she and I are not alone. Far from it: we are in the presence of the racial and phylogenetic cascade that begins way back in time then leads up to the very present. The NOW. This extraordinary event, a true fascination, of short duration, succeeded by the convulsion

and satiety of the *petite mort.* (*Grand mort* I will wait on; please, God, save
that for another day.)

Nascent Bard.

I WORK HARD, TOILING discretely at my notebooks while she is otherwise engaged. My encounters with the scions of esoteric thought — Lévi, Papus, Steiner, Sol Deutsche — are the palette from which I paint:

> *Master Rákóczi, le Comte Saint Germain, enjoyed his most recent incarnation as St. Germain, an 18th century polymath. He was adept at invention, alchemy, and music...and put his time in at various courts in Europe, where he made his mark as a courtier, a master of intrigue and adventure.*
>
> *I was drawn toward the Rákóczi legend on the strength of our common background. We were both native to Transylvania. The hills and dales of my youth once belonged to the legendary Count. I pored over several biographies of the man, including* Der Wiedergänger: Das zeitlose Leben des Grafen von Saint-Germain *by Peter Krassa, and* L'énigmatique Comte De Saint-Germain *by Pierre Ceria and François Ethuin.*
>
> *Master Rákóczi's scope and depth of influence were awe-inspiring. The word on the occult street was that Rákóczi would single-handedly usher in the Aquarian Age, subsuming the exhausted Piscean Age of the Christ. Not only that, but it is believed that his avatars included Roger Bacon; Francis Bacon;*

and not just the abiding genius, but the actual person of, William Shakespeare.

I had the good fortune to meet St. Germain during a sojourn on the Continent. Although guarded at first, I eventually found him to be quite affable and open to discourse. Over grog and kidney pie, I learned that his spiritual forebears included the nominative Queen Elizabeth AND Lord Dudley; he counted among his lineage a host of equally celebrated historical figures.

I was profoundly impressed. He described his metaphysical exploits with equal measures of passion and precision. Throughout our many conversations, he made repeated allusions to the fact that the utterance "I AM" was the bedrock of his spiritual platform. According to Germain, frequent reversion to this solipsism guaranteed free access to the Higher Planes. Further, his teachings were not only consistent with, but actually underlay, those of the schools of Theosophy and Anthroposophy. "Make no mistake," he averred — "I am the Real Thing."

If that wasn't enough to convince me, he said, he would lay it on thick. One time he opened a book of Rembrandt reproductions, pointing to the master's rendition of 'The Polish Rider.' He then explained that the painting was of Francis Bacon (actually known as the Count of the Cabala), another of Master Rákóczi's (i.e. St. Germain's) earthly manifestations. To his credit, Germain took no offense when I asked if the 'Polish Rider' might not also have returned as Pulaski, or Kosciusko, of Skyway and Bridge fame?

—⁓—

St. Germain, as I knew him, had an altogether dramatic appearance. His brown eyes sloped at the corners, giving his face a decidedly Oriental cast. His skin was the color of olives, light green and opalescent, not sickly at all. Together with his goatee and pointed beard, he might have served as a fellow at a Round Table, happily costumed in Elizabethan garb.

His tunic and cape suggested splendor, aristocracy. He further explained that he "had to make do", since the customs of our time would not take kindly to his former manner of dress, which included a hooded cloak of Tyrian purple joined at the neck by a seven-pointed [diamond-studded] clasp. These and similar accouterments waited in abeyance for him at his castle in Transylvania...

"When I'm dressed like that," *he said,* "the people can't help themselves. They get down on their knees and pray — to me!"

Reading the memoirs of Edgar Cayce, an American psychic healer, I found further reference to the Count. According to Cayce, St. Germain was sometimes present during Cayce's sessions of trance.

"No doubt about it," *Germain concluded at one of our meetings.* "I'm supernatural. I'm an Ascended Master. I can levitate; walk through walls; cure the sick; sometimes raise the dead. In my past lives, I helped the Americans draft their Declaration of Independence...their Constitution...and I helped Ben Franklin design the Great Seal of the United States. All this is given. In the historical record. If you don't believe me, ask Rowena [Blavatski.]"

I was starting to feel like I'd heard enough. I wanted to see if I could take a poke through his iron curtain of self-love.

"Remarkable," *I said.* "What else have you done?"

My weak attempt at sarcasm flew right past him, unnoticed.

"Glad you asked," *he said.*

"For one thing," *he continued,* "I designed the Maltese Cross...Know it by any chance?"

"Wow," *I said.* "Tell me more."

"I am Chohan of the Seventh Ray. You know, the Heresiarch, the Anointed One."

"Hold on there. Getting back to Francis Bacon. Didn't he die...in the year of Our Lord, 1626?" *[I threw the year out as bait. I knew Bacon passed sometime during that century, it hardly seemed to matter exactly when.]*

"Close, my friend. But not close enough. Bacon made it appear as though he died on Easter Sunday of that year. I say, Appeared. Once he attained the sixth level of initiation, he took on my name. You know — Bacon. As in, 'Bringing home the...'"

Considering the gravity of the matter, any attempt at humor, no matter how lame, was welcome. I guffawed and asked him to continue. Germain at last heaved a sigh.

"What else can I say? Seventy thousand years ago I was sent out from Atlantis...and founded the City of the Sun. I was High Priest in the Order of Zadkiel. I returned to the world as Hesiod. Plato and St. Joseph. Merlin and Christopher Columbus too."

"Many comings and goings," *I mused.*

"Indeed," *he agreed.*

"So how does one pin you down?"

He grew thoughtful at this, pulling at his beard.

"Hmm...underwrite a trip, I suppose. Believe it or not, travel still intrigues me. Sorry...still intrigues the one you see before you. The one known as me."

"I see," *I said.* "And where would me like to go?"

"Dunno," *he said.* "Cathay? You know I've always wanted to see the Great Wall. One of the few places I've never been."

"Say no more, St.-G. Pack your bags."

The twin-engine plane took us high over the continent — so high that what seemed like caplets were actually cumulus clouds in miniature, seen from above. The flight was long, interrupted only by two refueling stops en route.

St.-G. slept most of the time. He traveled light, an issue of Esquire Men's Magazine *his main companion. I buried my head in a book — dashed off two letters to my amanuensis Djuna — and realized that little could be expected of my travel mate.*

St. Germain dozed on, breathing in 4:4 time to the thrum of the engines. I wondered what a man like St.-G. dreamed about. On board meals and cigarettes — Germain revived himself for those — soon lost their entertainment value.

Still, things were looking up. We were on our way to China, to the accompaniment of polite chatter from fellow passengers, commenting on the virtues of Cochin pigs, rustic fare, and the ubiquitous staple, riz blanc. St.-G. himself had offered a few comments on 'Chinese food', stating unequivocally that he was 'bland, from bottom to top' and would I mind tasting the dishes beforehand to warn him off Szechuan and Hunan improprieties?

No problem. Things would have continued much like that — I even considered 'borrowing' his glossy magazine, Lana Turner in deshabillé on the cover — were it not for... the smell of smoke! Something was burning. The stewardess, unfazed, begged our pardon as she looked up and down the cabin for the source. I was admiring our hostess' rump as she bent over to peer beneath my seat.

Then she stood up.

"Oh my gosh," she exclaimed, putting her hand to her mouth. She signaled to one of the other girls.

"Mabel," she said, "tell me I'm dreaming."

"You're not, dearie."

Then in perfect unison: "THE WING IS ON FIRE!"

All hell broke loose. Trays and drinks went flying. The cabin upended, luggage spilling freely from the overhead bins. Cats and dogs mewled; children wailed. I shook St. Germain and against his better judgment he came to.

"Wha — ?"

"St. Germain. Holy Mother of God. For Abramelin's sake, do something!"

"Wha — ?" he repeated, looking around.

I gave him the benefit of the doubt. He was fresh from sleep. The guy deserved an explanation.

I mustered my best Romanian.

"Master Rákóczi," I said, "we're going down..."

Far as I could tell, we were alone. The island was uninhabited, untenanted save for the occasional stand of palm trees and limpid inland pools. Tiny fish pranced in these, scintillant stabs of color in the azure light. Tall beach grass blocked our view of the wreckage, which was now rapidly sinking beneath the calm waves.

Somehow we had made it out alive. But we were alone. I turned my thoughts from contemplation of the obvious — the miserable loss of life, evidenced by the twisted steel and body parts bobbing just beyond our strand.

If St-G. was aware of what happened, if he had any inkling of the extremity of our plight, he gave no sign. Instead he played with the Maltese Cross slung around his neck. He rubbed weakly at it.

"That will do us a lot of good," *I snapped.*

"Wha — ?"

I shut my trap. Enough out of me. My mentor was in a state of shock. Between the two of us, his situation was far worse. No matter, I thought. When he comes to his senses, that brilliant mind will rally. The Wisdom of the Ages will be our Guide.

Wrong.

As night fell, I became the quartermaster. I was the cook, the yeoman, the bodyguard, the monitor. I asked St.-G. to heap up some driftwood (fortunately, a box of matches had survived the crash intact), but he only stared. He turned to me — eight hours on that beach, and already he showed a three-day growth of beard — and pleaded. He wanted a kitten. A blanket. And something sweet — nothing else would do.

I speared some fish and roasted them over the crackling flames.

"Hey man, get a grip," *I said.* "All is not lost. We've got each other."

More of that blank Rákóczi stare. I had to remind him, had to recall him to himself.

"Hey mon pote," *I said,* "you are sitting on the Rock of Ages. No, cancel that: you ARE the Rock of Ages. Need I remind you of your glorious past? Standing on the shoulders of giants...Atlantis...the Chaldean Oracle...does any of this ring a bell?"

At that moment a mountain goat wandered into our midst. Fantastic! A source of milk, of clothing, of meat if need be...

St. Germain shrieked and jumped into my arms.

—*∿*—

The act of writing greases the skids. Once I begin, one story seems to follow hard and fast upon another. I take advantage of Djuna's frequent absence to ply my new trade. And why not? Why not turn these scribblings 'to account', as my father would say?

The Superfemale by Victor Hippolyte Rand

The Tour de France runs this year through the further removed peaks of the Alps and Vosges. Hundreds of cyclists line up, casting contemptuous glances at each other, dismissing the outlandish array of goggles, headgear, stretch pants and insignias as excessive, vulgar, hopelessly *ringard.*

I mount my *vélo.* That's v-é-l-o: velocity. In English, *bicycle.* The handlebars, the chassis, all of it luscious tubular steel, fresh from the craftsman's workbench in Lille or Marseilles, I'm not sure which. The seat, prong forward, perfectly adjusts to my height. It points, ever assertive, ever optimistic, always forward into the wind. Banter, the useless fruit of nervous anticipation, tarnishes the early morning breeze. Swallows take wing for the horizon.

The guy on my left looks around, takes one last hit on his *Gitane,* throws it aside, extinguishes it. No one seems to care — may he choke on his smoke! Competition is the name of the game. Last minute wagers are tendered, sponsors pat champions on the back, the rump, anywhere at hand.

I look up. A small flock of crows hovers in the near distance. I pay them no mind. I am not exempt from the jitters. I unfold my tour map and check the terrain. The race is legendary, mythic — for good reason. It is a bitch, a *putain de merde,* a living hell. Some have breathed their last rounding the final bend toward the finish line. So be it. Each to his own; each is here to win.

Off to a good start. We enjoy fellowship and ribaldry, watching the brisk play of clouds of a rosy-fingered dawn. The race is truly international in scope. Each rider contemplating the fate of the other, wondering who will survive the 4,000 km ordeal. The yellow bikes gleam in the pink of the sunrise and we laugh and joke and wish each other well. Jokes are tendered about the 'fair sex' and their exclusion from the race.

My cycling mate Alphonse Jarry snorts at this.

"Hah. They are too busy. They apply the makeup. And adjust the frilly undergarments. Hah."

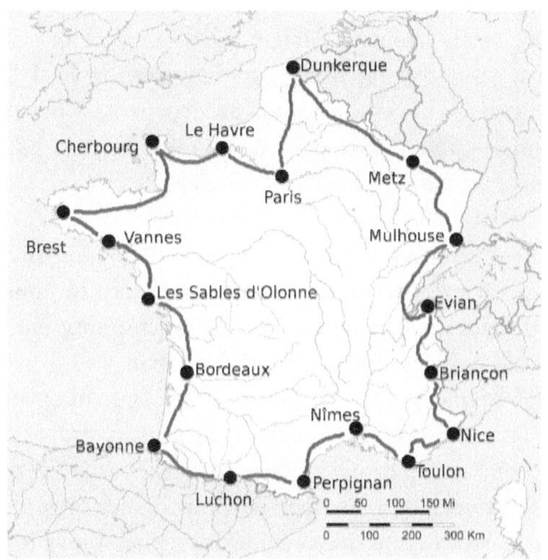

Route of the 1925 Tour de France followed counterclockwise, starting in Paris

The pistol is fired; the race is on. The peloton[7] moves as a single body down the indicated route, knowing full well that the transcontinental legs, followed by the perimetric stages of France, will test our mettle to the extreme. These men are my sole contact with humanity, my lifeline, for the next twenty-one days. Jules-Albert ('Zazi') and Didier Deschamps ('Samson') bring up the team's rear.

---

7   'Peloton' = Fr. for 'team'

I have been training for months. I have paced, timed and measured my endurance, building myself up, learning my weak spots, eating lean and healthy meals. Cigarettes and alcohol have fallen by the wayside, villainous companions my training self can live better without.

We pump, pedal, chuff and puff, hitting the 100 km signpost shortly after midday. The crows have followed, but we are accompanied now by flocks of other more agreeable (Scandinavian?) birds. My companions make great sport of 'portable' dining — munching on demi-baguettes, cutlets, and upending water bottles as they churn the road beneath their feet. Small islands of cheering fans greet us with a great show of applause and flag waving at 10 km intervals. This is a glorious enterprise — a beautiful thing! — and I'm glad of it, grateful to be a part of *sportif* humanity, humanity in gear.

Our enthusiastic debut is compromised for the moment by storm clouds; they are rolling in from the east. Drizzle turns to downpour. Instantly ponchos and macs appear — but there is no stopping now, no pause, not even in the eye of the storm.

With each passing hour, the catalogue of obstacles grows more ponderous. Laughable but grave: rain; summer hail; broken down lorries; herds of sheep and mountain goats; fears without name or number. My intrepid team mates *know* fear; they know it well. It takes many forms; always the challenge is to barrel through, pedaling as hard and fast as one can.

Dinner and Le Havre lie ahead. Few of us have appetites. We are too winded, too exhilarated, to eat. This too shall pass.

The Tour organizers gather the cyclists together for a word. Referees and team captains are unanimous: the remainder of the race will be continuous — there will be no more stops. We will bike the perimeter of France non-stop: no time for sleep, no time to think.

So be it.

To a man, we are in.

Truly, the race is on.

Several days later, practically rocketing from Metz to Mulhouse, I don't pause but I reflect. My body pedals, it is pummeled by the road, the wind, by the vapor trail each rider leaves behind. They are a grim competitive bunch and even at rest stops have very little to say. One fellow, pointedly anti-Semitic, pokes fun at the turbulent wake of the Dreyfus affair. I sit quietly, taking nourishment — I have nothing to say. Politics and the surrounding intrigue, the cabals, the innuendo: all of it leaves me cold. I am intent on racing. Racing and nothing but. I want our team to win.

The approach to the Jura and then the Alps is particularly treacherous. The organizers of the event decide in their wisdom that this year's Tour will *not* skirt these preposterous summits (yes, they are preposterous!) but will instead take them head-on. To a man, the riders protest loud and clear — but our cries go unheard. Do or die. Pedal on, boys...

The quality of mercy is not strained, however. We are not expected to conquer the Matterhorn, nor Mt. Blanc. Foothills and potsherd heaps will do.

Thirty kilometers into this stage Zazi develops a cramp. He lowers the wool stocking on one limb in order to scratch — rather furiously, truth be told — at the offending limb. Battling the wind, which at this point has grown fierce, I weave, narrowly avoid an escarpment...bringing myself up right beside Samson.

Samson pedals on, furiously, pretending I'm not there. In my haste I nearly topple off the cliff, a stunning drop and certain death the outcome of such a fall. The whistle, fastened to the lanyard yoked around my neck, comes in handy at such a time. I blow, I toot, I wheeze and finally — *le connard* — he looks.

He barely acknowledges me. Lifting a hand to his visor, he points ahead — where the dark mouth of a tunnel, bored deep into the mountainside, awaits.

I nod. Yes. I know about the tunnel. I point to Zazi, then to my calf.

Samson signs for me to ignore the other man. Incredible! Samson is so intent on winning that he is blind to — or simply cannot be bothered with — the suffering of others. *So be it.* His is a turn of the moral compass I am not willing to take. Instead, I sashay, at a breezy 12 km/hr, up to Zazi, hoping to learn more.

As team captain, Samson holds the (kit) bag.

I rehearse the application of dressings in my mind. Let's see: *iodine, Peroxide, gauze. Right.* I pedal on.

The tunnel is dark and meanders forever. None of us have slowed — that is suicide in a competition like this. Suddenly I hear a terrible crash, the certain crunch of metal and flesh, against the concrete wall. Looking back I see the dashed remains of a fellow from the opposing team, Germany or Luxembourg (can't tell which), too far gone now to cry for help.

"Fuck him," Samson shouts. With renewed vigor, we clear the damned space and are once again free.

Except perhaps for Zazi, who holds a bunched up tunic against his bleeding limb. He is bare naked from the waist up but clambers on, a hero in his own eyes and in the rabid eyes of his countrymen.

Before breaking out and moving ahead, I make another vain attempt to signal our captain.

Samson bows his head in mock deference and shouts, "Fuck him!"

Sadly, I begin to understand.

Days later, exhausted, deprived of nutrition and sleep, we leave the mountains behind — for now. The peloton rounds toward Nîmes...even in my depleted state, I am awestruck by the beauty of the coast. The lusty Mediterranean twinkles in this and in every kind of light. If I could, I'd gladly switch my place with any of those landlubbers I see shuffling lazily along the beach.

No matter. The race must go on. Only the strong survive. These and a hundred similar homilies ricochet stupidly through my head. For the last 60 km, Zazi has been hunched over his handlebars, veering from right to left, then back again, across the gravel road. No one seems concerned. I pull up to the fellow, thinking I will surely impress our captain with this latest disturbing sight.

Too late. Zazi's jersey, blazoned with the *Auto* and *Vélodrome* brands, hangs in tatters from his denuded ankle. The yellow tunic is now a sickly shade of prune, stained from repeated dousings with the poor fellow's blood. The wound is wide open, festering; I can even see the bone.

Samson looks back — why the unconscionable delay? He throws up his hands, but his trusty quadriceps do all the talking. He points at the sea — clearly he is annoyed. I pedal and pump, moving past Zazi who with his bike is lying all in a heap.

I know, I know: *Fuck him.* Tooth and claw it is — tooth and claw it will be.

I could sure use a nap.

Perpignon looms ahead. So do the punishing Pyrenees. Goodbye Mediterranean, somnolent sea, azure respite of my heart.

Up, up, up we go.. The foothills are entertaining but soon enough the way becomes steep. The grade alternates between jaw-dropping incline and near verticality. So what? Up we go.

My individuality, my sense of self, has long since evaporated. I am a husk, a shell, a carapace of muscle and grit mindlessly devoted to its grim task. I measure my progress and debility by stolen glances at Samson, but this is ill advised. He is stronger, he is captain. His persistence is nothing short of remarkable.

Then again, so is that of the lone rider several hundred meters ahead. This figure bobs and weaves against the near horizon. It is unclear which team this one athlete rides for. This champion is all vigor, vigor undeterred by obstacle. Accidents of weather, adversity, hazard — none suffices to bring the athlete down. With great effort I make out *Numéro 66* on the rider's back.

Word passes by chain of command from Samson on down. Word has it that something treacherous lies ahead. The fragrance of smoke on the air, at first welcome, turns bitter, then choking, telling all.

The peloton is headed straight into a blaze.

The terrain — mountain, path, thickets of knotty pine on either side — is consumed by flames. Roaring flames that lick the sky. Hanging back is not an option. 66 rides straight into the inferno, followed moments later by Samson, then by the rest. The conflagration consumes all available air, sucking the precious oxygen from the road in insane mouthfuls, depriving us of the substance of life.

My chest heaves, any effort to breathe is accompanied by terrible pain. I assume the others suffer the same. Samson's form — proud, unyielding, upright — leads the way. I imagine he is somehow following 66, who somehow skirts the flames, or rides straight through them — or both.

One fellow, a tall gaunt scion of the Danish team, bursts into flame. Bike and rider, trailing orange and blue fire, stop, then start, driven by the force of chance. Rider Denmark is crazy for water, anything to extinguish the blaze — which is now making short work of his jersey, his seat, his skin, his life — but the sea is long gone. The mountain is cruel and waterless.

Finally he explodes in a fireball of sinew, smoke and grit. I watch him convulse miserably, a sorry heap of cinders...a monument to the failed effort of wannabes reaching for the stars.

I look ahead and see a clearing. The climb before us is untouched by heat and smoke. For which I am grateful. 66, followed by Samson, followed by me, lurches ahead. Like the Danish rider, like the trees, the kilometers have disappeared behind us. There is only 66, Samson, me. A few stragglers bring up the rear.

The next town, Luchon, is our pole star. Infinities later we break through the mountains into a clear view of Bayonne. I am hungry, starved, exhausted beyond telling — but what else is new?

I could belabor the point. I could saddle the reader with the further agonies of the race. But I won't. Suffice it to say that Brest and Cherbourg briefly appear on the event horizon then are just as soon swallowed up. Samson has lost weight, his stocky profile now all muscle. 66, rider without a team, pursues a lone scout's path, leading the way. 66's reality becomes mine. What must it be like, riding like that, poised forever forward, always head of the pack? But 66, a solitary wraith, will not speak. For many kilometers now, this rider's posture has not varied: hunched at a right angle over the handlebars, never deviating from this dramatic pose.

But something has changed. Cyclist 66 shoots forward with an increment of fury. Le Havre, a welcome sight — it is the penultimate nonstop before Paris — looms, is upon us, then like all the rest becomes a thing of the past. The incline has leveled out and finally I am able to see 66.

Oh my God! 66 is a woman! My astonishment turns to awe. How on earth — ? Her hair, long strands of it, streams out behind her. I see an aviator's cap and smoked goggles. She is forever hunched over the bars, gripping them with unrelenting force. Samson acknowledges the mystery with a significant look.

First chance I get I take another look. She belongs to no team. Her legs are pistons, never varying in the depth and force of their stroke. Very strange...

The finish line is ahead. I know the Tour d'Eiffel will soon spring into view. I know this. Samson joins me, his curiosity piqued by the spectacle of the girl ahead. Together, Samson and I maneuver, making it so that we can pull up and catch a glimpse of the long-distance heroine.

What's this?

She is dead!

Gad...Samson takes his water bottle and hurls it at 66, whose body is yet a miracle, still pumping the pedals up and down, undistracted by the rude presence of death.

Dead. Samson's missile strikes the moving target without apparent effect: proof that the living soul of 66 has departed. When did she pass on? My visual memory draws a blank.

A sorry situation. The rider known as 66, whom I now think of as Jeanne d'Arc...the collapsed heap of her continually propelled forward by nonstop motion,

by ceaseless joyless pumping, by determination sur-
passing the limits of mere physicality.

She will hit the finish line first, dead or alive, no
matter which. This, of course, is unacceptable. I grit
my teeth, steel my resolve; I am determined to pull
ahead.

Paris at last. Samson is enraged; despite his best
effort he is still in second place. We watch with horror
as the cadaver on wheels breaks through the ribbon.

The crowd goes wild. Balloons fly, corks are
popped, festivity all around.

66 — Jeanne d'Arc, whoever or whatever she is,
transfixed by her bike — ascends to the sky.

There is applause all around...

I am proud of my work. I feel I have moved on to hitherto unknown
realms. My efforts at stage magic, such as they are, are passing, lukewarm.
They are stopgap, provisional — they put bread on the table and a roof
over my head. Stage magic gets me no closer to the ultimate Truth of
Things, which of course is where I want to go.

Ars medica — which I practice here and there, hither and yon — is
likewise deficient. Patients suffer and die all the time, despite (or because
of!) the best remedies of healers and quacks alike.

The stories, on the other hand, are my voice, my cry in the wilderness.
I labor over them, word for word, thinking of Djuna and the good life that
awaits. How proud she will be when she sees these!

I wander, I stroll, I sample the visual splendor of the city I call home.
The Pantheon, La Défense, Le Marais...each opening up with its cargo of
history and strife...the crazy surfeit of artistry and aesthetic combat that
makes Paris unique.

I have my own key by now, so I let myself in. Thin shafts of late afternoon sun percolate through the bare window, lighting up our bed — our
field of dreams. Djuna the elusive, Djuna the waif: I'm loving her, adoring
the very idea of her.

I wonder where she is.

In this pensive (almost elegiac) frame of mind, I reach for my knapsack.

A fresh look at my 'oeuvre' will remind me, along with the bed, the room, the utensils by the sink, of everything I hold dear.

The stories — my stories, all five of them — are gone. My precious work, the sweat off my brow, child of my loins, the blood of my marrow, etc., etc., — *gone*. Butterflies somersault in my gut. I feel I may faint. With racing heart, I grope for a nutmeg corn. Wrong. I grope for a chair. Then stand. Then I try to think.

Think. Where can they be?

Djuna won't be back till evening, late evening: she's off on another soirée. My patience runs out. I know she is at *Deux Magots.* It has been a point of pride with me to refrain from jealousy. At the very outset I vowed to never stalk, trail or otherwise make an issue of my...*needs...of* my possessiveness, which assumed monstrous proportions the moment she opened her arms to me. In the interest of self-interest...I should shield her, keep the green monster at bay.

But this is different: my stories are gone! Extreme circumstances call for hardy measures...so I head for *Magots,* covering the distance within minutes.

Two blocks...one block...I'm there. Then I see her, Djuna the flapper-manqué: marcelled hair, loops of costume pearls, half-slip bodice. A woman of her time, surrounded by admirers, who happen to be mostly men. Djuna holds forth, gesturing as she reads. A breeze kicks up and several pages fly from her sequined lap.

I deliberate then decide against a frontal assault. No. The circuitous approach is far more strategic.

I weave past the sidewalk tables into the bar. A drink is out of the question. I make for the side exit, placing me within ear- and eyeshot of the table.

God in Heaven, can it really be? The gentleman there, with the beard, the vainglorious one, the shit-faced Poseidon presiding, recently returned from the Spanish Civil War...the butch poetess, given to onomatopoeia, imbecilic word-play, vastly overfunded and overpraised...with her lieutenant 'e.e.', another promulgator of random inane verse...the Castilian satyr, six times a millionaire, welcome between the legs of every painter's model between here and Aragon...and that other famous alcoholic, scion of 'East Egg', whose adolescent scribblings place him securely in the ranks of reaction, privilege, and really bad writing?

Djuna sits among these, lording it over them, reading aloud. When they come up for air, during the rare intervals when they set down their drinks, they stare at her. In profound wonderment, no less. They are taken with her, with her *prose.*

I step closer.

Djuna, exhilarated at the attention, reads with gusto:

"I am Chohan of the Seventh Ray, the Heresiarch, the Anointed One."

Do my ears deceive? Can it really be?

"What else can I say? Seventy thousand years ago I was sent out from Atlantis...and founded the City of the Sun."

Those are my words! Djuna, with my story, basking in the adulation of the Inner Circle, has stolen my glory. Appropriated the thunder which should by all rights should have been mine.

Like Prometheus, I am chained to a rock.

I steal away, muttering: *Nevermore, nevermore...*

Come One, Come All!

"The unsatisfied need for the supernatural was driving people, in default of something better, to spiritism and the occult."

—Huysmans, *Là-Bas*

SIMPLY TOO MUCH. TOO much to bear, too much to live with.

I decide then and there to make good on Djuna's betrayal. They say living well is the best revenge.

She can have the stories.

I will have the women of Paris.

At first my strategies are freighted with impulsivity and haste. My thirst for vengeance obscures what could otherwise be a brilliant plan. I slow down — haste makes waste. I scout out likely venues and plan my attack.

I resume my one-man sideshow act — stage magic. This is a top hat I've worn before. But this time it will be different. I am committed to a purposeful campaign, an intentional campaign. My pincer movements will be staged front, right and center each at each step of the way.

The *zeitgeist* is with me, with no little help from my dad.

I show up at the butcher shop dressed to the nines, palms open. Ever the remorseful son. I present show bills, theatrical notices, favorable reviews: Father is duly impressed. He sets the meat cleaver down, jams a cigarette into his mouth, inspects my wares.

"Hmm," he says, "you've been busy. But with what?"

The business end of his *Gitane* glows (he works it like a cigar.)

"How much do you need?"

"Papa," I say, mock discomfiture dripping like an unstaunched wound.

"Tell you what," he says, reaching beneath the counter for his album of cheques.

"I'll give you five thousand — but strictly as a loan. One condition."

"Anything..."

"*Two* conditions: don't tell your mother. And don't expect me to show."

"Okay papa."

"I love you, Hippolyte," he says, then hands me the cheque.

Bank of Paris.

Ç est parti...

I hightail it to the bank, then to the printer. I've planned ahead. Equipped with an ambitious agenda — namely, rounding up the best and brightest occultists I can find — I proceed with my head-on assault. My reasoning goes like this: some of these 'savants' are phony, *but some are not.* If I can get them all in one place at the same time, get them to focus their collective energies on one goal — the manifestation of King Victor's dream — the arrows, including Cupid's, will surely fly. And no one, least of all the women, will be the wiser. Tally ho!

The flyers say it all. *Victor Hippolyte Rand, Magie de Paris.* The photo — me in top hat and tails, a bemused otherworldly look in my eyes — is grand. It is grand, it is specious; it is everything I want it to be. And the accompanying text promises the world: *Rand, sought out by Chancellors, Dukes, and Magisters alike, seeks the pleasure of your company. A Group Transubstantiation will be held at the Church of St. Sulpice, etc., etc....*

I consider the latter touch particularly inspired, St. Sulpice being the crossroads of many lines of force, of ley lines, of Huysman's Durtal, of innumerable cabals and illuminations before and since.

To spice things up, I also invite the dead and apocryphal, viz. St. Germain (of course!); Giordano Bruno; Galileo; Our Lady of Fatima; Hermes Trismegistus; Nicolas Flamel; Raymond Lully; Nostradamus; Paracelsus; 'pseudo-Agrippa'; Gilles de Rais; Robert Fludd; and last but not least, King Lamus (who does not show.)

Interesting how many members of the Paris illuminati are *women*. This suits me fine; the female vital energy will both equilibrate and supply the cosmic jolt I need.

—◊—

Come one, come all! Join 9th Degree Initiate Maître V.H. Rand, your host for <u>You Bet Your Eternal Life.</u> *Door prizes and honorariums for our worthy contestants.*

I'm pleased with the guest list. An additional perquisite leaps off the roster of the Chosen: namely, I may be able to approach — seduce! — some of the female invitees. The convocation I have in mind will pump me up in Parisian esoteric circles, elevate my reputation beyond reckoning. As top dog, I plan on sniffing out any and every bitch in heat...

Dismissive, banal, coarse: granted! What I have in mind goes beyond mere morality. It is a coming out of 'etheric' power — the best Europe has to offer.

Anticipating the event, I grind my teeth. There is much work to be done. My funds will not last forever. This may be my last shot at Eternity.

To the Society of Priests of Saint Sulpice:

I will soon be well known to you as benefactor, congregant, and faithful devotee.

I am truly blessed — the fortunate recipient of many years of Jesuit training. In exchange for the enclosed donation (the first of many), I hope to use the Church as a meeting place for a congregation of the Elect. If it please you Fathers, we can discuss this matter at your earliest convenience.

> *I am and shall remain,*
> *Your devout & humble servant,*
> *In recognition of the One True Christ,*
>
> *Victor Hippolyte Rand*

Money talks, money walks...Not long after, a tousled-hair choirboy shows up at my door bearing a personal invitation. Father Germain-Cohen [sic] has graciously placed himself at my disposal...

—⁕—

The church is ponderous, aimed at the sky like a missile in granite repose. Parishioners and clergy file in and out, paying homage to this Mighty Ark of the Lord. What we have here is more like an amphitheater or an arena than a house of God.

The name itself is redolent; it stinks of tradition. Perdition too... *Sulpicus Severus* (360-420), biographer of Saint Martin of Tours, preceded *Sulpitius the Pious* (d. 646) who survived *Sulpitius of Bourges the Severe* by fifty years. The Society itself, founded in 1646, has been dedicated ever since to the education of priests...and so much more.

Huysmans' Durtal tells us so. In *Là-Bas*, Huysmans describes another society altogether, a horde of overread, intoxicated, purblind initiates pursuing recondite pleasures of the flesh and spirit. Sulpice is an ideal setting for their diversions — a sacred backdrop for their less-than-sacred sport.

I am tempted to describe the many wonders of this building. In the interest of time I will refrain. Suffice it to say that each mullioned pane, each stone flag, roundly and soundly confirms my choice: St. Sulpice, a true spiritual arena, will suit.

—⁕—

Germain-Cohen is tall, of indeterminate age, shabbily dressed. His office, strategically placed above the transept, is practically inviolable. Clouds of smoke — a toxic spume of pipe tobacco, accumulated over many decades — curl from beneath the door. He admits me to his sanctum, studying me with rheumy eyes. He'd like me to have a seat.

"Where, Father?"

The question goes unanswered. There is no seat. He points the tip of his meerschaum at me, at the roll top desk, indicates I should sit. The tiny office, redolent, windowless, admits very little light. Stacks of paperbacks, about to topple, are arranged haphazardly around the room: *Simenon. Gérard Dixe. Black Mask.*

My interest is evident.

He tries to explain.

"It's a complete mystery," he says. "My mission as priest-detective is to solve it."

"Mystery, Father?"

"The greatest mystery of all time: who killed Jesus?"

"Everyone knows — "

"Everyone knows, everyone blows," he says. "Forget what you learned in school. The received wisdom is foolishness. *Une bêtise,* nothing but. Nothing but...How can I help you?"

I tend my offer — a monthly subscription of 500 francs, in exchange for the one time use of the premises — which beyond the first payment I have no intention of ever supplying. The matter is concluded.

We settle upon a time and date. He offers a hand.

A stack of yellowing dog-eared pulps leans precariously toward me.

"Watch the books," he says. "They topple."

—◦◦◦—

The good Father has agreed to help, even beyond the loan of the facility. We have planted at least a dozen of his flock in the audience, as shills, encomium-gatherers, founts of hearty applause. In top hat, tails and gaiters, I assist at the door, eying the rank and file of the Inner Circle as they make their way in.

They are an assorted bunch, some elegant, some dog-faced, but safe to say *civilized* as they make their way across the nave to find their seats.

I hand out business cards, paying particular attention to the women. Women...in evening gowns, in costume dress, some in street clothes...I see them all. I love them all. I lick my Astral chops...

The evening begins with an exercise in mind-reading: *What's My Sign?* We hand out nibs and paper, asking the lucky recipients to jot down the date (but never the year!) of their birth. This business of...*mingling*...of *making nice*...consumes several minutes, each more tedious than the last.

The ladies and gents scribble away. I descend from the stage, walking among them, winking my Third Eye. I exult in the moment — I am empowered. I am mighty, more capable this moment of seeing through them, through whoever dares to bar my way.

My 'sixth sense' frightens me though.

I'm learning too much — as I walk among the pews, 'a 'killing look' takes on a whole new meaning. Some of the assembled are paladins, Illuminati and Knights Templars of occult circles diverse and/or unknown. I feel in my pocket for my lucky charm: a particle of The True Cross, there in a phial among the loose change and lint of the day in my trouser pocket.

The silence of the gathered horde, such as it is, is misleading, specious: *these people don't need to talk. They can read each others' minds.*

A silver-haired gentleman in the first row, a wholly respectable type (a 'Monsignor' of the Church of Satan, as it turns out), moistens the tip of his tongue and smiles. I peer into his soul and find it grievously barren. I see a garret filled with *gamins,* with children plucked from the streets, waiting to be packed off to slave markets abroad. Two rows over, a wealthy abortionist, proud as a hen, discusses the going price of afterbirths...and heaves a discouraged sigh. Purveyors of sham news consider their next bold exposé, up to and including that of yours truly, and the present event. (This is unsettling.) Cabinet members, in the guise of masked revenants, hatch plans for pilferage, recalling an aphorism (from the cradle? from Spengler?): *Unrest is best...*A woman in tight satin broadcasts seduction; she will have her way with me first chance she gets. I cringe at the thought: not at all what I had in mind. A neocolonial type broadcasts an entirely different wavelength: *Rand is not an Oriental, far from it. He will pay for the error of his ways. I will cannibalize his business and give it a distinct*

Chinese flavor. A soignée lady in black has a parlorful of clients in bondage, awaiting further applications of the rod...

Enough! The spigot is dammed, corked, finished; the torrent of ideas stopped up. The show — my show — must go on.

Compared to this Niagara of mental detritus, the next phase is relatively tame. I catch my breath, gird my loins, and approach my shills. (Each wears a costume jewelry crucifix and so is easy to pick out.)

Mirabile dictu! Not only do I guess their sign, but I get each and every birthday (day, not year, remember?) right. Devious, *n'est-ce pas?*

———

The audience is pleased but restive. These top guns of esoteric 'science' want more. Admission is free, but they still want their money's worth.

Which they get, served up first as *Jehovah Jeopardy,* a competition in which players guess at the identity of mystagogues, demiurges, and satraps. Awards, *faux*-parchment scrolls honoring the occasion and the Master of the event — me — are handed out.

Grumbling is heard throughout the house.

"Ladies and gentleman, hold on to your hats," I tell them. "I have saved the best for last. In recognition of your valence, your indubitable power, allow me to present what is arguably the most dangerous yet most thrilling bagatelle of all: *Bardo Ball!*

"Those unfamiliar with this 'game' — and I use the term cautiously, for it is hardly a game — need not take part. Consider yourselves automatically excluded. And fortunate!

"Seekers after the Light — and the more rarified pleasures of the astral realm — know instinctively that it is wrong, always and deeply wrong, to call down a curse. Maledictions and the evil eye inevitably turn back on you, incurring a karmic debt that is all too often paid by the sender with death — and sometimes even worse...

"That being said, I now turn to you, *Mesdames et Monsieurs*, in my hour of need. I need two teams...of three courageous members each. Who will answer the call? Who will stake life and limb to promote a Noble Cause?"

I bow, I scrape, I manage a smile. From the sea of raised hands I quickly assemble a team, some of the characters familiar, others downright strange. Papus and Eliphas Lévi, followed by two women and a dog, shamble onto the makeshift stage.

I need two more bodies....but all hands are down. I consider streamlining the spectacle, reducing expectations and team size, when a man in circus tights strides onto the altar.

"I am Peloton, Joseph," he says, his considerable girth a statement in itself.

"And — " I begin, but am drawn up short.

A terrible racket, that of metal wheels abrading stone, interrupts the introductions, then rolls on, growing louder. A truncated woman, the upper half of her 'body' attached for better or worse to a platform, the whole unhappy affair on casters, steers itself toward our little group.

"I am Belle Hélène," she says, "darling of stage and screen. Please don't mind the wheels."

I scramble for things to say. I reach deep into my verbal bag of tricks, my sac of social savoir-faire, pulling out the big guns: heavy-duty conversational ordnance. The contestants line up. The onlookers, happy with the collection of freaks and psychic strongmen, finally quiet down. A hush descends upon the crowd.

All eyes — expectant, dewy, moist — are now upon *us*.

The spectacle unfolds.

—〰—

Here was a new side to Lévi, a side I had not seen: a conniving predator whose eyes, ferocious and dark, bore right into you, right into the skull. Likely he came to the event already prepared, of a mind to make short work of his opponent, Encausse (Papus.) These two, facing off upon the small stage like that, quickly become the center of attention.

Belle Hélène is not pleased but there is little she can do. She rolls a bit on the casters but at a glance from Lévi she desists.

I too am humbled. But I persist in my folly.

"Dearly beloved," I begin, "the object of the game is to disarm your opponent. Each team member will marshal his or her psychic abilities to the utmost. You must inflame, exhort, scare, incite — call it what you will — your adversary."

Papus' female companion raises her hand.

"Oh, is he here too?"

"Pardon. Sorry — ?"

"The Adversary," she says, "You know, with a capital 'A'..."

"Ah, rest assured madam, nothing of the sort," I say, casting a quick glance at Lévi. "Unless of course we *choose* to call Him forth."

Nervous laughter sounds across the room...

We hear from Papus next.

"Master of ceremonies," he says, "why not cut to the chase? I suggest a match between the, er, *Titans,*" he says, casting a look of pure vitriol at Lévi. "Lévi and myself. The Two Titans."

"Unless, of course, he in any way objects," Papus adds.

"Excellent idea," Lévi says, smoothing back the opera glove of one hand. "I was about to suggest something of the sort myself. This way the ladies — and the dog — can safely sit it out. It's going to get ugly, you know."

I study the crowd. Mild applause turns to fanfare. They want a match to the finish.

But Belle Hélène is not done.

"I can help," she squeaks, raising her voice over the fingernails-on-slate noise of her conveyance.

"Er —"

"I know these guys," she says. "Someone has to pick up the pieces. Lightning bolts, body parts, you know the drill..."

The audience is clapping in unison; now they are stomping their feet.

"What say you, gentlemen?"

"Agreed."

"Agreed."

"May the best soul win," I conclude. "Now shake hands and come out writhing..."

—∿—

We dim the lights and a hush falls over the room.

A somber other-worldly radiance shines from the sweat-drenched brow of each contestant.

Each has fallen into a deep trance.

Papus is the first to speak. The portentous syllables that emerge are no longer Papus. In fact they are hardly recognizable as human. Instead, Papus is the mouthpiece for The Dark Force, a force older than human time, that speaks through him. In clotted and choked syllables, it directs its wrath at Lévi.

"Eliphas," it intones, *"I know you! Lévi, Levite, tribe of Abraham and Sarah...miserable cur, you wander the earth alone. I know your fatal infirmity. Now it can be revealed."*

Lèvi's amusement turns to perplexity. He seems to hang on every word.

"Simpleton, curmudgeon, yardstick of despair, disease, distress...your weakness is revealed: you love to eat!"

Lévi is unprepared for this. He recoils.

Belle Hélène rolls back and forth, emitting a continuous low squeak. Papus continues:

"Viands, legumes, fruits de mer...Baguettes, broccoli, bouillabaisse, brioche, beef bourguignon; confit, cassoulet, croissants...and we still have most of the alphabet to go. Should I go on?"

Lévi is incensed, furious at the public disclosure. He rolls back a sleeve, moves toward the podium and announces that the baton is now his. It is his turn to strike.

"I tell you M. le President," he says (no idea why he calls me that, but I like it, definitely like it), "my opponent will stop at nothing to sully my good name."

Lévi waves at the pews. "Let the gracious among us pardon what comes next. What, in a word, I must do. Forgive me, one and all."

Something tugs at my pants leg — it is Belle Hélène. I *shush* her and return Lévi's stare. Powerful magic is coming our way.

———⁂———

Eliphas Lévi draws himself up to his full stature — all 1.7 meters of him, elongated and elaborated by his pronounced beard — and snarls at the crowd. He cups his hand and announces, "Close your minds. Shut your hearts. What I'm about to bring down is for *his* ears only."

A murmur of disaffection ripples down the room. He is sparing them. They don't yet know from what.

"My learned adversary," he begins, directing his remarks at the other bearded man, "Huysmans describes you as *le gentilhomme qui se contente de ne rien savoir* — the man who is happy to know nothing. Joseph Boullan is of the same opinion. As am I. It is high time to draw our psychic swords."

Papus manages a sneer, a snort, then winks in derision.

"Faites vos jeux, mon cher," he says.

"I speak to you from a deep place," Lévi continues. "The place of your dreams. A place you can no longer call your own. It is now populated by phantasms, by sigils and devices far beyond your knowing."

"Ha! I'll believe that when I see it," Papus says. "Is that all you've got?"

"Not really, *mon vieux,*" Lévi retorts.

Lévi flashes a silver tipped wand at him, makes circles in the air.

The atmosphere grows heavy, dense, almost fetid. Papus sprouts feathers from his belly and chest. The onlookers are stunned — tickled pink at what might come next.

"I draw down from the Infinite," Lévi explains. "The Etheric is at my command. Check this out..."

Papus, feathers and all, is considerably ruffled. He scratches at his backside. Just in time he lowers his trousers and drawers. A large egg, bigger than an ostrich's, drops from his ass.

Lévi chuckles. "Is there a nest in the house? Bed of straw, anyone?"

Belle Hélène, on top of the escalating situation, is about to lend a hand. Suddenly all vestige of poultry disappears: egg and feathers are gone.

"Just a portent," Lévi says, "of what lies in store. Lots of gore which you shall deplore. I can hex you so hard you won't know which end is up. I'll wager you can't tell false from true."

Papus has heard enough. Hitching up his pants, he signs with his free hand. Immediately his opponent is surrounded by vipers, coiling and snapping at their intended prey.

Lévi outsmarts. Instantly the wand becomes a flute, a bagpipe, a clarinet. Lévi toots on each of these in turn; the writhing tatterdemalion dissolves.

The crowd is stupefied.

Still they want more.

Papus senses this; he knows the moment is right.

With glee he points a finger at Lévi.

"Cicada season!" Papus cries; a horde of locusts, ten thousand crazy mischief-makers, invade Lévi's privates.

It's Lévi's turn to scratch.

"Turn it off, Gérard, turn it off," he pleads. "I'll be your best friend..."

"Too little, too late," the other says. But Lévi has more than one trick up his sleeve. Reaching nether-deep, he hurls a handful of the critters across the stage. They hop, they leap, some of them fly...right into Papus' open mouth.

"A pox on you!" Lévi intones. Then, confiding in his rapt listeners, "cancel that. Forget about pox. A full Biblical plague is what you deserve... and is what you're going to get!"

Heaps of bugs melt into thin air, replaced by pustules and weeping buboes: flocks of them, fighting for space on Papus' hands, neck, face. Papus shudders, then reminds himself that this manifestation of wrath is an illusion, that the power of mind can also make them disappear.

"Harrumph," he bellows, "take this!"

Papus claws at his face, glaring — always glaring — then hurls a terminal oath at Lévi.

"A curse on your first born, to the seventh generation," he says.

Lévi, a quick study, snaps right back.

"No fair!"

The situation is out of hand. Those in the front rows cast imploring looks my way: *do something, anything*...salvage the situation, make a difference...

I muster my most soothing, conciliatory tone.

"Gentlemen: please. No name calling. We'll have none of that."

The entire building, roof included, trembles.

Billows of sulphurous smoke paint the aisles yellow and black.

General pandemonium, accompanied by a great deal of coughing, ensues.

—⁓—

The sequence of events that follows is hard to describe, let alone believe.

The Mage known to the world as Éliphas Lévi Zahed totters, falls in a heap, instantly replaced by a glowering, glittering Phoenix, a mythical bird of fierce aspect and giant proportion. The creature scries its whereabouts, makes its way to the cathedral's double doors. Hinges creaking, beams protesting, the doors fly open at the eagle's approach.

Gérard Encausse (Papus), a Mage in his own right, is likewise soon replaced. The grizzled gentleman, still smarting from his sores, makes his way to the steps of the church. No one objects. No one bars his way. In the blink of an eye he is transformed: a sloe-eyed green skinned dragon, its scales and wings rippling lazily in the breeze, takes his place.

Were it possible, battle lines would be drawn. Instead, shopkeepers fly to shield storefronts with cardboard, with stanchions, with whatever comes to hand. The battle is about to start. Fire will be breathed; buildings toppled, lives lost.

No one can be sure.

The resemblance of the pair (Lévi, Papus) to statuary is remarkable. The bird's beak, a hook-like promontory extending a full two meters beyond the body, snaps at the air. It seems to *savor the moment*. Its opponent casually lumbers up beside it, unclenching its reptilian jaws, threatening, only threatening, a torrent of scathing flame.

The griffin (that's what it is: part lion, part eagle, all quadruped) beats a wing, acknowledging the presence of the other. For the moment it does little else. The dragon uncoils a serpentine neck (actually, there are three), pulls back, snaps at the bird. Who, outraged by the vicious attack, fans its wings in protest, toppling dragon...who for a moment lies akimbo, belly up, belly exposed. The griffin dives, making for the lizard's soft parts. The griffin lunges and pecks.

A brown smudge of reptile liver oozes forth.

This is more than the dragon can take.

(Meanwhile, police have cordoned off the church. Only firemen and ambulances enter the scene. Women and children are led away. The authorities do what they can.)

The dragon shows his true colors (ambergris green, toad brown) breathing fire, the nostrils twin Hellesponts of flame.

An apocalyptic roar fills the district, outdistancing the sirens of *pompiers* and police. Rising on the currents, the dragon suddenly ensnares the eagle in the coils of its middle neck. Wings slam up and down, fluttering in insane counterpoint to this primeval *pas de deux.*

Payback time. The mighty dragon hurls its winged prey against the stones of Sulpice; several are dislodged. Without pause, the phoenix regroups, hurling itself, a veritable missile from Hell, straight at the dragon's flank. Said body part instantly whips back, avoiding another painful jab.

The dragon rears on massive hindlegs, bracing for another assault. Wisps of smoke then actual flame arc through the sky, toasting the bird but not bringing it down. A calculated wing beat (dragon's, not bird's) grazes the errant griffin, tumbling it ever closer to its enemy, still waiting for it there in the public square. A sudden clawing action rakes the griffin's flesh, three rivers of bright orange *ichor* flowing forth.,

Maddened, the griffin ascends to the level of the tallest building top. Taking the measure of its opponent, it delays no further and dives, catching the dragon completely unaware. The griffin's beak sinks to the hilt deep into the dragon's eye. The dragon, now stunned, swipes like a dazed gladiator at the empty air.

Another precious moment forfeited to the game. The griffin, who seems to beat a hasty retreat, in fact does the opposite. Griffin idles for a moment, then swoops, once again catching the larger creature completely off guard. The yellow beak plunges, plunges in full throttle, transfixing the dragon where it really hurts — its bursting liver. The dragon screams in protest, its mammoth heap collapsing down upon the spindly legs beneath.

Griffin takes to the skies. I am relieved: we have been spared further spectacle, (human) loss of life, certain disaster.

The tumult in the street tells me otherwise. Who will be held accountable for this primordial circus? What to do with the massive carcass bleeding out on the church steps?

I look around.

This would be a perfect time to start smoking.

I dismiss the thought at the sight of a very familiar face: my father!

There he is, in all his drab glory: blood-stained apron, beret, fixed grin.

He runs right up, takes my arm.

"I saw the whole thing," he says.

"What do you think?" A stupid question, if ever there was one...

"What do I think? A butcher's son, and you have to ask me what I think?"

Father points at the still quaking mass of the dragon, its green hide now turning a salacious blue in the lamplight.

"I think you have a public health situation here," he says. "And a once-in-a-lifetime opportunity."

"Opportunity? How so?"

Père Rand rises to the occasion — majestically. He signals to a truck (*Rand et Fils* stenciled in tall letters on the side), which weaves through the traffic and stops. Two smiling butcher boys — my surrogates, I suppose — emerge at the curbside. The gleam in their eyes matched only by the gleam of their sharpened cutlery: saws, knives, axes.

Father takes a closer look. The 'opportunity' is already thick with flies.

"Hack it up, boys," he says.

Tools in hand, they set to work.

My success is instantaneous. Occult circles near and far ask for subscriptions, beg for an audience — five minutes, *anything* — with 'Maître Hippolyte.' The floodgates are open.

Students flock to me like fleas to a mangy mutt.

I surprise even myself. I am puzzled, confounded actually, by the lack of publicity. No mention of dragon or phoenix, conflagration or cosmic battle, in any of the morning papers. The unlikely appearance of Père Rand a gilded lily in the garden of apparent hallucination...

There remains only the gentle zephyr of springtime, wafting the sweet taste of last evening's performance, of my awesome victory.

Once the smoke clears, it comes to me.

I have somehow magicked the gathered initiates of Europe — convinced them one and all that the evidence of their senses — raptor and saurian locked in combat — was completely real. Hence my popularity, my charm, and my infinite appeal!

Contributions flood the offices of *Figaro* in my name. Would-be benefactors clot the mail with inquiries and donations. This is good, very good. I lease office space — there is an immediate administrative, logistic and didactic burden; I must be equal to the task.

The following day I send the following notice out — *Maître Hippolyte, Occult Acolyte, Seeks Clerical Support.* The candidates, who arrive by foot, by wagon, by limousine, are a variegated, bimodal lot: they are Seekers After the Light, or Seekers After Centimes. I make a game of this, but this is a game I cannot win: candidates from opposing camps are functionally indistinguishable. Most are female; all want *something...*

—⁓—

Nothing casual about any of this. My Hippolyte College of Higher Learning: *All Will Be Revealed,* is dead serious in intent. What began as fancy, mere ambition, is now alive and kicking and very much wanting to thrive. There are hundreds of seekers clambering for light. My responsibility is enormous; I am determined to see it through.

I study the boulevard from the 'French' doors of my expansive (and very expensive!) office suite. Merry children on bikes; merchants tending shops; lorries (will I ever be rid of these?) clattering along...

The broad sweep, the sheer plenitude of it all, hits me at once.

I must rise to the occasion. I need a philosophy. I need words — not drivel

— to live by. In order to teach, I must learn. The learning must be inspired.

This is where book knowledge comes in. The hours spent hiding from the Brothers, buried among my books, hours devoted to insane bouts of reading, finally make sense. The *Massif Central* of information I received at one address or another, the pamphlets, white papers, feuilletons, almanacs, the rag-tag instruction in the mystic arts: all will serve. I thank my stars for these, even for the misaligned contacts with the lesser lights of the esoteric realm. Ultimately it was all useful; all will serve.

William Blake had it right.

The Road of Excess leads to the Palace of Wisdom...

—⁓—

I apply myself to the task. I construct a System. The Hippolytic System begins where neo-Platonism leaves off, effectively streamlining the wisdom of the Occident, bringing it into mystic harmony with the yogic practice and wisdom of the Far East. (The homilies of King Lamus find their way in here too.)

—⁓—

This is what I believe, this is what I teach:

The physical universe, and the metaphysical one which surrounds it, are governed by Cause and Effect. For every Cause, there is an Effect. For every Effect, there is a Cause.

Not all causes and effects are visible.

Each of us is a Center of Light.

Light has many wavelengths; some are perceptible, some are not.

Each being is driven by Will, conscious or un-. We *will* things to take place, through active or passive desire.

Example: I decide to decorate my office. I want a painting by Max Ernst on the wall. Money changes hands at a gallery; hammer and nail are recruited; the picture is up. My desire is actualized.

Some effects require more arcane — that is to say, less visible — methods. Courtship of the woman of my dreams unfolds in a sequence of both visible and (para)visible behaviors. The array of proximal causes becomes manifest...once she is in my arms!

There is nothing supernatural about any of this. Far from it. The argument from cause to effect is scientific and amenable to observation.

It can even be reproduced.

The mind is an engine of terrific force, the repository (they say) of all the power in the universe. The same atoms and energy that populate the stars course through each of us. Harnassing that energy means tapping into the motive power of the universe.

And that's not all. The ancients taught that the Grand Design of the planets and stars is replicated in the microcosm of man. The mind interacts with other minds (and with the world around it) in myriad ways. 'Powerful' thoughts and feelings — specifically, *thought-forms* — are the motive force behind action. Thought-forms are expressions of concentrated, sharply-focused Desire.

Supremely focused Thought, accompanied by strong feeling (i.e., passion), acquires the momentum of comets. It charges forth into the world and, metaphorically speaking, can even raise the dead. Each of us is a Creator. Actively or passively, we send out mind-missiles — *thought-forms* — and in so doing change the world.

Those who do this actively, volitionally, are *the* true magicians. Those who do not are victims of their appetites and their misguided (because unfocused) ambition.

It's simple: *Create;* don't *react.*

Simple, abstruse and arcane.

Got it?

—

Echoes of distant thunder. All across Europe rising prices, unemployment and inflation rattle nerves. Devotion to my newfound mission keeps the blinkers on...but certain developments are hard to ignore.

General strikes and unrest are in the air — particularly in Germany, where men in brown shirts are fomenting discord, pointing fingers, calling for a new order. The former Adolf Schickelgruber, reemerged as 'Hitler', has burst upon the scene, promising a return to that nation's imperial past. The German economy is poised for re-armament; the continent is unprepared for the brewing maelstrom, for the storm that is sure to come.

I have other fish to fry. My curriculum, my school, my reputation are on the upswing, each a blazing success.

I burn through a series of receptionists, assistants, office managers. None are to my liking.

Then I meet Her. I meet Her in the most unlikely way...

Traffic on the Boulevard Haussman is crazy. Citizens wave fists and sticks, threatening to take matters into their own hands. Horns, sirens, and whistles so loud they shatter the morning calm, percolating through the windows of the office suite. Even the lorries grind to a stop.

Finally I take a look.

Why the racket? Rather officiously, almost in a lather — after all, I am chancellor and headmaster of Hippolyte Higher Learning — I step out into the day.

A vision in cambric greets my eyes.

A woman, no older than twenty-five, carefully dismounts her steed — actually, a camel, freighted fore and aft with fabrics, jewels and flowers of the season.

Moving toward her, I catch my breath. None of this comes easy. Her voice — charming, questing, intelligent (all at the same time) — eases my pain.

"Maître Hippolyte?" she says.

"Indeed," I say.

"So formal!" She laughs, extends a lovely hand.

I glance at the camel. "Well, it's not every day — "

"Oh, that?" She makes light of my awe. She waves a hand; a sherpa steps forward.

"Geraldo," she says, "please. We're creating a disturbance."

"Ma'am," he says, leading the sleepy dromedary off.

I see that her eyes are brown, almond shaped, quite perfect. Still smiling, she bows.

"Alexandra," she says. "Alexandra Peel." She notices the building behind me. The sign over the door captures her interest.

"Well," she says, "I'm here. Ready for an honest day's work." Her innocence is disarming. Her smile, her affability, her poise — are sublime. Clearly, she is in charge.

"Good," I say. "So am I. Right this way."

She/Her/Djuna/June

The interest, love and otherwise, is mutual. She knows all about me. I know very little of her.

That defect is soon filled in.

Her knowledge of Tibet, including the language (written Sanskrit), is phenomenal. Already in her young life she has been everywhere. She speaks a half dozen tongues. She has charmed the pants off seneschals, dukes and kings. Her knowledge of books and occult traditions is alarming. Yes, she knows Lamus — after all, she is from England. What else do I need to know?

She skirts over her wants, her needs, hardly explains why a woman like her might want to work for a man like me.

Alexandra is an 'empath.' She sets my accounts — literal and otherwise — completely in order. Attends to me in the greatest and smallest of ways. Tells me how to dress, how to speak, when and where to appear. Grooms me. Encourages my dependency on her in every way: *La petite mère.* I love it.

Her fits of self-doubt slay me. Alexandra looks down at the floor, tenders an insouciant half-smile, looks away. The first kiss, a hurricane, ushers in all sorts of tempests... we are supreme lovers, matched souls, twin cargoes heaven-bound...

One thing disturbs me.

One thing leaves me unimpressed.

I share.

"Alex," I say. "One thing leaves me unimpressed."

"*Cheri,*" she says, "only one thing? Tell me. What it is? What could be so bad?"

(Her months on the steppes betray themselves in the rearrangements of her occasionally fractured French.)

I mention another Alexandra (whom we left to the Hereafter, tumbling down a frozen Himalayan crevasse.) I mention this Alexandra's strange resemblance to the doomed mountaineer.

"Mere coincidence?"

This Alexandra doesn't miss a beat.

"*Alors,*" she says, her smile so all-embracing I want to kiss her. "I knew that was coming."

"Here," she says, "Read this and weep."

She hands me some pages, loosely cinched with a riband. The words, familiar to me, run together through my tear-filled eyes.

Cagliostro! My story!

"Where — ?"

"Lo-lo," she says, moving closer with every word, "take a better look."

All I see are words. Rivulets and streams of words I wrote what now seems a very long time ago...

"At me, not at the page..." she says.

The gods on Olympus clap and cheer. A thunderous tumult rising...my chest is heaving and about to explode.

"Djuna!" I shout. "Can it be?"

I can't believe what I see. Alexandra — the intrepid explorer, championess of international suffrage — and prodigal Djuna, are one and the same! We embrace.

Djuna showers me with kisses and love.

—⁄\/\⁄—

Later, much later, explanations emerge.

Alexandra — now Djuna — delicately explains.

"Alexandra was lost somewhere in Tibet...only to resurface — apocryphically speaking, mind you — as the Fiji mermaid. That's neither here nor there. Bottom line: 'Djuna' — *me* — is the latest avatar of 'Alexandra'. Formerly known as Ishtar, Esther, Nefertiti...I am SHE. Must I go on?"

"Please don't," I say. "I'd rather kiss you."

"By all means," she says.

So I do.

—⁄\/\⁄—

We have really set up shop, occupying not only the suite of offices but splendid apartments opposite the Luxembourg Gardens, paid for by our growing revenue. Djuna the Visionary, Djuna the Spectacle-Monger, decorates the place like a sultan's palace.

—⁄\/\⁄—

A contemporary sultan. Glass brick, mostly blue, sits well with zebra woods and mahogany décor, illuminating two very grand pianos...Metal accents shiny with mirrored surfaces fairly cover the place. Art Deco and Bauhaus galore! All well and good; a much-needed woman's touch, I tell myself, pocketing the loose change...

With expenses like these, there isn't much. Add Djuna's afternoon '*faire des courses*' at Avenues Montaigne and shopping at *George Cinq*, and I'm one foot in the poor house. (Well, not yet anyway...)

Her newfound taste for *haute couture,* for costume, for expensive evenings at the opera and the most *recherché* spots in town — doesn't surprise me in the least. This is the same woman who breaks bread with expats and surrealists in the demi-monde; the very same woman who unflinchingly dismounted a camel not too long ago outside my office door.

What does surprise me is the sharp detour in her musical taste. I find her hunched over notices of Wagner festivals this (and every) time of year at Bayreuth...in the guise of tomfoolery, she brings home carloads of opera gear, tridents, Valkyrie hats, breastplates...

I confront her but she only laughs. Didn't I know that she hails *from a long line of Teutonic royalty,* on her mother's side?

She giggles, fastening a horned helmet to her head. Which oddly enough seems to fit.

"I am Brigid von Ribbentrop, Princess of the Vulgarians," she giggles. *"C'est drôle, n'est-ce pas?"*

Not really — *non.* What happened to my *petit chou-chou,* happy to crawl into our bed with a bottle of cheap wine and a handwritten poem?

As if to soothe me, to chill my inflamed nerves, Djuna strikes a new pose — she reads to me in bed.

⁓⁓⁓

At first I protest. The last thing I want after midnight (we rarely hit the sheets before morning) is a whopping dose of fairy tale. No matter how fetching the reader...how charming the Scheherazade...the main thing at that ungodly hour is *to sleep.* No matter. Princess Djuna gets her way. With minor variations, from one night to the next, the story she reads (poem, fable or lullaby) runs like this:

Great Odin, mustaschioed ruler of Asgard,
Valiant Über hero come to claim his due,
Vanquish the lily-livered weaklings,
The notary, the gypsy, and the Joo...

"The Joo?" I ask. "What means — the Joo?"

"Oh nothing, silly. Just a word."

She replaces the book — *Grimmoire's Fairy Tales* — an edition I have never seen, incidentally; then turns over in the bed beside me and stares up at the light.

I reach for the bedside lamp but she takes my hand.

"No, *mon coeur,* there's more."

There's always more.

"Please, listen...I so want your thoughts on this. You're so good at these *bookish things.*"

A better man would silence her. Or toss her out on her ear. But there she is, pouting, mawkish, hardly a woman but no longer (was she ever?) a girl.

"I'm tired of *Deux Magots.*"

Could this be the good news I've been waiting for?

"Hemingway bores me," she says. "The man lives inside a bottle. Pound is crazy. And Picasso..." She sighs. "Simply cannot keep it in his pants."

"Agreed," I say. I'm liking this — very much. "Tell me more."

"Life is about change, *cheri.* Half the battle is knowing when to move on. It's time I moved on."

Bon sang — sounds good to me! I hope against hope she is referring to me...to us...to our ever-shifting arrangement.

She is not.

Art, and artistic circles, she explains, are not matters of *life and death.* Only philosophy, philosophy and politics and philology, will answer. These are the true calls-to-arms.

What do I make of...Schopenhauer? Nietzsche? Heidegger?

Can I relate?

I know these names. As she recites them, the harsh syllables gliding so easily off her tongue, I shudder. This is my girl? This, the woman who shares my ambition, my dreams, my bed? Celebrating the ascendancy of the Ur-Man, the Ur-State, the *Führer?*

She immediately recants.

"Oh darling," she says, looking into my eyes, "it's nothing as serious as all that. But when it comes to foreign affairs — the march of the Reich, that is — I think we can be gracious enough to mind our own business. And turn the other cheek."

—∿—

Hitler in Poland, Belgium and France — *'foreign' affairs?* Hardly!

Across the border, things are heating up. The National Socialist (a.k.a. Nazi) takeover of Austria is a festive event, celebrated in beer gardens across that land. Adolf Hitler, *Wundermensch*, in his side-car, shuffles merrily along...

JOURNAL OF ELDRITCH SCIENCES.
Journal of Eldritch Sciences (Silesia, 1952)

Looking back, historians and journalists alike recognize that Adolf Shicklegrüber, a.k.a. Adolf Hitler, may have belonged to a so-called 'Black Lodge'. This was the Thule Order of Tibetan Black Magicians. The Lodge was formed to further the nefarious aims of the Third Reich, and stopped at nothing — including satanic rituals, and animal and human sacrifice — to ensure the victory of Hitler's Wehrmacht.

What to make of Evil in the world? What would become of those who actually opposed the onslaught of tyranny and fascist rule? One Czechoslovakian mage[8], deported to a camp for his refusal to collaborate, imagined he was working off 'bad karma' earned in a previous lifetime as Hermes Trismegistus, a Mahatma whose legacy includes the Emerald Tablet, and a complete reworking of sympathetic magic.

---

8   This was Franz Bardon, a Czechoslovak occultist whose life and work run curiously parallel to Rand's. In the introduction to his minor masterpiece, *Initiation into Hermetics* (1956), Bardon writes: "Anyone who should believe to find in this work nothing else but a collection of recipes, with the aid of which he can easily and without any effort attain to honor and glory, riches and power and aim at the annihilation of his enemies, might be told from the very inception, that he will put aside this book being very disappointed. Numerous sects and religions do not understand the expression of "magic" otherwise than black art, witchcraft or conspiracy with evil powers. It is therefore not astonishing that many people are frightened by a certain horror, whenever the word "magic" is pronounced. Jugglers, conjurers, and charlatans have discredited this term and, considering this circumstance, there is no surprise that magic knowledge has always been looked upon with a slight disregard."

METAPHYSICAL TECHNOLOGIES.

*Homesick for homeland, Daedalus despised Crete
And his long exile there, but the sea held him.
"Though Minos blocks escape by land or water,"
Daedalus said, "still, the sky is before us,
And that's the way we'll go. Minos' dominion
Does not include the air." He turned his thinking
Toward unknown arts, changing the laws of nature.*
                    —Ovid

...The purpose of art is not the release of a momentary ejection of adrenaline but is, rather, the gradual lifelong construction of a state of wonder and serenity.
                    —Glenn Gould

Evidently some people will come to the conclusion that several of the political movements or parties are performing an indirect magical action with the gesture of salute, and in this manner supply the general reservoir with more, however small parts of the vital power, by constant repetition. We shall remember the salute of the German Nazis, consisting in a lifting of the hand and certainly representing a certain gesture of power. But if such an increased collective power reservoir

> *is used for greedy and questionable purposes, this mentally strained power is turning against the founders because of its polarity, and decay and destruction will follow, apart from the fact that the curses of the absolutely innocent victims pining in prisons, sentenced to death or sent to hopeless battles in the field, will invisibly produce an opposite polarity that will also contribute to the decomposition of the power reservoir."*
> —Franz Bardon

Piece by piece, I construct a technology. Yogic texts, handbooks of meditation, precepts of the ancients, all agree: the mind can be honed, razor sharp, into a tool of inconceivable power.

———∿———

I start, end and fill my days with self-mastery. Breath control, muscle relaxation, and active perception are key.

Each morning, and each night before sleep, I gather my senses, in-fold my awareness, visualizing a spinning cone of white light that shields me from the tumult of the world. I sharpen my senses, appreciating tastes, textures and sights as I never have before. Walks down the boulevard are an exercise in memory and acuity: what have I just seen? Can I recall, down to the finest detail, the shape, color and sound of each passing car, lorry, pedestrian? I practice the art of heightened visualization, of intense recall. This is of inestimable value during the evening, when I do my trance work.

I dedicate — and sanctify — a corner of the library to this work. The room, its artfully arranged bookshelves and *fauteils,* is conducive to trance. Arranging myself comfortably, I inhale...each breathe fortifying, as it were, the column of silver light that encloses my spirit, my labor, my astral girth. Aiming for emptiness, for the boundless, I eventually achieve my goal: the absence of thought, of sensation, of awareness. I have created a blank canvas. Now I can paint.

The work is sacred — and dangerous. With the aid of active imagination, I invoke — and see — the Four Archangels, investing them with power and spinning light. Breathing in, I summon mightily: Michael,

Raphael, Gabriel, Uriel, each in their robed and flaming glory, protecting my magical work at the four cardinal points — North, South, East and West. They are here to protect me, to guide me, to support my crusade beyond the etheric divide. All of this achieved, I can 'fill in the blanks'. I can summon what, and whomever, and whatever I want at will. The Power of the Universe courses through...

A further digression, if I may. Proper understanding of religion, of mythology, across all historical epochs and lands, yields fantastic fruit. Pantheons of deities, gods and goddesses — whether Hindoo, Jain, Greek or Roman — ultimately sort out the same.

The centers of force — 'gods', 'goddesses', 'chakras', 'sephiroth' on the kabbalistic Tree of Life — are one and the same. This is potent knowledge, knowledge that can be immediately harnessed for the betterment of self — and mankind. The Moon power, for example, located at the base of the spine, governs reproduction...the unconscious...the element of Water and the ebb and flow of the tides. The Solar power, at the umbilicus, identified with the Christ, harmonizes the activity of the powers above and below. Kether, the *Summum bonum,* located in the brain/mind, is the site of highest possible attainment, where union of the microcosm of man is achieved with the macrocosm of the universe. Contact with these centers, and masterful orchestration of their energies, facilitates magisterial control over the self — and the world.

Need I say more?

Consecrating my magickal space, I evoke a host of sylphs, salamanders, faeries and gnomes. Over the course of many evenings, by candle or lamplight, I invoke a demon horde, knowing their accumulated spoor will advance my cause: *Abraxas, Agailiarept, Manu, Alal, Alastor, Apophis, Asmodeus, Azaz'el, Baal, Banshee, Baphomet, Beelzebub, Belial, Chemosh, Damon, Demogorgon, Furfur, Hag, Jinn, Kokabiel, Legion, Lucifuge, Nar-as-sammum, Pazuzu, Satanacia, Sut, El Tio, Tengu, Wendigo,* and *Zachan.*

Believe me: there are more.

—⟡—

How this might play out will become clear in short order.

Effective magic — successful transmutation of the will toward a given end — relies on *passion;* on frequent repetition of the stated desire; and most of all, upon *specificity*. Violation of any of these cardinal principles will result in a 'working' gone awry.

The following serves as an example:

I've already described the somewhat *louche* spending habits and pastimes of *mon amour*. Thinking I had successfully arraigned and trammeled Djuna's profligate spending, imagine my surprise at finding three closets' worth of brand-new gowns...slippers...robes...and undergarments, still unopened parcels fresh from the best shops in Paris. To prevent fresh assaults upon our finances, I had girded up my own spiritual resources... applied them night after night in conjurations of the deities of *Malkuth,* the 10th station on the kabbalistic Tree of Life. Malkuth: the sphere of Earth, of ground, of 'the buck stops here.' Night after night I applied myself to the task, appealing to the Malkuthian spirits, winning their favor with the deepest of trances, with heartfelt *simpatico*. Gnomes — furry little things, spirits of the earth, weevils really — clambered about the room, applauding my not unreasonable demand.

"She will stop her spending NOW!" I roared, to the general approbation of these tiny spirit familiars.

"Henceforth her wallet will be FROZEN!" I bellowed, the shutters and chandeliers resonating in seraphic harmonic accord.

I was shocked at the sheer mass of needless expanse, of unabashed self-indulgence, thrown open to my eyes as I stood before those infernal closets: my foxy hellion once again had made the rounds of every boutique in the city, helping herself to drawerfuls of lingerie, *mouchoirs,* haberdashery, hats, mink stoles, gloves...you name it.

Where had I failed? Where in the grievously acquired habit of magic had I let myself down? Once I questioned her, the answer appeared.

"My dear," I ventured, holding myself in check. *Too much rides on this*, I think. Can't lose control now...Thrift can cost a pretty penny too...

"We need to talk."

"What about, my love?"

I was so angry the words caught in my throat. I extemporized.

"About that — " I said, my outstretched hand cutting a plaintive arc through the air, around and about the accumulated damages...tulle and silk and nylon in mad profusion everywhere, spilling over from half-open boxes and paper sacks. Sashes and ribbons and string, webs and cradles speaking to an appetite gone mad...

Silence. Nothing. Soon enough she got impatient. As in, *How long will Victor go on about this?*

Finally she spoke.

"You made it very clear, my darling: I'm not to spend any more money."

"Exactly." So far, so good. I held my ground.

"I didn't," she said. Was she actually capitulating?

"I bought it on credit, you see. In your name."

Me see? *She* didn't buy the goods — I did!

Unless the arrow of will, coupled with clear desire, is pointed toward a very *specific target* ('Djuna will shop no more'), no good will come of the conjuration — no good at all... The mage must be painstaking in his description of the outcome — or anything can happen, anything at all....

Consider the following anecdote, by way of further illustration.

A young man, desirous of great wealth, devotes every waking moment to the pursuit of money. He thinks money; he imagines money; he *smells* money. To live his dream, he finds work in a bank, thinking he is about to realize his goal. Five years later, he is still struggling to make a wage. His problem: *he was not specific enough*. He rehearsed his desire; thought he knew what he wanted; but he neglected to foresee that handling hundreds of thousands a day — *as a bank teller* — would get him no closer to the throne of gold.

Have no doubt: in the proper hands, with the proper intensity of thought and will, magick will work. Thoughts and desires, accurately focused, become realities.

The rest of my life stands as sorry proof...

—◆◆◆—

Djuna's irritation at being reined in doesn't show. Not right away, in any case.

When it finally does emerge, it takes on a whole new cast. More flamboyant, more volatile than ever, she imports a stunning new element into our lives. She is charting new waters. Djuna is now a double celebrant, a resplendent Aphrodite — and a daughter of Sappho.

This new chapter begins innocently enough. My Tuesday morning workshop on 'psychic self-defense' — a long-winded excursion into the pitfalls and dangers of astral travel — is winding down. A knock at the door rouses the students from their reverie.

Djuna, and another young woman — both dressed as men in fedoras and matching double-breasted suits — peer into the room.

"May we?" Djuna says, entering the classroom.

She leads the other woman by the arm. She doesn't have to knock twice. I nod in grave assent.

"Don't mind us," she says. They hitch up their trousers, adjust their cravats, take their seats.

"Please, continue..."

Which I do.

"Aristide," I resume, adding drama to my remarks with a rubber-tipped pointer, "made a grave mistake. By publicizing the secret ritual, he betrayed the Lodge. This was unacceptable to the membership. By unanimous vote, and a pact with the Prince of Demons, a curse was mounted on Aristide's head. Don't you know, within twenty-four hours he was dead."

My students are familiar with this terrain. That doesn't stop them from *ooh*ing and *aah*ing at the fatal conclusion of the tale.

Djuna's companion — a pert, somewhat officious blond, with a raspy voice and a perfectly Aryan nose — pipes in.

"How would that work, Professor? What exactly killed him?"

Djuna is enjoying this. She nudges the other woman, elbow in the ribs; both break into similar smiles. Their mirth is barely suppressed.

"I'll tell you how," I say. "The fellow was literally bombarded with toxic energy. Death rays, threats, imprecations, poisonous visualizations and workings that finally did him in. *Capiche?*"

The two women, thick as thieves, nod in unison. They rise, bow, and make for the door.

The rest of us stare in disbelief.

—◦◦◦—

Later that day, perfectly within my rights, I demand an explanation.

We are lolling at a sidewalk cafe, enjoying the remnants of the day. Djuna sips at a *Kirchewasser*, now her favorite drink.

On the corner, a man with a calliope and a monkey on a string entertain passersby. A turbot-laden lorry makes a great deal of noise bouncing by.

"What was that all about?" I say, referring to the spectacle in my classroom, not to the passing truck.

"Meet Leni," she says, who suddenly appears on our event horizon, in top hat and tails, reaching for a seat.

I take a closer look. The crisp tuxedo blouse suggests the treasures that lie beneath. Djuna notices my wandering eye.

"Two hundred point Egyptian cotton," she says.

"Duly noted," I say.

Leni, a promising young film-maker, is over from *Bayerische*, on a 'shoot.' She wants to know if I've seen her work. I haven't, of course, but I've seen something else. Something that to my mind is far more important than her celluloid. I've seen how her man-tailored pants somehow embrace, announce — and pronounce — her very womanly hips.

Hmm.

"Darling..." Djuna again. She has taken Leni's hand.

"Leni has something to show us."

Wunderbar, I think. *Bring it on...*

"She'd like to screen a film. Just the three of us. Tonight, in the home theatre. *Ça marche?*"

Who am I to object?

—◦◦◦—

A waiter, wheeling a cold *table d'hote,* sashays into the room. *Maxim's* is catering; *we* are putting out the dog. Bowls of sevruga, beluga, and osetra — little mountains of the stuff — await their turn, in the good company of an ice sculpture (*The Little Mermaid),* three bottles of Moët, and enough vodka to keelhaul the entire Russian navy.

I smirk.

"What's the occasion, luvs?"

"Places to go, things to do. *We thought we'd break the ice.*"

Leni, who has slipped into 'something more comfortable' — a black silk dressing gown — rushes to my side, propping me up with some ostrich feather pillows.

"Comfy, Monsieur Rand? Mark: once the lights are out, we'll need your full attention. Eat, drink and be merry. But remember: not a peep out of you!"

Everything but the projectionist is provided for. Leni the film maker takes care of that, leaving Djuna's side at opportune moments to adjust the sound, splice a reel, slather a toast point.

The lights dim and the ladies light up, thick curlicues of smoke trailing from cigarettes (in ivory cigarette holders) and mounds of hashish (stuffed peremptorily into hookah bowls.) I'm fine just like this, plus or minus the occasional sip of Moët Chandon...

The hatch marks and digit counters betray old stock: 16 mm, lovingly duplicated onto wider more modern film. Emil Jannings, the stodgy greybeard professor, is lovelorn, helpless, hapless — practically a beggar in his mad pursuit of Lola (Dietrich), every man's dream girl chorine. Marlene had it even then — the killer legs, the paralyzing vacuous stare, the cheekbones. F.W. Murnau's professor doesn't stand a chance. Who among us would have? Who among us would have it any other way?

I feel compelled to speak during a rare pause in the action.

"They don't make them like that anymore," I venture. As it stands, my statement is ambiguous. Am I referring to the movie, or to the goddess? *My* goddess-in-residence places a cautionary finger on my lips.

"Shh, darling," she says. "We warned you, no talk. We'll have none of that! Here, have another drink."

The last reel plays out. We hear its tail end slapping in the projection booth behind us. Each is humbled in the presence of film art. *The Blue Angel* stands triumphant, flapping goose down wings...standing the test of time. We applaud and finally Leni gets up, making for the rear.

"Uh-pah!" she squeals. "Please, let me."

Djuna leans over, drinking my champagne from the crook of an arm. Cute. Definitely cute.

"There's more where that came from," she says.

Things grow more ambiguous by the moment.

Djuna pecks at my cheek. A solicitous, wifely peck. *Good,* I think. *I'll have more of that.*

Leni fusses with the lights, adjusts the sound...and we're off. Outside, another world marches stoically in place. Streetlamps illumine the gathering dusk. We're here, safe, replete, ensconced. What could be wrong?

A grizzled but savagely noble face stares out from the screen. The physiognomy is starkly Prussian.

Djuna whispers, "Thomas Mann...I'd know that mastiff head anywhere..."

Mann, waving for silence, reaches for the microphone. Camera bulbs flash, reporters hurl questions; he hardly dares speak. Finally there is an opening. He clears his throat.

In his best English — fraught with a charming Silesian accent — he manages, "It is with the greatest sorrow that I leave this country behind. The land of my fathers is stained with hatred, with calumny..."

Leni is beside herself, up in arms.

"*Gott im Himmel!*" she hisses. "How did that reel get in there?"

Then, rushing from her seat, "You didn't see that, kids. *That man* is a lunatic, I tell you, a complete lunatic!"

In a tizzy, she forages among the film cans, searching for the right — the remedial — one.

"Okay, found it," she announces. "Sit back. Now you're in for a real treat."

Scratchy music, evocative of a not quite bygone era, fills our little theatre. Cabaret music plays out to the easy smiles of *danseuses* and *flaneurs*: this is a 1931 movie version of *The Three Penny Opera*, Brecht and Weill's tribute to the dubious and degenerate elegance of late Weimar society. I catch refrains from *Mack the Knife;* for the first time I really listen to the words... The song drips with violence, decadence and world weariness.

As the snap of the celluloid announces the film's close, the debate begins. Three bottles of champagne down, and we are each in our cups. I take the lead.

"That one song has to be the most forthright condemnation of Aryan culture I've ever seen," I say.

"Whoa, Mein Herr," my common-law wife chimes right in. "Who appointed you culture vulture? *Hein?*"

Leni, right behind her, could not agree more.

"I feel your pain," Leni agrees. "Putting up with Monsieur *Je-sais-tout* over here!"

Leni continues, much in the same vein.

"Look at the evidence," she says. "It's as long as your nose."

A low blow if ever I heard one. No doubt Djuna has filled her in on my background, my heritage — on my Jewishness — on everything.

Leni smiles.

"Kurt Weill is a Jew. His father a cantor — that's no lie! What do you expect from *der Juden?* That he's going to praise Germany? Think again, *boychik."*

Again with the smile. A smile as ambivalent as the day is long. (And this day and night seem to be getting longer by the moment...) Djuna softens the blow with a sweet caress.

"Don't mind her, darling. She's coming off a tough affair."

I twist and turn, gnash my teeth. I don't see that I have much choice in the matter.

Djuna checks her Swiss diamond-mounted watch.

"Getting late, kids. What say we turn in?"

—~—

The next night we dine on truffles, lobster thermidor, and Vichy water, chased down by flute after flute of *Perignon.* Leni and Djuna are in identical trench coats, two gun molls working the trade.

Things start out slow.

———✺———

Tonight's movie menu leans heavily toward documentary, favoring pedantry and life lessons yet to be learned. Which is all right with me. We settle into our seats — love seats, actually, provided by my prescient and occasionally thoughtful partner, now named June (*?Djuna, Jeanne, Jane?*). Our small but dedicated group lingers over the 'modest' fare — oysters Rockefeller, steak tartare, peacock eggs — then we hunker down for the show.

A master intellect, a spokeswoman for the analytical psychology school of Carl Jung, appears on the screen. She speaks from an institute in Zurich and she speaks from the heart. Professorial to a fault, this woman has given a great deal of thought — actually dedicated her life — to the subject at hand. Severely efficient spectacles riding down her spare nose. A Swiss or Bavarian twinkle in her eye, she expands on her theme: the confluence of symbol in fairy tales and alchemy.

Brothers Grimm, hold on to your hats. The learned doctor, leaning toward the camera and winking conspiratorially, explains how the retorts and familiars in the medieval laboratory — and little Red Riding Hood — are archetypal reminders of one clear and abiding truth. The folk heroes, the *Gotterdamerung* and *Erlking*, are clarion calls from an eternal source: Norse and Aryan mythology, in her view are the only true religions for man.

"Suspend your disbelief, *cheri*."

I do. I swallow my ethnic pride. And while I'm at it, another beluga-slathered toast point. (These are rapidly becoming a habit.)

Next up: a former monastery on the Nile, brought to you by an infinitely gracious host, Gunther Schiller von Franz, a very wealthy colonial and purveyor of fine art, etc. During the guided tour, von Franz takes great pains to point out the kabbalistic dimensions of important architecture: his home, Notre Dame in Paris, the Pyramids in his beloved Egypt. He is a practicing alchemist so he knows whereof he speaks.

I begin to doubt the wisdom of Leni's choice when von Franz reverts to casuistry. He insists that a 'deeper' and more penetrating understanding of numbers, of architectural and ergonomic proportion, leads to one startling conclusion: the mythos of the Fatherland is here to stay. Sumerian temples, the tombs at Luxor, news photos of the promising young Chancellor 'at home': these are, are avatars, iterations, of the true and permanent Reich.

A bit much, wouldn't you say?

My good manners lock horns with my restless displeasure with June. Why has she brought this discord into our lives? Are the women now lovers? Has June gone topsy-turvy on me, descending headfirst into a slipstream of quasi-religious propaganda?

As though reading my thoughts (see *Rand College of Higher Learning* Seminar #14: Thought Broadcasting, and What to Do About It), June and Leni, seated at my right and left, begin soothing me. Giggling, stroking me, whispering sweet nothings in both my ears.

"An open mind and an open heart," June whispers.

Leni changes the reel then reappears right at my side.

"Maybe you'll like this one better," she says.

That remains to be seen...the grainy stock, the raspy sound, surrender to titles and credits. *F.W. Murnau...Nosferatu...*the grand-dad of all Draculas. Max Schreck, a wiry hook-nosed freak, plays Count Orlok, a vampire who preys upon his wife (Greta Schröder.) Murnau's Nosferatu, anemic, pasty-faced, and predatory, is everyone's worst idea of the Jew. He emerges from hidden cabinets, always at night, slinking from room to room, rapacious talons and oversized nares bared for the kill.

A captive audience: Leni and June, and petulant horrified me.

When the lights go back on, I mount my attack.

"Guess what? If that was meant to offend...it succeeded."

"No, no, not at all," Leni reassures. "Only intended to *depict*. How the rest of the world thinks..."

"Daarling, you must admit: the evidence speaks for itself."

"What evidence?"

Then in unison, I hear, "The killing of Christ. The shedding of Christian blood. The Protocols."

"Protocols?"

"...of the Elders of Zion," Leni says.

"And you actually believe that crap?"

A finger to my lips. Leni's. She stands.

"Hey," she says, "Shh. Take a look at this one. Last film of the night. Promise."

—∿—

A line all in unison of flaxen haired girls in jumpers fills the screen. Rows of them, accompanied by a boisterous brass band and dour-faced cadets. *Following suit* is the name of the game. The kids march — goose step — in deep cadence, in lock step, to the music. Their armbands tell the story: these are the Hitler Youth, a new generation of stalwarts, future firebrands, dedicated to the purification of the Homeland and the Race.

Leni commiserates but sticks to her guns.

"Honestly Victor, do you really think they'd be kicking up such a fuss if there wasn't something to it?"

"She's right, you know," my increasingly common common-law wife says.

I'm speechless: *Anshlussed*, if you will. At a total loss for words. Djuna's sudden plunge into this specious alliance with a card-carrying National Socialist has me on edge. I change tactics and push back.

"I suppose, Leni, you think you're furthering the cause?"

Djuna butts in.

"You bet she is," she says.

"How so?"

"I'm a filmmaker," Leni says, the Swabian accent more pronounced than ever.

"I make films. About the workers...the children...the racial cleansing...surely you've seen my work?"

"Can't say I have."

The women gaze at each in other in disbelief — which rapidly becomes suspended disbelief.

"I'm working on a new feature right now," she adds. "It's called *Triumph of the Swill.* Look for it."

With that she nudges Djuna who, rising to her feet, follows her out the door.

"Leave him here. Let him stew in his own juice."

Which is exactly what they do.

Later — I don't recall the exact time, save to consider it a *witching hour* of some sort — I stumble, in an alcohol-induced torpor, from the bed. Djuna's side is untouched, the sheets crisp as a newly printed Deutschmark. She and Leni are at the armoire, making hasty decisions and drinking in the dawn.

"No, leave it all, I tell you," Leni whispers. "The main thing is getting out. I'll take you shopping once we're home."

Home? Where might that be — Bonn, Berlin, Cologne, perhaps?

Roused by now from my torpor, I tear at the sheets.

"What is all this?" I demand.

"I don't owe you an explanation, *Schatz,*" Djuna says. "But here it is. I'm leaving. Leni and I are off to the Fatherland. Together. You may hear from me — or you may not. *Auf wiedersehen,*" she says — pitch perfect. Then, perfectly rehearsed, they bow.

That night — and for many nights after — I sleep alone.

Eat, Sleep, and Pray.

"If God gives you lemons, make lemonade.
 If God puts you in a gas chamber, breathe deep."
—Sol Deutsche

My sleep is troubled: nothing but wrack and ruin, and hands-down despair. What has my life come to? High practitioner of Workings, canny receptionist on the EtherPhone, fancier of astral retorts and alembics...where has it gotten me? Despair, nothing but despair...I pace, fingering the silk and brocade drapery of my Special Operations Room, hefting the cones of frankincense and charcoal in their braziers, each and every object staring back at me in dumb reproof.

The Way is difficult, the Way is long. I know this. I also know that I must soon return to the Higher Plane, to the Akashic realm, to renew my spirit and sharpen my purpose.

I must commune with the Ancient Masters.

Surely a spirit guide will appear.

Triply rehearsed in the magic arts — an able petitioner of Thrice-Blessed Hermes — a witness to a cosmic battle between phoenix and dragon — I am, nonetheless, perturbed beyond reason at the prospect of *sleeping alone.* Inwardly I shudder, imagining the white nights yet to be painted across the Berlin sky by Leni and June...

Ah. Achhh. Ouch. *No rest for the weary...*I wrestle with the bed clothes, gathering up the fine dumb linens we once shared...

What little sleep I get is set upon by the most grotesque dreams.

...A woman in white, a nurse I believe, ministers to the sick and dying. Perhaps I am one of them.

"Who are you?" I stammer from the wings — the wings of dream...

"I am Clara Barton, founder of the American Red Cross...An angel of mercy, a vision in crinoline, tending to the wounded in the American Civil War. I don't suppose you know me. But I believe you will. I was only eleven years old when my brother fell off the roof from a barn. I rushed to his side, I cared for him for two whole years. He was my first patient! You will be my next."

"Not sure how I feel about this, Ms. Clara," I say.

"That's what they all say," she beams. "Now relax, young man. There's God's work to be done."

Clara Barton

My knowledge of American history is scant, the little I have of it supplied by snatches of school lessons and from *feuilleton* images glimpsed along the way. What other unlikely cargo could I now expect to see in my dreams? Susan B. Anthony? Harriet Beecher Stowe? Florence Nightingale?

These names are strange and unfamiliar to me. So be it. I pound the pillows, prosecuting my just cause: another hour or two of precious sleep.

Which arrives, just as the magpies and starlings become *boulevardiers* and start chirping like mad. I descend, gratefully I think, into the open arms of the void...

Somewhat renewed — stoked on coffee and *pastis* — I intentionally return to trance.

This will be an invocation, a call to arms, a signal cry for clarity and resolve.

I must align my will with that of the Universe. As of late, you see, the Universe and I have been working at cross purposes.

The candles are lit, the curtains drawn. Fragrant myrrh and charcoal leavens the room. Breathing in the proper manner, I call forth the archangels, assigning each to his quadrant, invoking the Conversation of My Holy Guardian Angel (this is spelled out, step by step, in the latest edition of Lévi's *Rituel et Dogma de Mon Haute Magie,* Pleiade Éditions.) They may carp, they may mightily object — but their presence is guaranteed. I am Grand Master of the Seven Planetary Planes, Magister of the Three Worlds, and as such, they are each and every demon Jack of them subject to my Will.

Ablutions done, circumambulations performed, I assume the lordly pose, the preferred posture, my thoughts honed to a fine point. I burn the flame of my desire into an Egyptian scarab, the beetle unresisting, astral, hallucinatory, and as ever, mine to command. As the smoke clears, I see a hovering visage, an all too familiar face.

It is Sol Deutsche, revenant of East End pubs and of roads less traveled.

Sade in Hell.

I recount the following in the heartfelt hope that this record of my serial misdeeds will serve as both lantern and decree to any who might contemplate pursuing a similar course of misadventure and folly.

The ordeal began, I suppose, during my very first year among the Jesuits. I was young. I was young and foolish enough to assume that each and every mentor, proctor and professor would welcome with open arms my autodidact's surfeit of learning. Learning which, *in toto*, scarified the persona I so guilelessly foisted upon the world. I was reading psychology. My tutor was a reticent, somewhat frightening, creature called Brother Joris. He had made a name for himself in certain academic circles as a major contestant in the never-ending quarrel between those advocates of 'nature' and those proponents of 'nurture.'

What began as a simple ivory tower *contretemps* soon took on life-threatening tones. With laborious research I attempted to demonstrate that the kindest, most innocent of souls could, given sufficient environmental impetus, become a hardened criminal, murderer, or rapist. I supported this thesis with mountains of information, related specifically to the younger ('formative') years of the Marquis Alphonse Donatien de Sade. This 18th century French gallant is known for his obscene and unseemly narratives of furtive couplings, sodomy, more sodomy, murder...and just about any other deviant behavior that would blaspheme man, angel, and our Lord in Heaven alike.

My question was this: how many were aware that prior to the *letter de cachet* that sent him packing to prisons and insane asylums, the Marquis had been a man of exemplary character, writing, and teaching?

To this day it pains me to recall Joris Moorcock's abominable handling of the deeply researched biography I had placed in his hands. I was further shocked at the outrageous challenge the ill-informed academician next threw my way.

"Stuff and nonsense!" Brother Joris roared. "Do you actually believe any of this crap?"

I held my ground. I envisioned my glorious career taking a nose dive into the ash heaps of history...anomie...disgrace.

"Sir," I managed, "with all due respect. I stake my honor and name upon the veracity of those words. Every word of it is true."

Joris Moorcock pulled at his cabbage patch of beard, reflecting not so much upon the parabola (or flat line) of my career as upon the Jesuitical sufferings he could, with professorial bemusement, watch me endure.

"Are you willing to defend your thesis — no matter the cost?"

"Indeed, sir, I am."

"All right, then! I ask no more of you than this: armed with paper and pen, you will enjoy the identical fate of your mightily researched hero — the ramshackle 'humanist' de Sade. I have already taken the liberty of signing you on for a six-month sabbatical...at La Salpêtrière. If and when you emerge from that dungeon, we will be better positioned to scrutinize the prose you have written in gaol."

<center>~~~</center>

Incarcerated 32 years of his life, including ten years in insane asylums. Ten years in Paris in the Bastille.

Sade was incarcerated in various prisons and psychiatric institutions for 32 years; 11 years in Paris, a month in the Conciergerie, two years in a fortress, a year in Madelonnettes, three years in Bicêtre, a year in

Sainte-Pélagie and 13 years in Charenton. During the French Revolution, he was an elected delegate to the National Convention.

Many of his works were written in prison.

A sadness [he wrote] deeper than the deepest chasm in the remotest part of hell. The sadness of looking back on a life mostly lived in pursuit of something else. A lifetime of days thrown to the winds, subject to and abject with the passion of the moment. Surrender to the vain appetites, appetites of the lowest common denominator. Yet a hero to many, a healer, a source of comfort and light. To himself, a lonely prince, a certified fool, lost in the carrels of an infinite library, certainly lost in the dense traffic of souls above the ground. He filled his head with visions, squeezed painfully like pustules from a realm where it was a foregone conclusion that his relationship with his own kind would always be less than perfect, pathetically short of oceanic bliss. Came to the point where life held little sweetness for him; 'life' meant oceans of pain and worlds of regret. Bring children into this world of pain? No thankee — he saw the pain that would unfold as certainly as the coming dawn in all these lives...and he would especially regret the day they would suffer the pain of his departure.

Tried to soothe his pain...with the thought that he and we were here for a reason. Doing overtime in enemy territory — no sleep allowed. The dead and dying only overshadowed by the quick and living, who suffered more than their decaying brothers and sisters. Who wouldn't regret bringing more children into this world? Who regrets more than I the terrible loneliness of this realm? Who sees more deeply than I, more piercingly than I through the hollow and frivolous, through the sweet distractions that sometimes fall into place? Who tarries as long as I in the hellish groves of regret and nostalgia? Who aims more than I for a Neverland of Parnassus, a heaven of meaning and light and bliss? Who more than I falls in love every possible moment, falls completely on his knees before fleshed and blooded extravasations of his own overworked dreams? What can I teach any children except — to suffer in silence? Should I provide the bare sustenance that prolongs in mere comfort this wretched stroll on the strand? Is that truly *humane?*

Who more than I resembles, to his utter horror, his sire; the bane of his existence — his *dad?*

To laugh, to love, to lose, to erase oneself...all consubstantial in the river of words. The riveting transfixion of being the priest. The daily crucifixion of helping and healing while poking at the sore that is 'me.' Is there nothing larger, nothing greater, nothing mightier than this fear and trepidation that grows like an evening shadow, that falls upon the tinsel town of our tiny empty selves? Better an empty cosmos than this impermanent tease! Better to flash the wings of one's soul at the moment of release, to fly away all at once in the arms of a lover, in the thrall of a chord, in the thunder of the well-crafted phrase. To fall in love again and again and again and to be forever denied the illusion one seeks. Truly this is the foyer of hell, not purgatory by any standard I know. Nothing will be undone — everything will be undone!. My lovers and my children will become rotten corpses, mere flesh appended to bones, a hearty meal for the worms and maggots that will for all eternity become us, as we become them.

My Demon Familiar.

He appears in my trance like a spiritual Apache, in a many-feathered head-dress, offering dubious 'spiritual' wares and quondam counsel. He would shriek and whoop if I did not threaten to consign him to the smoky margins of the magical circle, where a host of incorporeal entities wait, hoping to devour whatever offal I throw their way.

"I am Deutsche," he says, "and my name is legion."

"No it's not," I counter. "Your name is Conversation with the Holy Guardian Angel. " (I know this from the treatises and grimoires I've taken great pains over the years to learn.) "So unless you're prepared for a discussion or, a meeting of the minds, you're out of here. And that's that." (The handbooks advise taking a strident, imperious tone with astral visitors. They are like mad dogs, these visitors: the moment they sense fear, they fall upon you, all jaws and slobber.)

"All right, all right...*be that way.* But don't fence me in..."

"Now then: where exactly are we?"

This elicits peals of otherworldly laughter.

"You're asking *me*, pontifex? Hardi-har-har."

Deutsche then reconsiders, lightens up.

"Last you left me, we wuz a-grogging...in an English pub, as I recall.

Well, I've moved on. 'Crossed the bar,' you might even say. You're none too shabby yerself, Aladdin."

"How I wish..." My voice, no longer the stentorian trumpet of former days, trails off. "Reversal of Fortune. The Hanged Man, you might say."

The graybeard ponders this, grabs at a salamander who happens to be darting just that moment between his bowed legs.

"Damn thing!" he cusses. "Can't live with 'em — "

I finish the thought.

"Can't live without them. My thought exactly! I'm down one woman, as things stand..."

"I see," Deutsche mewls. "Down one woman..."

A thought — an aberrant moment of passing coherence — lights up his face.

"So what? There's plenty more where she came from."

My guided meditation is like a slot machine. My turgid encounters with the Real flash before me, so many cherries and lemons and ducks not in a row. I see it now: my bank accounts, now longer flush, a line of gutted sows bleeding cash. Worse still, I remember our last night together — when, in the company of Leni and the local prelate, June and I took vows.

The absconding harridan made off with half my fortune...

The writing is on the wall. (In fact, a cloaked and hooded death's head, scythe in one bony hand, scrapes my funereal finances on an interior wall. That's how transparent the situation is. Deutsche reads this, but does not yet weep.)

"Yours is a tough row to hoe. As they say. You have been most fortunate... up until this point... You consider yourself a Mage among magicians, a Winged Victory without canard."

"Lay off the jokes, lose the word play, Deutsche," I moan.

"That I cannot do."

In a gesture of sympathy, he waves off the grim reaper.

"Enough scribbling on the cave wall," he says. "That will do! Take your skeletal self and hither-yon thee, and make it fast! Hear?"

"Thank you," I manage.

"Under the present circumstances, the least I can do. Now then."

"I'm all ears..." Suddenly a hundred organs of hearing sprout, grotesquely adorning my deep-in-trance arms, legs, chest.

"Solomon!" I cry. "You promised..."

"So I did. So I did." With a whisk of his crooked scepter all but two ears, the God-given ones, are gone. Leaving poor penniless me, awaiting the master's next brilliant word.

"As your Guardian Angel, I will say this: my, but you are bereft! Empty pockets and empty heart."

"Tell me something I don't already know," I squeak.

"Your magic isn't all it's cracked up to be. You ascended on the planes, worked the Steps, followed in the footsteps of the Ancient Rite. Where did it get you? I'll tell you where: it got you locking horns with the universe."

"Horns? What did I leave out? Did I fail to hoodwink the Eye of Horus? Have my desires not been pure? Are they not refined, pointed, *penetrating* enough?"

"No, no, no. That's drivel. You're banging your head against a wall, spouting foolish nonsense. There are Things One Cannot Change, you know."

"So what do I do?"

"Simple," he says. "You make change. You go around the wall."

And with that riddle, he was gone.

—◦∿◦—

We are caught up in the tumult of events. Did I mention that France, honoring the guarantee of Poland's borders, declares war on Germany? (My passion for the work at hand, the work of occult initiation, is largely to blame for this lapse of attention to international events. I am so preoccupied with things at home that the big picture, of things abroad, continually goes out of focus.) I could go on and on, apostrophizing the efforts of right-minded citizens of Great Britain and France to put things right. That is hardly the focus here. To properly tell my story, I adhere to the facts — as I know them. First and foremost I am a Magician; my story is about Akashic conquest, triumphs of mythic proportion — and not about current events.

I leave such matters to the journalists and rabble-rousers of our day.

—◊—

As if by magic, promising events begin to tumble my way. In a letter from Berlin, Juna catches me up on her Sapphic progress. She *pooh-poohs* the significance of her adventure with Leni, going so far as to invite me to join them at their country retreat.

I feel exonerated. Following Juna's departure, the 'home office' — the Institute — gets back on its feet. I find an administrative replacement for the wandering light of my life, a mousy but dreadfully efficient older woman who immediately takes our business — the catalog, the rolling admissions, tuition collection — well in hand.

One day, as I'm admiring our growing Magickal Artifacts museum — the collection includes historically important wands, censers and natal charts — my musings are interrupted by a knock on the door. The new secretary, Mme. Fortinbras, fairly bristles with immediacy. Seems she is in a lather...

"This man insists on seeing you, Master." (Yes, *Master:* this is the name I insist on at the School.)

She looks around, a little crazed by the seeming urgency of the moment.

"I think it's important. I cleared your morning calendar. I hope you don't mind."

Never one to balk at fate, even importunate fate, I make the ring toss.

"Please," I say, "have a seat."

I dismiss Fortinbras; she's endured enough.

My irritation with his presumptuous entrance shines through.

"State your business, sir. State your name."

"The name is Deutsche. As in Deutschland."

"As in *Über alles?*"

"Precisely," he says.

Two can play at this game.

"Related by any chance to Sol — Solomon Deutsche, lately of Cardiff, Findhorn, and Finisterre Way?"

This last remark catches him unawares, offering me a chance to study the unlikely features of this uninvited guest. He is tall; clean-shaven; dressed like a spy. A white silk cravat peeks out from the narrow hinterland between his neck and his coat. The mackintosh, fastened to the collar against the rain *(...what rain?...)*, speaks to a borrowed sensibility. So do the seven league boots, laced up to the knee.

"Let's assume I *am* Sol Deutsche," he says, somewhat fatuously.

"Why?" I say, pushing a box of Havanas toward him. "Humidor?"

"Thermidor," he says.

"Okay, let's assume," I say. "But why?"

"Because that," he says, "guarantees your complete cooperation. And enthusiastic participation in what follows next."

He's got a point. The connection to Deutsche somehow validates the entire operation. He clips the end of the cigar and accepts a light.

"Can I be honest?" he asks.

"I insist."

"I am prepared to bail out your operation." He screws up his features, looks me over. "At no small expense, I might add."

"True, true..."

"I've heard great things about you."

"Go on."

"All I ask is an open mind. And access to your enormous talents."

"Tsk, tsk," I counter. "Please, go on."

"*We,*" I notice the imperious first person plural, now dominating his spiel — "We offer a once-in-a-lifetime opportunity to turn your gift to our mutual advantage."

"Turn my gift...to *account?*"

The praise begins to rankle.

"What gift...what talent?"

"Why everyone knows how you recently tamed the Griffin, and slew the Dragon, saving Paris and its grateful citizenry."

I feign humility.

"Ah yes. That. I do recall. Please — go on."

"We need spiritual forecasting. Rather soon, I might add. We need a Paris-based seer who can tap into the life force, predict population movements, the march of time. All like that."

"Exactly whom do you work for?"

"I am an agent of historical change. Let's leave it that. The only thing *you* need to know is this..."

Pseudo-Deutsche reaches into his sumptuous pocket, extracting a fistful of cash.

"Deutschmarks and francs. Whichever suits. And there's plenty more where this came from."

He sweeps the bills across the desk. I eye them, perhaps a little too covetously.

This is Deutsche's cue. He extends a gloved hand. (Is there a sidecar waiting?)

"Are you in? Do we have a deal?"

The hillock of cash will float my rent and my credit for the next two months.

He's got me. I suppose I'm in...

—ᴧᴧ—

The other Deutsche — in my view, the real and only Solomon Deutsche — becomes a regular feature of my dreams: my dreams, my waking meditation, my city walks and reveries. For the sake of exposition, I will telescope these sightings into two or three visitations. (The oracular, preposterous pronouncements are what count. And that figure heavily in the remainder of this tale.)

"Don't mind the tiara," he tells me during the first of many visits. "The baobab doesn't apologize for its diadem. Neither shall I."

Hard to ignore the coiling serpent adorning his headpiece, or the jeweled scarab fronting his brow. All in a dream, as they say. To continue:

"Want to succeed in this life? Then make peace with the Devil."

"The Devil?"

"The absurd, boy! Deal with it!"

More than I can stand, even within the relative safety of my visualized cone of light. I was running afoul of Deutsche in particular, of conjuration in general. Quickly I invoke the Pole-Star, at once poleaxing my unwelcome mentor right where it hurts: POW! Right in the Akasha! With the aid of a celestial choir, in a flowing glowing robe of white, I banish him to the South. With a wave of my mental wand, and his barely suppressed groan, he is gone.

...Only to return the following night.

I take many precautions, hoping to avoid a repeat performance. Lo and behold, Deutsche is back, in all his glory: appearing first as a trapper, a lone denizen of some primeval forest, then as a Merman (aqua, not Ethel.) I think: *Douse his spirit with aqua vitae, that will make short work of him.* But my supply of the precious elixir has dwindled to nothing; so my guest makes himself comfortable, finding himself a comfortable durable place in my mind.

"Cheer up," he says, "all is not lost."

"Don't know about that, boss," I mutter, from some disconsolate place within my trance.

"Victor!" he shouts. "Pay attention. I've sampled the best and brightest, bringing you *professional* opinion on your plight. You are suffering, no doubt about that."

"No doubt," I say. "The bitch's name is June...Juna...Djuna...she is a warrior princess who has truly tanned my hide."

Deutsche's rant continues.

"You are not alone — far from it. You have been attacked by a predator, a dimorph...a psychic and sexual worm, as it were."

"Actually we haven't done *it* in quite some time..." I remark.

"You're on well-known territory. Listen up. Here, verbatim, is the very latest on your lamentable condition. Which, incidentally, may be reversible. Who says one can't shed astral larvae?"

He laughs and launches further into his madness.

"In the February, 1934 number of *Psychiatrie,* a journal for the trade, there appears a paper on the seemingly obscure subject of intercourse with demons. 'Cacodemonomania' (both the title of the paper written by Ludo and Finstermacher, and the term given to the practice) reviews the subject and provides several case studies of more than passing interest.

"Their citation from *Malleus Maleficarum* (Grand Inquisitor Torquemada's broadside on the diagnosis and spiritual treatment of demonic possession) makes it plain as day: the subject matter is grave, disputatious, dangerous. And not trivial in the least. Countless thousands lost their standing as respected citizens in the community — not to mention their lives, perhaps their souls — as a result of prosecution for demonic *coniunctio.*

"Here is the briefest sketch of such a case.

"The patient (victim? rube? *schlemiel?*), a 50-year old physician, came to the office in a near-terminal state of anxiety. Hector P., otherwise successful in his professional and personal dealings, was most unhappy with his wife.

"H. — Hector, that is — was like a rodent, one of those tenebrous creatures peering from the canvases of Hieronymus Bosch.

"*This?* H. asked, *"This is the girl I married? This is the quincunx, the Ophelia I have wrested single singlehandedly from cruel Stygian waters?'*

All crimes, every form of violence, had been committed in the name of consanguinity against him.

You ask, *To what extent did H. bear the telltale stamp of the paranoiac?*

"Defamation, deforestation, moral defloration, derogation, rupture of limbic hymen [Editor's note: men have these too!], slander, libel, verbal abuse, taunting, mockery, belittlement, emasculation, strangulation, vagina dentata, character assassination, devaluation, ball-churning, betrayal, poor diction, bad taste, negligence, and cruelty beyond words were palpably present — just to name a few.

"*This harridan*, this hideous belch from the dyspeptic gullet of Satan — whose rantings, whose 'words' are fecal bastinadoes — has robbed me of self, of dignity, of moral valence. Yet still she walks the earth. Still she breathes God's good air!'"

"Hector P. felt he had suffered every one of these abrogations of common decency.

"Many among the professional and lay community still believe in witchcraft. Heaven help those whom they serve! Examples of common mental disorders misdiagnosed as demonic possession are legion. We have already witnessed the pitiable outcome of 'professional' interventions, intended or not.

"Sol Deutsche," I interrupt, "is this a rant—or what?"

Uncomprehending, he continues.

"The extant literature on modern demonology is sparse and begs for expansion.

"Cacodemonomania has been described in children. One paediatrician often delivered a diagnosis of satanic stomatitis or told already distraught parents that their baby would be born 'Beelzebub breech.' Hastily organized bake sales, under the covert Satanic imprimatur, are not unknown. A spiritual leader in Kew Gardens, USA, guided his (kabbalistic) congregation through raffles, bingo tournaments and — get this —exorcisms!

"I ask you: what is to be done?"

All I can do is stare, which disturbs him not in the least.

"First," he goes on, displaying a new and virulent pedantic tone I had never imagined possible in the miserable wraith, "the diagnosis of cacodemonomania should never be made casually. Recognize that parallel psychic anomalies exist. Unwonted incursions by werewolves, vampires, salamanders (alchemical salamanders, not literal ones), gnomes, sylphs, faeries and wendigos are rare but factual.

"The most insidious form taken by invaders from the other side is wrongly considered secular. 'Routine' marital conflict, 'routine' interpersonal strife may be anything but routine. We are here on this planet to seek happiness, garner wisdom, and to give to the poor. Those saddled with adversarial spouses, friends, grocers and pets are very likely experiencing spillover from a darker, far more remote realm. Get help! Recognize the devils for what they are. Avoid pre-nuptial agreements with such creatures; you may find yourself signing decrees far more weightier than those tacked to the walls of Wittenberg by Martin Luther himself.

"Oh yes — one more thing. Stock up on garlic. The efficacy of the so-called 'elephant' variety — a variety that has adorned tables rich and poor for centuries — remains to be proven. But most important of all: *Never marry a bitch."*

—◦◦◦—

I was chafing at the bit. Chomping at the bridle. Not pleased with my interlocutor nor with his mouthful of *fantôme* 'good news.' The latest bout of reportage left me sorely wanting. The next time we meet — in full trance, the disc of the moon pendulant in the vitrines of my sacred room — I pretty much tell him so.

'Lighten up V. H.," he says, "hold on to your hat. There's more where that came from — and believe me, buddy boy, you'll be thanking me when the time is right."

I'm near incredulous.

"What is that supposed to mean? Is that a threat? Now you're threatening me?"

"No, merely your friendly mentor — *cum*-Wise-Man — avatar of a thousand faces, talking..."

"Look, Sol Deutsche...or whoever you, whomever you claim to be. We need to get something straight."

That will-o-the-wisp, the face of Deutsche, suddenly now in flames, throws me a cheery grin.

"Go on, lad, let it fly..."

"Are you Deutsche — or are you not? How'd you come by that stupid moniker, anyway?"

His turn for a show of contempt.

"You really don't get it? After all this time?"

"Get what, Mr. Lunatic Fancy Pants?"

"Reincarnation! Atavism! Iteration without cease! Was the lesson of St. Germain entirely lost on you? I'm gravely disappointed..."

"You're disappointed? My sweetheart traipsing around the Sudetenland, probably having the time of her life...my Academy teetering on the brink of financial ruin...you barging in here, on my private moments, casting doubt on all I've come to hold dear...How am I supposed to feel?"

"Now, now," he consoles, extending a gauzy hand, only partly materialized, from the Other Side. "We can work it out."

A hush falls on the gloom.

I step on the gas of my Spiritual Accelerator...musn't lose a beat. Must keep up with this conniving wraith.

His next explanation beats me to the punch.

"There have been many Deutsches," he says. "Different iterations, morning and late edition Deutsches, hitting the corner newsstands at all different times and places. Surely you caught the discrepant spellings of the name?"

From my thought-form cocoon, I glare. Glare, then finally relent.

"Okay Bright Eyes...which is yours? Do we go with the Low Country, the German, or the American English?"

Again with the proffered hand.

"Wolf," he says, "Wolfgang Helmut Deutsch. Deutsch is the name, bricolage is my game."

"You're sure now?"

"Infinitely," he says. "Or at least indefinitely. I suggest we move on..."

I'm flush with Deutsche(s). The most recent Deutsche — Deutsche the confidence man, offering steamer trunks of cash for God knows what insidious purpose — seems to always be at hand.

I decide to play it cool. Rather than squeezing more specious names and explanations from him, I go for the gold. Thanks to Djuna, I'm still in arrears. There is still the College to consider: a lifeboat for humanity I am determined at all cost to keep afloat.

I'll take his money...and let my sleepy conscience be my guide.

Rheingold.

My new patron — Hans Lamprecht du Plessix Deutsche — insists I keep it simple. He shows up frequently, raising not a few eyebrows with his perfectly tended Erich von Stroheim appearance. Monocle, cravat, riding crop — the works.

I look the other way.

"Call me Helmut," he says. "Or Rheingold or Dietrich. Whichever you prefer."

I go out on a limb — mentally. In my fevered imagination, I sing,
Let me call you Sweetheart/Let me call you Deutschmark...

"Deal," I actually say. "Okay, 'Rheingold': what's the drill?"

He extracts a deck of playing cards from his neatly cinched portmanteau.

"We need to establish a baseline," he explains. His polluted French — dappled with distinct Swabian diphthongs — betrays his Österreich origins. At this point, Rheingold puts a pseudo-scientific veneer on things, trying I suppose, to impress the vigor of his project upon me.

Let me call you Deutschmark...

"We have here the four suits...the spades, the clubs, the hearts, the diamonds...Let's see if you can call them, unseen..."

"Ah," I say, "remote viewing, eh? I'm rather good at that. Especially when I've invoked Thoth."

Rheingold places a cardboard barrier across th glass-top desk.

The conjuration goes smoothly, despite (or because of) the presence of this bizarre guest. From where I sit, deep in the cone of light, blanketed in a cocoon of emptiness, I see him set the cards up.

Systematically, from where I sit, I call them. With obvious and increasing pleasure, he jots down my tries. (*Thoth*, known to some as *Mercury*, to others as *Hermes*, gleefully assists me throughout. With such an assistant, this 'work' is mere child's play.)

I'm about to call the next set of five cards when Rheingold rises, triumphant and beaming, from his seat.

"No need to go on, my friend," he says. "Your guesses far exceed the statistical threshold. The odds of your correct hits — in this case, 6 out of 9 — are something less than six million to one."

"Six million, eh? I'll take that," I say, a bit full of myself at this point. "What's next?"

He removes then instantly sets the monocle back in place. Is that perspiration on his furrowed brow?

"Pattern recognition," he says. He extracts a second set of cards. These cards are larger, each featuring a different shape.

"Here we have easily recognizable forms. A circle, a square, a rectangle, a triangle. You recognize these, of course?"

"I wasn't born yesterday."

"Most assuredly not."

He hands the cards over. His 'geometric forms' hint at something more. The rectangle, for example, is bisected by an upright: a boat? The triangle has tiny protuberances at its base: are these feet? What — ?

"No time for reflection," he says. "All will be revealed. For now, I want to see how well you can *burn* these images into your brain, then project them *here.*"[9]

---

9 Rheingold's project for Victor Rand may have been a precursor of Kirlian photography. So-called 'Kirlian photography' began with the work of Semyon and Valentina, Soviet scientists who in 1939 experimented with capturing mental 'thought forms' on unexposed photographic film.

—◦◦◦—

The man comes prepared. He pulls out an Agfa Speedex camera, no doubt the top of the line, and proceeds to point.

"Here," he indicates, poking a tobacco-ruined finger at the lens.

"Whatever you say, boss." He either ignores or dismisses my contemptuous reply — this being characteristic, actually, of all our exchanges.

The experiment begins. Holding fast to my inner focus, I visualize in turn each shape. Rheingold is the model of patience, sitting through this laborious undertaking as I intensely study, recreate, then project my imagination into the Agfa's dark maw. One by one, I mentally devour then regurgitate each symbol on the cards. As I proceed, with great effort, the shapes become increasingly recognizable: planes and boats and men.

At last we're done. I ask Rheingold if he'd like to dine. He apologizes — he must be off to the lab. He is eager to develop the film...

"Here," he says, handing me an envelope filled with cash. "Feast on this."

—◦◦◦—

One night Djuna calls. The call is from Berlin. She is solicitous, tender, her cagey voice sewing up the miles with breathless repartee, questions, advice. A second woman's voice, in the near distance I suppose, keeps trying to interrupt. This would be Leni, no doubt...

"*Ask him* — " Then I hear, "—No, tell — "

"*Shh! mein liebe,*" Djuna remonstrates. "*I will, I will...*"

"Ask me what?" I say.

"*Dis donc,*" Djuna finally says, "have you heard from Rheingold?"

I bait her on.

"Not one of Wagner's best," I say.

"*Carrément, ma puce,*" she says drily. "I'm referring to our man in Paris. Who brings you...the gold."

"*Your* man? I see... You mean Rheingold was your idea? Was your *man?*"

"Who else?" she says. "Isn't he a dream? A dead-ringer for von

Stroheim, *non? Listen, cheri, please do whatever he says...or the bills simply won't get paid."*

Handoff of receiver, then muffled sounds, with more words hurriedly exchanged. Then she is back.

"Oh, I nearly forgot..."

"Yes?"

"I miss you. I want you. As in, When can you come?"

Silence. At last I stammer some reply.

Silence. She reads me an address. Slowly, twice, so I can copy it down.

"We're waiting...*Bisous.*"

The work with Rheingold proceeds apace. He visits regularly, always with cards: patterns, symbols, some simple, some more complex. Which I commit to memory then discharge, like some psychic Napoleon, into the muzzle of his lens. At a certain point my curiosity overrides my strictly pecuniary interest, so I ask how I'm doing. Am I on target? Are the images coming through?

At first he is loath to respond; but with continuing success (I imagine), even this ironclad Hessian will relent. A hint of a smile breaks through the storm clouds of his facial hair.

"Not bad, not bad at all," he says. "Let's not muck things up. Let's not contaminate the results with expectations. Or hopefulness. Let's just say *you're doing fine."*

Meanwhile, all is not fine. German troops have overrun Poland, defying treaties, provoking international outrage. The British temporize, hoping the Anschluss will mollify Hitler's world-lust. France mobilizes; there is a general call-to-arms. The word on everyone's lips these days is *war,* and the ripple effects of this despotic tide are felt far and wide. Borders are closed; security is heightened; supply chains, now precious life-lines, are guarded by soldiers and guns.

For me, the forces of conscription are held in check — for the moment, at least. Recall that I am married; I can entertain the troops (with stage magic); last but certainly not least, I am Jewish. Personal survival is the least of my concerns. I think instead about Djuna, out there in the Aryan wilderness, and I think about posterity. My posterity. The Academy must survive!

My benefactor, *guter Schweinhund Rheingold,* maintains appearances, the embarrassments of cash arriving intact and always on time.

He shows up one morning, lines of worry etched more boldly than usual across his craggy face. He winces as he screws the monocle back in place.

"Here," he says, handing me a single sheet of foolscap: not money, but a list.

"What is this?"

"Remote viewing points," he explains. "Tourist attractions across your country. Visit each, take mental snapshots, and launch them to me. In the way you know how."

I'm puzzled.

"The camera?" I ask. "Where's the camera? Where are you?"

"I'll be out of the country," he explains. "My departure necessitated by historic events. My Rolleiflex and I will be just over the border, ready and waiting. The etheric currents will propagate your mental snap shots."

Then, as an afterthought, "The work should be quite pleasant, by the way... Put yourself up in hotels, order the best meals, buy yourself company — it's all on me."

On me. Hmm. And I'm off, my wallet stuffed with the latest surfeit of 100-franc notes, my spirits soaring high. Bills paid, a motor tour through the countryside, the prospect of seeing my wife: these lift my spirits, as does the prospect of not seeing Rheingold's grim mug anytime soon in the days to come...

The Huns have invaded. Ingloriously dubbed as 'the Battle of France', my beautiful homeland, plus Luxembourg, the Netherlands, and Holland, are taken by the German war machine.

Think of it: the *Wehrmacht.*

My work with Rheingold takes on a new and eerie meaning.

I follow my instructions to the letter, dutifully debarking at each town, registering at the local hotel, then taking mental "photographs" of the particular site and environs. (With Rheingold's pinpoint specific coordinates, I use only a minimum amount of "film.") My dutiful efforts are interrupted at my third stop — Criqueville — by a young man, a young man obviously hot around the collar, who runs up to me on my glorious perch. (I'm seated on a rock overlooking the sea.)

"What are you doing there, Citizen?"

I study him. His breathing slows, but his complexion is still red. A red bandana is tied around his upper arm. His self-importance, clearly the biggest show in town, shines right on through. I wax cynical, hoping sarcasm will win the day.

"What is this, the Paris Commune?"

"No, Monsieur. This is a forbidden zone. A site of strategic importance — an airport. See?"

I do see. Just beyond the sea grass, exactly where I had trained my second sight, there is a modest airfield, where a small flock of single and twin-engine craft are cozily parked.

"Hand over your camera," he says.

This is his heroic moment.

"No camera," I say, smiling, holding out my empty hands.

"My camera is up here," I say, tapping my head. He grins. We are co-conspirators.

As he leaves, I ponder the evidence. Much to my chagrin, a lorry (this time filled with soldiers) bumps and grinds its way down the runway of the narrow coastal road.

My patience with the situation, with the mission, with Rheingold and his blood money, wears thin. So much for Criqueville! I drive, I arrive, I check in.

My worst suspicions are confirmed. The next two towns — and

presumably all the remaining stops — are military installations. Hangars, warehouses, depots for munitions and personnel.

Cash or no cash, this simply won't do.

—◦◦◦—

Finally I understand. My work with Rheingold makes me a snitch. A treasonous, money-grubbing snitch.

Goodbye, easy money. The time has come to turn my sights toward better things. A broad horizon, possibly a life of dignity, a life well-lived, stretches before me. That much is up to me.

I deposit the remaining cash (half in my vault at home, the remainder in the bank) then move on to higher ground. I must come to terms with myself, with all that has happened, with what I have done. Once I do, other projects — rescuing my wife, apostrophizing my life, saving France — will come into focus. I won't need a Hasselblad for this. I've got my heart, my soul, my etheric double brandishing a spirit camera as we scale the heights.

I think, *Go deep within yoursel, Victor.* Whatever lies ahead, whatever came before, must now be dwarfed by that which lies within. Trance work is an ancient venerable practice. The deeper I go, the higher I climb...

I begin my session at the witching hour, just as the clock strikes twelve. My breath slows, becomes regular, even, on the count of *1-2-3-4...1-2-3-4.* Systematic tensing then relaxation of every set of muscles in my body follows. The breathing, together with the restful poise of my body, eliminates physical distraction. I stay here, vigilant, relaxed, alert, as I spin a whorl of light.

The light cocoons me, revolving faster and faster around a stationary core: the living, breathing subject, me. It is a blazing wall of energy, spun from gossamer thought, a barricade between my meditative self and a thousand unwanted intrusions. Intrusions, including street noise, half-remembered songs, sudden thoughts, physical sensations, are jettisoned wholesale, far beyond the luminous wall. Discarding these things, these entities and thought forms, is salutary in the extreme, a far-ranging process of cleansing and self-directed *auto-da-fé.*

Auto-da-fé, not *cassoulet!* Psychic barrier erected, breathing and body in tow, the good void in place. This is where the truly fascinating work of meditation begins. A stream of bare consciousness — words, feelings, somatic stirrings, images — threatens to inundate the shore. The watchful observer, ever vigilant, will let it flow, will allow these slips and shards to meander where they will, so that the stirrings, the parturitions, the shadows, will ebb and flow...and finally desist. The movie screen of the mind, busy with random snatches of yesterdays and today, cluttered, haphazard, like so: *a lemon peel...citronella wax...owl in the eaves...Biarritz tide...tank turret...Montgolfier...the setting sun.*

Get the picture, catch the drift? To the extent I detach from the torrid spectacle, from the compost heap of every passing sight, sound, and smell between now and then — to that extent my spirit, untrammeled, can soar. (An intelligent guide to these mental workings is found in *Liber XII* of my Academy of Magic Bulletin, intended solely for the use of novices, wannabe initiates, and aspirants dedicated to the Path.)

Parked in the clamor-free void like this, I am all dressed up, with nowhere to go. Now what? What comes next?

This is where a schematic — a roadmap, as it were — comes in handy. This terrain has been thoroughly mapped out by the generations of seekers who came before. Kabbalists, alchemists, initiates of yore, with the aid of pentagrams, magic circles, and pantheons, left a living (inner) house plan for generations of indwellers to come.

The immediate goal is rescue, salvage, damage control. Call it what you will, I must employ every sigil, device and incantation known to man in the service of one goal: saving my wife. With that in mind, I turn for assistance to a moon maiden. Circe (Luna, Hecate, Ishtar) may be the only lunar goddess equipotent to my adorably histrionic Woman of Wiles, Djuna. I operate this working in the sphere of Yesod, the Ninth Station of the Kabbalistic Trees of Life. I conjure (and sacrifice) the requisite *chauve-souris* (vampire bat), dedicate coins and imprecations to demon and archangel suborns, my third eye sighting true North.

The operation is a success. Tethered by a silver cord, my astral body soars aloft, ever forward, on a noble quest for house and home. Will I live to tell the tale? Or will inexorable fate sever my vital attachment to earth, and wife, and the life below?

Operation Wife Rescue.

...IS A BLAZING SUCCESS. In my etheric cocoon, I hunker down, spin the filaments of light about me until they aggregate, coalesce into something more substantial. In my trance I feel I can reach out and touch everything I see. The trance state lives, it breathes, ripples with authenticity, with the subtlety and grace of real life.

Where am I? Where I am. At first I don't really know. Two stone pachyderms, trunks poised, stand guard at a gate. It is well past midnight. *Elefantentor,* the elephant gate to the Berlin Zoo, is untended at this hour. A motorcar chugs past in the distance; it chugs alone. Pedestrians have fled; the *Alexanderplatz,* stretching far in both directions, is untenanted.

Astral flight — don't knock it until you've tried it. I hover, I circle, I weave and bob. With feints and comet tail jabs of light, I approach — or rather, am ineluctably drawn toward — a residence on the opposite side of the street. (There are no lorries in this state of mind.) A single window illumines the otherwise somber facade.

Someone or something is awake — I know it. My archangels and devils, a pensive bunch at best, sit it out on the sidelines of my trance. Somehow they are cheering me on — I feel it. The cold vapor condenses in the trails of my flight.

I swoop in to take a closer look. My astral body, more or less a pancake now, flattens its disc-self against the window, hugging it close. The sight of Djuna — of course Djuna, whom else would it be? — stops my heart, clutches at my throat, practically severs the silver cord. This is Djuna in full sacrificial mode, her hair unwound, a penitent's tunic wound tight around her straining mid-section by a ceinture of early medieval design. Every gorgeous inch the virgin maiden, lowering herself onto a platform, no, actually it's a life-sized crucifix, her arms and legs offered in submission to some vampiric oneiric rape...in the person of Leni.

Leni, at this point my least favorite person on earth. Leni the succubus, Lilith, She Who Must Be Obeyed, standing imperiously before my woman's open thighs, licking her lips, studying her prey. She sweeps her floor length cape over Djuna's supine form. Leni draws a dagger — no, wrong again, actually it is a phallus — with gargoyles and other ephemerata carved up and down its horrible length — and laughs.

"Ever the willing victim, eh? No need to tie you down..."

Djuna, very much the eager celebrant, plays the scene out...to the hilt. She whips her lovely head back and forth against the cross's unyielding wood. Mock despair, fatuity, enough genuine sensuality to make me want to puke. Then she pauses, staring up then out the bay window, staring at me and through me, far into the stupid night beyond.

"Leni, I forgot my lines. What comes next?"

"Then you say, *Victor, you cannot resist our sex magic. We summon you.*" Then, "Gad, June, we rehearsed this last night...Maybe this will jar your memory."

Leni transfixes her victim, her tongue leading the charge. No amount of training in psychic self-defense could prepare me for this. Mortified, I accordion my astral self and beat a hasty retreat.

Something must be done.

—〰—

We're not the closest of friends..., but we are definitely friends. I actually look forward to his visits. Unruffled by the Occupation, Rheingold arrives unannounced, unscheduled, an Erich von Stroheim look-alike, always bearing gifts.

199

Under martial law, Paris is no longer a city of lights. Paris is a city of darkness, dour under the weight of curfews, food and clothing shortages, and the ubiquitous presence of the Hun. A stranglehold, aggravated by overt acts of complaisance and collaboration, hangs like a shroud over the capital of the world.

Our recent contretemps notwithstanding, Rheingold is patient with me. At his insistence, the experiments in 'spirit photography', albeit diluted, continue apace. He is pleased with my progress. We make occasional forays into more pleasant conversational realms. One afternoon Rheingold shows up with a small box of books.

"A gift," he says, deftly slicing through the cardboard with an Italian stiletto (handcrafted, only the best).

"For me?"

"Pour toi," he says thickly, his Silesian underbite making a laughable mongrel mess of the words.

Books, books, books. Some are leather bound, others have spines worn down right to the glue. I recognize them right away, the precious reads of my childhood: *The Count of Monte Cristo,* Captain Haddock and Professor Calculus (*Tin Tin*), Jules Verne.

"Where did you get these?" I'm stupefied by the gravitas, by the sudden intimacy of the moment.

He flashes a toothy grin, mostly gold.

"I found a little butcher shop, not too far from here. *Rand et Fils,* I believe it's called. Know the place?"

The question, not entirely innocent, hits home like a punch to the gut. I've been out of touch, out of reach, for far too long. Deprived my mother and father all news of my success. Must be ages since I've called. Absence makes the heart grow cold...In my self-absorption, I have neglected the loving wellsprings of my life. Worse still, how have they fared under the heel of the new regime?

Rheingold isn't an empath but he can read my thoughts, each a white flag, an emblem of surrender, abasement, self-loathing.

"He wanted you to have these," Rheingold says.

"Who — ?"

"Your father, man. Your father."

Further astonishment then further questioning. According to Rheingold, his 'superiors' honored their commitment to me by moving my parents to a safer — ergo, unoccupied, department — of France. Moved them and their business, minus yellow stars of David, out of harm's way.

Rheingold hands me another book, this one even more tattered and ancient than the rest.

"He especially wanted you to have this," he says, screwing that ferocious lens of his back into place.

The volume is handwritten, a memoir in tiny cursive script, hundreds of pages long. It feels strange, like nothing I've held or read before.

"Not mine."

"I should hope not," he says. "What you have there is some of the most vile — vile, execrable, and precious — writing on earth. Your father... he is a collector, *nicht wahr?*"

I study the first pages. In overblown block letters I make out *Confessions...of Alphonse Donatien de S.*

"No," I say. "It's not possible!"

"I thought so too. But I have it on the word of not one but three persons in the know, three experts in the field, mind you, that this is in fact the real thing. Hold on to it, Victor. Guard it with your life."

I thank him, assure him I will.

"And my parents? When can I see them?"

"Soon, very soon. Now then — smile for the spirit camera. Say *Cheese!*"

—ᴠᴠ—

*Let me count the ways...*Along with the exercises in awareness and intense concentration, with all these experiments in consciousness of one form or another, I conduct fearless moral inventories. I plumb the depths of my emotional 'feeling' self and find it grievously wanting.

Not only have I neglected my parents but I fear I have sold Djuna short as well. Her 'experiment' with Leni, for example...may be entirely my fault. Why has she absconded like this, departed with such fury of intent, with such finality? Her seeming dereliction of conjugal duty is anything but. The shrinking bank account: my purview, my lapse of home economics and home husbandry! Wherever she is, whomever she is with, I still feel a glowing ember of kinship, intimacy, love.

It was Djuna, after all, who insisted on marriage. Looking back — looking ahead to the uncertain future — I see that her insistence was not casual, not whimsical. Far from it. Somehow she sensed the looming intrusion of harsh reality. Hey: marrying me spares me, at least for now, from the doomed association with the Yellow Star. In this way, stumble as I may, I can still plan, envisage, strategize; I can shoulder the Academy and carry it forward. My better half, Djuna, is actually looking out for me. I sense this. I feel this. Her continuing devotion means the world to me.

Random insights, haphazard gleanings...I distract myself by coloring the Tarot cards. I apply pastels and earth tones to the major arcana, filling them in as tradition prescribes. Every morning, following two workshops and the self-communion of deep trance, I paint. I daub, I touch, retouch, always careful to stay within the lines. The cards, formerly mute, take on the personality and vibrations of the ink. The life force — the sex power, chakras, kundalini — is always scarlet. Its mastery and redirection is white. Colors in between correspond closely to the gradations of matter between gross matter and the unblemished light of attainment.

This activity propels farther and faster than I imagine. (This has always been the case with occult work — the return far outweighs the initial investment of energy and time.) One day it hits me, with the force of truth: Filling in the blank spaces is a sacred act, essentially an act of creation. I recreate the strokes and image-ination of the first six days on earth. What a feeling! And then a day for rest...

Another card, this one a hand-lettered invitation on fine paper stock, arrives one day. The invaders' hereditary love of music carries the day: a performance of *Das Rheingold,* organized by the occupiers, will be held at the Palais Garnier. I am invited. The event appeals to me on several levels: they are reaching out, currying my favor; the choice of this Wagner work may be more than coincidental. I dust off my top hat and tails; clear out my calendar; and hope for the best.

A box seat has been reserved in my name. I see that I am not alone. A shapely woman, barely acknowledging my presence, peers over the balustrade, studying the hall. Her empire gown, hemmed tightly beneath the bust, is perfectly pleated, all taupe and silver and silk. Her hair, barely contained, falls in an avalanche of waves and curls.

Finally she lowers her lorgnette. I know this woman.

"Djuna!" I exclaim.

⟿⟿

Das Rheingold — or is it *Lohengrin?* — bleats away in the opera hall, a suitable backdrop for our tears, our laughter, the *Sturm und Drang* of our heartfelt reunion. I can hardly believe my eyes, Djuna there beside me, glittered and garlanded, but much the same over the top festival-woman who clambered into my disordered life from the back of a camel. There is a pretense of restraint — the velvet curtains pulled aside for the next ponderous act — but our best efforts are lame, shabby, soon we are in each others' arms and out the door.

We gather our wits in the back of a hansom cab, one of several coach and fours patrolling the district *entr'acte*. I jam a rose somewhere north of her bosom, in the silken verge of her gown; she jams her tongue down my throat. *Why hello! I like you too!* A welcome incursion, to say the least...

Not much has changed: she has endured the tutelage of Leni and Leni's Berlin like a trooper, she is buoyant, festive as ever; she compliments me on my resilience, my savoir-faire, asking "How did you ever make it (i.e., without me)?" I answer, "Did I have any choice in the matter?""Cheri, bitterness is unbecoming...unflattering to you...I'm here, right now, here in your arms. Can't you see?"

The street scene is an afterthought, a sideshow to the main act. Djuna has more than cafes and dappled horses on her mind. She wants to know if Rheingold *behaved.*

"He kept his end of the agreement, if that's what you mean. Paid me in cash...as long as the camera obscura kept clicking."

Right away she detects the hesitation in my words.

"And then?"

"And then I had to stop. Just couldn't go on. Whatever you may think, I'm no rat. No amount of money can justify treason. Sorry *mon coeur*...I'm not working for the enemy."

Her next volley floors me. Although it shouldn't have — considering the company she keeps...

She titters."Oh *you* — enemy, *shmenemy*...we're all brothers under the skin." A pause. "Even if you are Jewish."

"Unacceptable," I counter. "Risqué. You married a Hebe, now deal with it."

The grinding of wheels in the distance...a lorry? A freight car, loaded with terrified kinsmen, rounded up, headed to points unknown?

"Besides," she says, running a finger through my hair, "our very own government is running scared. Preaching and practicing collusion. I know — let's relocate.... How about Vichy?"

"Face it," I say. "We're star-crossed."

"More like Star of David-crossed, I would say."

Djuna — who is she? where did I find her? — gets more precious, ever more inane, with each passing moment. A change in the conversation will do us good. That is, if anything will...

"Things may be looking up," I say.

A Real Find.

We make it past the entranceway, tumbling into what once was our home. She sniffs, on the lookout, I suppose, for any sign of change... the presence of another woman...then she abandons the effort, decides I'm hopeless, concludes, from the predictable arrangement of things, that I haven't been with anyone else.

I take the crook of her elbow, leading her up the stairs.

"Ah," she smiles. "Are we in the mood for love?"

She sags, and throwing back her head, lets a lone shoulder strap descend.

"Hold on," I say. "I want to show you something."

"Ooh...golly..."

I reach for the sideboard, extracting the weathered notebook of de Sade.

"Take a look at this."

"Hardly the time for a good book, *mon amour.*"

She pouts, puts lorgnette to eye, then does as told.

Her jaw drops; the lorgnette hits the floor.

"Where on earth did you get *this?*"

"My dad," I tell her. "He gave it to your pal. Who gave it to me."

"Do you have any idea — ?"

"Not really," I say. "Tell me."

"Why this book is worth its weight in —"

"Rheingold! I know."

She sums up. The couturiers will have a field day...

"Darling," she says, "you simply must have it appraised."

The harried husband — me — flashes her a textbook look.

"*Gott im Himmel*," she sighs, once again forgetting herself and her country, "we need the money."

We kiss, we make up, for a time we even cavort. For now we leave it at that.

—*∿*—

She looks so innocent in her sleep: a jejune Marianne, a nod and a wink away from a carefree run in the field. I know different, of course: she breathes like a baby, lying there, *but I know different*. Three valises spill over with *raffiné* contents, representing plunder, ill-advised purchases, purloined bank accounts from God knows where. Before surrendering to Lethe, she makes light of these, tossing a string-wrapped bundle of receipts and bills my way.

"You'll want to look at these," she says, the all-commanding second person *you* hitting *me* where I live. My heart ricochets in its bony prison. Then she passes out.

What to do?...the choices are few and far between — abandon this expensive flotilla — or float it?! My reasoning goes like this: With Djuna at my side, I am inspired (actually *forced)* to go the distance; to maintain, somehow pass muster and bravely forge ahead.

Twinkle, twinkle, unlucky star...the gleam in Djuna's eye suggests that all is not lost. Or that perhaps it already is. My lovely dark swan rushes in, pretty tail and feathers bobbing. The de Sade peeks out from the lip of her handbag.

"Where has that been?" I say, a drowning sailor, wariness clouding my smile.

"Fulcanelli, the bookseller," she says. "The supreme antiquarian. Sought out by collectors far and wide. Fulcanelli wants it."

"For a very fair price," she adds.

I don't mince words.

"Sold," I say.

—⁓—

The deal is done. Fulcanelli explains his risk: he wasn't aware of the existence of such a notebook; collectors will kick and scream for a chance at it; he will offer the book at closed auction and hope for the best.

"I'm assuming it's authentic," he says.

"Most assuredly," I say. "In my father's library these fifty years past."

Good enough for him. He harrumphs, hawks up a gob of phlegm, then hands me a check.

For a very healthy amount! That night, Djuna and I are beside ourselves, jumping each others' bones for joy.

—⁓—

First thing we do is buy a roadster: a gleaming black sports car that lives to eat up the road. With the top down and the wind in our hair, we are King and Queen of the road. That's not all. Djuna, self-indulgent as ever, particularly elated at this reprieve from the bottom line, wants to go 'shopping' — which has always meant a personal tour, expense account in hand, of the finer outlets of Parisian *haute couture*. I insist on a not unreasonable tightening of the belt (in this case, Balinese crocodile, three thousand eight hundred francs, handcrafted from choice reptilian parts.) The sky's the limit — but we stop there. Wisdom, including the financial sort, comes with age, comes from weathering the storm. The lion's share of the de Sade will secure the future: I pay off arrears on the home and apartment mortgage. A budgetary sleight-of-hand guaranteeing many halcyon days ahead...The roadster runs like a dream, purring, basically driving itself, handling the miles like the extreme toy it is. Djuna, jubilant, beside herself, has gone the limit, preparing a picnic basket for the day. Imagine! Ever the playful *cocotte*, in an excess of enthusiasm, she comes up behind me and slips a pair of touring goggles over my eyes.

"Ha ha!" I cry, pinching her bottom, settling her in beside me with a trail of endearments and sloppy kisses.

À La Maison

The weather, the woman, even the carrion crows in the trees: auspicious, the perfect start of what could be a perfect day.

'Vichy' turns out to be another jewel in our crown. A countryside commune with everything but a beach. As we approach the lane to my parents' new home, I try to catch Djuna up — on some thirty years of back story, all told.

"Silly man," she says, impertinent, glib, raucous — her usual self. "Do you really think any of this is really *necessary?* They sound perfectly adorable. Hush. I'm sure we'll get along."

Speaking of adorable...a classic French farmhouse swings into view. Blocks of hay. Chickens, goats, a happy dog. A far cry from the city.

"I'm not eating those," I protest.

"Shh," Djuna says. "Here we are."

Elation flows like wine. Yes, here we are, reunited in safety, no yellow stars, the prodigal son returned with beautiful wife in tow. Immediately my father breaks the mood. He looks at my wife's flat belly and sighs.

"It's wouldn't be too soon," he says, the inimitable bull in the china shop.

"Romain!" my mother protests. "Hold your tongue. Not now..."

Feathers are ruffled but not plucked. We endure an afternoon of innuendo, separated by tiny islands of civility — touring the house, looking at photo albums — and I apologize for my lapse of filial devotion. My mother makes light of it, so sure she is that I had "better things to do." And how about that Stutz Bearcat parked outside!!!

———

Dinner that night is festive, memorable; a coming together of good times and bad. Mother and father are of course shocked at the irresistible roll-out of the German war machine and its imponderable effect on their lives. At the same time, they are pleased, even delighted, at their new surroundings.

They are country squires, removed from historic necessity, no longer bowing beneath the yoke of social Darwinism. Their concern about the plight of French Jewry is tempered with an insouciance born of distraction and the pleasures of the moment. Together they concoct a banquet fit for a king: endive, watercress and citron salad, the *de rigueur* smoked salmon, vichyssoise (of course!), crab legs slathered in garlic (flagrantly non-kosher), and a marvelous turkey floating on a bed of truffles and escargot. Father is especially proud of his wine, a 1935 Burgundy aided and abetted by cocktails, champagne and many rounds of Armagnac.

———

There's no stopping us, once we set our minds to feast.

Djuna makes the attempt.

Happily she accepts another glass of Pouilly-Fusé then the conversation changes gear. Against my better judgment, in between conjugal tempests and tourneys between the sheets, she has been devouring Freud. Never one to be sidelined, she flaunts her new imprecise knowledge.

"Remarkable, Victor's recent success," she says.

"June..."

She is entrenched, hard put to not go beyond this and expand on her theme. We are in store for uninvited wholly gratuitous dilation.

What comes next surprises even me.

"You're a butcher, Monsieur Rand. *N'est-ce pas?*"

"You've got me there, sweetheart. Always have been. Always will be. What's your point?"

"Simply this, Monsieur."

"Call me Poppa. Please."

"Poppa Please...Nine out of ten psychoanalysts would agree: Victor here is scared to succeed. In fact, he's *terrified*. His success comes at great personal cost. The inner man, sensing doom, trembles in fear. I know this. I live with him."

Sensing that her brilliance has fallen on deaf ears — worse still, on stupid brains — Djuna gets up, makes for the kitchen.

My astonished parents bow their heads, completely at a loss.

"Where is she going?"

"I'm back!" she says, exulting in her sense of *a triumphant return*. Djuna brandishes a butcher knife in one hand, a gleaming meat cleaver in the other.

"Think about it, Monsieur Rand.. The obvious question. It's sooo obvious. How many of these" — brandishing the cutlery — "has Victor seen in the course of his short young life? What lasting effect —" she lands the ax deep into the table — "do you suppose that might have had? *Hein?*"

Next thing, she primly takes her seat. Finishes her drink. The profundity resumes.

"Oedipus complex, folks. Each success a setback. The poor man is terrified that someone, something, will cut IT off."

Three cheers to my father! Forty years in the *boucherie,* trading quips with whomever came through the door, has well equipped him for badinage. He rises to the occasion — and to our collective defense.

"Oedipus, *schmoedipus,*" he says, prying the blade from the riven wood. "How about some *schnapps?*"

—⁂—

Cuban cigar in one hand, tumbler of cognac in the other, I am back to myself. Once again alive, alive and in love. Djuna, dressed like a flapper, is radiant, her sequins and smile catching the light and, infinitely generous, throwing it back to the room.

—♦—

"You've done well for yourselves, I'll say that." My father leans back, pulling on his cheroot. Is he actually leering at my wife?

"In large part thanks to you," I say, dismissing my observation. "The de Sade volume caused quite a stir. Imagine the scribblings of that old reprobate fetching such a price!"

My father is genuinely impressed.

"The one you so thoughtfully sent to me, along with the Robert Louis Stephenson, the Jules Verne, the Dumas. The de Sade was a masterstroke."

The metaphorical meat cleaver — the sword of Damocles — descends.

"Wasn't me," he says.

I look at Djuna but she is hardly there. She toys with a crab leg, applies the lit end of her cigarette to the dead vacant eye of the crustacean.

"Djuna," I say.

Finally she looks up.

"Wasn't me," she says.

Once again a pall descends on the room. Something is up. Conviviality bows out, making way for silence and gloom. Something clutches at my innards. Only Herr Rheingold can shed light on this. But Rheingold is absent, away, tending to the Reich.

And to all a good night...

Walking Papers.

When it rains, it pours.

Marital bliss, a respite from reality and the other events of the day, is soon shattered. Djuna comes to me, disconsolate — not like her, not like her at all — with telegram in hand.

"It's Leni," she says. "She needs me."

"She needs you. What am I...wood?"

This brings her back to her fatuous self.

"Silly goose," she says. "You know Leni. She — they — are making another film. More important than ever."

"Right," I say. I know all about Leni's films...I don't even ask where, or how; at this point, the details are beyond me. All I know is that, once again, she is dropping the crystal ball.

"But I'll be back. Or better still, you'll come with. You'll join us, won't you, dear heart? Say you will!"

⸺∿⸺

No camel at the door this time, no turbaned dromedaries bearing a jaded empress. I put her in a taxi and she is gone.

Later that day I'm still crying. The end of France, the death of romance... insufferable indignity, unpardonable loss.

Then the telephone rings — a klaxon call from hell.

"Rand?"

I know the voice. From a distance, the pretense of authority grates horribly on my nerves.

"She's gone, Rheingold," I sob. "Find her!"

"I'll see what I can do," he says. "But first things first. Listen up."

I collect myself, put my mental house in order, enough to field the call. Rheingold wants to 'test' my powers of clairvoyance. Clairvoyance, clairaudience, extrasensory perception. Wants me to track down the source of some 'troublesome' radio transmissions originating in France.

"No, Rheingold, I won't do it. Now you've gone too far. I'm not spying on the Resistance. Do you finally understand?"

"I'm afraid you don't understand, *liebchen,*" he says. "You don't really have a choice. That manuscript you sold. Take another look. It is a forgery, plain and simple. Bankruptcy, humiliation, public censure —tell me: is it really worth it?"

"Blackmail! How cruel. How very *sadistic!* You can't be serious..."

"Oh, but I am," he says. "Here — " he says, " — listen to the voice of reason."

The receiver changes hands. Now it is Djuna, remorseful or playacting, I can't tell which...

"What are you doing there? With *him?*"

"Oh my God," she says, "I'm so sorry that it's come to this. But Rheingold is right. You've got to flush those transmissions out...for the greater good of all. If you don't, the reprisals will be far greater. Unthinkable. That's why I'm here. For you. And for France."

Again, the phone changes hands.

There is a ring tone, then there is nothing.

—⁓—

A fine kettle of fish, I'll say that. My recondite leanings, my glorious

Institute, my encounters with sages contemporary and past — all use-less, null,empty, hopeless. Enfeebled, desperate, I return to the only far-seeing promontory I know. I retire, retire deeply to a single point of awareness.

I summon my inner Sol Deutsche.

"Ha ha!"

He cartwheels, bounding across the floorboards of my heightened imagination like a dancing bear...but this is no Moscow circus. This is dead serious...

Finally upright, Deutsche is something to behold: his costume an ata-vistic tribute to a pantalooned past, the jacket four sizes too small, the pockets of his pants turned inside out in a lampoon of penury, he laughs, he cavorts — again he jumps, then sighs. How his Geppetto hat remains on his head through all this, I'll never know...

More to the point, he offers advice.

"Think Victor, *think*...You are poisoned by phenomena, paralyzed by events. *The antidote should be within easy reach.*"

"Come again?"

"Use your power, Victor. *Take a closer look.*"

With that, Deutsche is gone. I'm about to call it a day, shut down the trance, pack up my *asana* and the rest of my mental gear, when suddenly it hits me.

Of course: remote viewing!

If I could use it to betray France, I could certainly use it to save my sorry hide.

With some minor adjustments, a turn of the Inner Dial, deep in trance, I call up Djuna. I am an old hand at this so she appears as more than an image. This is the same living breathing woman who only recently left my bed.

She is not alone. Rheingold, assisted by two officers of the Reich, sur-round her struggling form. She is captive, straining against ropes; would cry out if not for the wad of cheesecloth trailing from her mouth. The vision flickers, fading in and out, my heart pounding hard against my ribs. The vision wilts, flares, a horribly unwelcome sight...

Rheingold leers, imprecates, waves a crooked finger. I can see the ridges and whorls of alluvial tobacco deposits along the finger's filthy ridge.

"If you care to see her again...anywhere on this side of eternity...I suggest you rethink your...*approach.*" I imagine that I see the hemp cords cutting into her tender flesh.

"Enough," I say (or broadcast or remotely transmit). " I'll do it. Just leave her be. Untie her, set her free...and I'm all yours. Okay?"

A mourning dove appears, a tiny parchment scroll in its beak. The precious bird coos in appreciation as I unfurl the message (These events transpire in trance but they portend what will soon enough be real.) A lieutenant of the *Einsatzgruppen,* disguised as a peasant, will collect me at my office door at the break of dawn. 'They' have big plans for me.

Djuna and her captors fade out.

My nerves are frayed.

Here comes the next hairpin turn.

—◦◦◦—

Victor Rand? Victor...? Or victim?

Perhaps both...

My poker-faced companion, in black beret and fatigues, has little to say.

This is no Frenchman, I think. I keep the thought to myself.

We are professionals. I will spring Djuna, and that will be the end of this nasty business...

The country and its people are tense, tight-lipped, scurrying for supplies and sometimes for cover. The changes, the devastation, the widespread paralysis — they truly break my heart.

Back to Berlin! This city is also changed, dressed in the bellicose bonnet of war. I recall my last time here, my dream visit, frightful yet somehow inspiring...and now I'm back. Inside the city proper, my appointed driver insists on hooding me — a black balaclava without eyes. I submit to this latest indignity. What choice do I have?

Wolfgang (*Fritz? Hans?* all those miles, and I never learn his name) deposits me at the door. Each step of the journey — up to and including this last one — is freighted with enormous protocol. Border crossings, mountain passes, sentry boxes — each attended by grim young men barking at each other in a guttural language that deeply offends my ear. The requests for papers are legion...

They hand me off, saluting and barking, checking papers (they have a madness for papers, it's obvious) and finally I'm inside. This is it: deep in the bowels of the earth, beneath the Reich Chancellery, in the concrete and steel hive of the Big Man and the Big Man's High Command.

Taciturn becomes tactful. Suddenly I am surrounded not by soldiers but by strategists. Men with severe, perfectly groomed faces, faultless posture; impeccable opprobrium presiding over all.

Then I see her, my queen bee: my Djuna. Looking natural, carefree, in army fatigues; the way I like it.

Hall of the Mountain King.

"Welcome to the *Führerbunker,*" she says, throwing me a guarded wink. "Your home away from home."

Djuna takes my hand, leading me away from my High Command imperial escort.

"Play along," she whispers. "These guys love a good show."

Still no sign of danger. No scimitar or revolver leveled at Djuna's snow white throat. Far from it. Two levels down, three chambers in, we are feasted...fêted...set loose on a banquet fit for a king. Or a Chancellor. The classic dishes — *schnitzel, sauerbraten, blutwurst,* head cheese — elevated to artistry by flagons of Rhine wine and heady steins of bock beer.

Off to the side, a string quartet cranks out the strains of *Hall of the Mountain King.* Meanwhile, The Big Man is nowhere in sight.

"And here I thought you were in trouble," I muse, savoring my second or third joint of freshly slaughtered lamb.

"Hardly. In fact, once we sleep this meal off, we are in for a real treat... our very own side car!"

"I don't want a side car."

"Shh," she says. "Just play along."

"This is perfect for a couple. *Wunderbar*. Perfectly designed, with young people like you in mind." And, to eradicate any lingering doubt, "The Americans have nothing on us. Tell me: have you ever seen such craftsmanship?"

The salesman — Otto, or Friedrich, or Gunther, it's hard to say — practically swoons, he is that pleased with himself. The showroom speaks for itself: a dozen or so 'late' model sedans plus sidecar, the officious little numbers only the Germans could ever devise. 'Sedan' is overly generous: the vehicle part of the contraption is more like a tube, a sausage, a rocket, ingeniously or precariously retrofitted onto an upholstered box built for one.

In France we have a word for this: *Ringard*. Meaning 'corny', 'tacky', in utter and obvious bad taste. But there really is no accounting for taste, particularly in a nation obsessed with world domination, anthropometry, and racial hygiene. Gracious, perhaps unaware of my Semitic origin, the gentleman encourages us to 'take it for a spin.' In my mind's eye I see him applying the calipers to my cranial vault, then examining my privates.[10]

---

10 **Editor's note**: The following monograph, 'A Sidecar Named Desire', was found among Rand's surviving documents:

The Knowledge is out there. It always was. Timeless Wisdom consoles. An avuncular Guardian Angel, luminous wings beating the cadence of eternity, kept constant watch, a kind presence over and behind and around me. Someone to Watch Over Me.

I read widely. I scoured libraries, databases, talked to rabbis and gurus. What I found was deliciously consistent: you are what you think. *Tap into your True Self and the rhythm of the cosmos will be yours. As above, so below. I'm dancing as fast as I can. Etc. & etc...*

A paunchy gentleman in top hat and tails handed me the Key to Aphorism City (Think: the dashing little man on the Monopoly board...)

God, grant me the courage to change the things I can.

Hermes Trismegistus, King Solomon, John Dee, Paracelsus, neo-Platonists galore: the whole bloody lot of them chanting in unison, *Use the force, dude, Use the force...*

So I did. (Or thought I did.)

I achieved trance states, following upon the rigorous application of tried and true methods:progressive relaxation, breath control, visualization, Active Imagination...

In one of these a testy apparition (think: Vincent Price in *The Tomb of Ligeia*) appeared: winking, munching cheerily away on a celery stalk.

"Say there" the sprite said. "I'm your *demon familiar.* I'm here to advise."

A beat.

"Go on," I said.

"Well," he said, "you can forget about your Higher Power. 'Taint no such thing. As a matter of fact, you can pretty much do whatever the hell you want!"

The sober light of Truth was dawning.

"You mean Ayn Rand...Friedrich Nietzsche...Muamar Qaddafi...were right?"

He beamed.

"You got it, kid. *Do what thou wilt shall be the whole of the Law.*"

I came to with a start.

A whole new world of possibility was open to me. No moral, ethical or spiritual guidelines; no constraints whatsoever. I could be anything, do anything my heart desired.

I had a new outlook on things. I was radicalized. No one could challenge my imperial stance.

The sky was the limit.

So I bought myself a swanky sidecar:

Turncoat.

THEY WINE AND DINE me: *Putting out the dog,* one might even say.

My companions at table — the scenario painstakingly realistic, meant to resemble four-star dining in every way, with candle light, *sommelier,* chamber music and all — are Djuna and Leni. And two high placed intelligence officers of the Waffen S.S.

Djuna is radiant, the black evening dress cut low, her pearls resplendent in the light. Even Leni, in butch field uniform, looks crisp and sparkling tonight. A violinist does his reasonable best with *Liebenstraum.*

The crispier and more starched of the officers raises an eyebrow, adjusts a monocle. Offers me a smoke.

"So. Can we go forward? May we count on your help? The time is right to make your move, Victor Rand. Mars is in the seventh house."

I smile — a flattered, foolish, perfectly vacuous grin. I say nothing.

The coffee and *schnapps* arrive. Djuna throws me a significant look, taking me by the elbow. She knows I rankle at the thought of cooperating in any way.

"The loo," she says, *sotto voce.*

"Pardon us," I say to all and sundry, rising and taking a bow.

We make our way down the corridor — less restaurant and more citadel, I see, the further we walk — and Djuna leans close.

"Play along," she whispers. "Convince them you have a plan."

—∿—

Erwan Pfennig-Strumpf, a big wig in the Nazi hierarchy, comes across as a *softie.* I suppose the guise is intentional, a piece of theatre rigged up through the infinite cleverness of their war machine. The costume is what I've come to expect: the *de rigeuer* monocle, the paisley ascot, the leather riding boots. The jodhpurs as if chronically carrying a load. If the fellow wasn't directing my personal Inquisition, he'd be right at home on a movie set...

Kaffee, strudel and conversation — under hot lights, at three a.m.

The gentleman proceeds.

Business as usual.

I beat him to the punch.

"Erwan," I say, "may I call you Erwan?"

"By all means. Please."

"After careful reflection — and a good deal of soul-searching — I've made my decision. You have won me over. I've decided to play with the winning team, as it were."

"Ah. The voice of reason. Finally you have come around, I am absolutely delighted."

I step away from the table and move to the blackboard, which has been conveniently placed there for my treasonous designs. I pick up a piece of chalk and use it to emphasize my talking points, stabbing at the air (always toward Erwan) as I digress...

"My meditations reveal stunning opportunity...in the enhancement of one of the Reich's already estimable areas of strength.

"For years, Germany has been unrivaled in manufacture. Your nation puts out the most powerful and efficient machines on earth."

"And — ?"

"Automobiles, gentlemen, automobiles!"

My auditor adjusts his eyepiece, carefully inspecting me (as it were.) Am I damaged? Am I mad?

"Hear me out," I say.

"What I'm about to tell you is bold. Not only bold but beautiful too. Hot off the psychic press. Stamped with the promise — and inevitability — of tomorrow.

"The car," I say, "has always been a handy designation for the body... and the spirit. Way before the genius of Karl Benz, or my countryman André Citroen, thousands of years before, *Phoebus* rode his chariot past the sun...dependably...every morning, in fact. Mystic *car*-tographers — believe me, the word is not casual, not coincidental — depicted the soul's journey as a chariot, a chariot fronted by rocketing, frothing steeds. A Tarot card of the very same name, The Chariot, tells it all. Perhaps these mystagogues knew what was coming. Perhaps they already knew what would put Germany on the map."

"As it were," Erwan adds. Humor, from a wan Pfennig-Strumpf, at four a.m.?

"My demon familiars advise us as follows. We need to capitalize on your country's greatest and most appealing strength."

"Which is — ?"

"*The sidecar!* Man! The sidecar's potential role in the Great Aryan Unfolding is indubitable, already revealed. My demon familiars have spelled it out.

"You may well ask, *why the sidecar?* I continue.

"I'll tell you why. The sidecar, in particular the German sidecar, has to be the ultimate symbol of authority, subordination, submission, paternalism, hierarchy, the Fatherland. It is a bullet-shaped phallus, a motoric sidearm, an arrow poised at the heart of the future.

"It may well disappoint — but comes as no surprise to me — that the concept was originally French. Legend has it that a French army officer named Bertoux designed a massy contraption to carry one passenger — this was way back in 1893.

"Obscene ornamentation? Gilding the lily? I think not." I move closer to the board, spelling and drawing out my thesis in broad bold strokes upon the slate.

"The M-72 bike, with turret-mounted gun, based on BMW's blueprints, was Stalin's attempt to modernize the Russian war effort. Motorcycles manufactured in Irbit by Irbit Motorcycle Works came to be known as 'Urals."

The shoe is on the other foot. Now *my* audience is captive. Erwan yawns and rubs his unguarded eye.

"I could use a drink," he says.

His comment gives me pause. Was my delivery anything less than brilliant? I look at my watch.

"At this ungodly hour? What kind of drink, if I may ask?"

"A sidecar!" he chortles. "I can practically taste it."

I chime right in.

"Of course," I say. "What we have here," I say, trying my best to stay on point, "is neither a coupe...nor a sedan...nor is it a roadster. We have an eminently useful, supremely practical conveyance, with bolted-on wicker chairs, cargo boxes, or missiles...as the case may be.

"Each model is different: uniquely striving for, and uniquely attaining, the very acme of the grotesque. Sidecars are a slap in the face of bourgeois punctiliousness, of Judeo-Christian self-righteousness. Friedrich Nietzsche, may he rest in peace, would have loved one.

"Tubular steel frame; passenger car; or utility box — the choice is always yours. Leaf spring suspensions soon caught on. The car box, aesthetic nightmare that it is, lends itself readily to any number of iterations: single or double seats, *pompier* apparatus, chimney sweeping equipment, what have you..."

The major domo arrives, briskly sweeping away the remains of our now forgotten meal. Erwan signals the man. He clears his throat briskly."I require something,"

"Sir — ?"

"A sidecar, please. And don't spare the cognac."

The man looks my way but Erwan anticipates."Nothing for him."

Some remarks are better left untouched — *let sleeping dogs lie.* I continue, spreading the Good Word. (I'm just warming to my subject. I'm a teacher, after all...My enthusiasm will melt Erwan's hoarfrost like a warm spring rain...)

"Harley-Davidson in America came out with its own sidecar in 1915.

The sidecar achieved real notoriety the following year when the United States Army ordered some Harleys to flush out Pancho Villa in Mexico. That's when Bill Harley further sophisticated sidecar engineering by introducing machine gun mounts.

"Sidecars featuring turret-mounted machine guns saw action during the War to End All Wars."

"You can thank Versailles for that one," Erwan interjects, drinks in hand, fists making a broad sweep of the room.

"Never again."

"Duly noted," I say. "Shall I continue?"

Erwan is silent. His body language says it all: he is desperate for the major domo. He wants another drink.

"Hugo Young's Flxible Sidecar Company of Youngville, Ohio — the competition — is for a time the largest sidecar company in the world. The Swallow Sidecar Company — of Britain — re-emerges as Jaguar Cars. Few know that. In response to diminished demand, Flxible now makes ambulances and hearses of renown."

—◦◦◦—

"Then your BMW and Zundapp got in the game. Which brings us full circle."

Supplied with fresh liquor, for the moment renewed, Erwan wipes at his monocle. He's about to upbraid me — we're here for a reason, for military strategy, not for a history lesson.

Once again I beat him to the punch.

"Here's the plan, sir. I have canvassed demon hordes, archangels, pored over grimoires, and I can tell you this: the Wehrmacht need go no further.

"The thousand-year Reich, and beyond, are virtually guaranteed by massively increasing the presence of this killing machine. Every commando worth his salt will want one. My transports in the Astral Realm reveal a grand design, a Cosmic Blueprint if you will: a splendid vision, an endless network of German sidecars shuffling to and fro across the globe...carrying soldiers, sensitive information, ordnance...an unstoppable accretion of Teutonic engineering, multiplied to the nth degree...the realization of ancient dreams...a Fatherland composed of busy sidecars... *happy sidecars* navigating thoroughfares, brooking all obstacles, honking merrily away...blasting their way through people and outposts like there's no tomorrow...carrying a message of authority, of invincibility... finally proving to the world that the technological know-how of Germany far outshines that of America, of Ford, of Chrysler...and always will!"

I'm radiant. I'm on a tear. I'm incandescent.

"What do you think, Erwan?

Erwan puts down his drink.

"Guard!" he shouts, "take this man away. He is out of his element. He is out of his mind!"

—⁓—

Dream of the Sword of Damocles?...On 30 October 1940, Pétain makes state collaboration official, declaring on the radio: "I enter today on the path of collaboration."

—⁓—

More feasting, more dilation, more time spent waffling among the *Waffen* in the corridors of German power. What it finally comes down to is this: in exchange for Djuna, for a shot at our life together as we knew it (solvency included), I will carry the gauntlet...renewing my estimable efforts on their behalf, including remote viewing of troop movements, bombardments, aerial missions...

In short, I will make my best effort to influence the course of the war.

I will psychically attack Whitehall and Churchill.

The plans are spelled out, rather succinctly, in a two hundred page 'brief' that would have done von Clausewitz proud.

The more I hear, the less I like. I take great umbrage at these demands. They defy every notion of what I hold dear. They violate my basic sense of what is right and what is not.

But Djuna is already there, tugging at my pragmatic sleeve, reminding me about Romain and Stella, now ensconced in bourgeois comfort and relative safety. Reminding me of the evaporation, thanks to Rheingold, of our bills, our mortgage, our outstanding debt at *Maxim's, Deux Magots, Dior, Chanelat,* at every boutique in the land...

The trade winds blow fair, blow east of the Maginot Line. I'm about to surrender it all — my integrity, my commitment to the spiritual high road — to the inexorable pressure of the moment.

That same night, right before bed, I overhear her: Djuna in hushed tones on the phone in the next room.

"I almost have him," she says. "He's about to give in."

A pause.

"Yes.......(mumble, mumble)...*der Führer's* plaything...and then I can be with you."

Softly, she replaces the phone on the cradle, tiptoeing into the room. Comes up to me, hovers, delivers a soft kiss.

"Good night, my darling," she whispers.

Good riddance, I think.

Coup de Foudre.

THIS IS WAR, *WAR* in every sense of the word. War, with belligerents facing off on killing fields, facing off with cannon, sword, animus and lead. War, featuring death and gore and the horrid plaints of the wounded and dying. Entire nations in *extremis*, making ultimate sacrifice for the greater good...Mobilization, recruitments, oraisons and field calls, battle cries on the field of Mars...This is a time to distill, to sublimate, to refine: a time to set aside my merely human concerns in the service of a far greater calling — the dignity of man, the survival of men, women, and children beneath the cudgels and ploughshares of hatred, division, and blood lust.

Djuna's advice — *just play along* — is sound. Exactly! Leni and her Obersturmführer, on the highest authority, hope to install me in a glorious lakeside setting, where I will marshal sufficient force to roll in the Reich's next thousand years.

So I play along. Sounds great, I tell them. Consider this, I say. *I can do far more damage with a full complement of willing souls. I need my student entourage to invoke the rise of your new Dark Age.*

They hear me out — and ultimately, they agree. In exchange for a massive prospectus of the invocations and conjurations to come, they will release me. The obligatory show of crocodile tears, the demonstration of tenderness and longing compassed — Djuna and I professing eternal love, renewing vows and saccharine versions of the Eternal Return — I am on my way.

———✳———

Paris is a shadow of her former self. Metro stations serve as bomb shelters. Harassed citizens don't know where collaboration ends and resistance begins. Every gesture is fraught with double meaning. Paniers of pastry may conceal nests of vipers, poisonous complicity and murderous intent. I encourage these images; grow them, nurse them. The images flow smoothly now; they will be useful in my experiments in sabotage and regicide.

I hatch the plans covertly, with no visible assistance. More than once, Sol Deutsche, more clownish than ever, puts in a appearance. (Mystically speaking, of course.) Deutsche's bereft careworn appearance is welcome to me: the trances are lonely, plaintive summonings on interior windswept plains. He spells it out, in plain English and French. I will need a *minyan* of kindred spirits, celebrants capable of raising sufficient force to invoke Ares and attendant demiurges in a massive show of strength.

Ares. Mars. Martial vehemence. Firebrands by any other name...Kali, Arjuna, gods and goddesses of war, standard bearers of devastation...With this operation, we will wipe the slate clean. The repeated application of force will replace darkness with light. Deutsche, in the guise of psychopomp, hierophant, and spiritual arbiter, assists in the plans. Deep in trance, I select my best students to orchestrate the music of our righteous *coup.*

Coup: 'Cut', 'blow', 'severance'...bloodshed in the name of life. Psychic slaughter — execution of the Big Man, a.k.a. decapitation of the German Wehrmacht — is the name of the game. I anticipate with relish the consequence of our concerted astral attack, as in: *So long, cloaca-face! I bind you, I scythe you, I winnow you with the blade of my psychic sword. I have personally reached out to the Prince of gnomes and salamanders in order to strike you down...*

I approach the Academy differently now. There is a certain springiness, a marked lightness, to my step. The floorboards, the slate boards; the kabbalistic diagrams, the tapestries and charts — these speak to me in clear tones, shine with renewed brightness, a brightness lost upon me before.

FASTING. ABSTENTION. INTENSE MENTAL FOCUS.

I handpick the team.

I enter a period of fasting, abstention and intense mental focus.

Five of us embark on the grueling process of ritual magic execution. My team is hand-picked: each celebrant has demonstrated superior skill in the playing field of the mind.

I have tested them mightily, without respite they have come through with flying colors. Each is capable, by means of sharply attuned pinpoint concentration, to invoke; to evoke; to sit in the eye of a hurricane while directing the traffic of the world.

The chamber flies the adversary's martial colors: red, white and black. Swastika-festooned draperies and flags hang from the rafters. A single crucible sends clouds of dark smoke from the center of the room. We will call forth Mars — Ares — the god of hellfire and war. His lieutenants will bow and scrape before us and do our bidding. The ceremony will wipe clean the global slate. In the center of it all is the main object of our intention — a ju-ju doll to wreak our collective fury on.

This is no ordinary *poupée,* not a plaything to elicit squeals of delight from little girls...No, friends, this is an Adolf Hitler doll, this is the man himself in exact miniature effigy. A tiny armband holds a tiny field jacket sleeve in place. I have seen to every detail. The conjuration and dispatch

— the vibration that will send this monster into the next world — must have a specific, exact target, must be precise in every way. The replica's features are painstakingly modeled in wax; the miniature mustache, handcrafted from the black whiskers of a dozen rats, are our final solution, our finishing touch.

Passion, and vehemence, and the blue flame of righteous indignation go into every step of the operation. I have seen to it personally.

The ritual slaughter proceeds swimmingly, each step unfolding as carefully rehearsed. We reach somber accord in our visualization, in our chanting, in our hearts poised as one. We want this man dead, we want him and his henchmen banished from the face of the earth. In the flickering light of the tapers (five candles — five cloaked initiates — five being the mystic number of Mars), the Hitler's wax face yellows and melts.

And Soror Paracelsus — whose name, I later learn, is actually Annelise Spielverderber (*'spoilsport'*) — suddenly breaks rank and runs screaming from the room.

The circle has been broken. Sighs, murmurs and protests replace the grave tone of malediction that came just before.

By the time I catch up with her, it is too late.

Annelise is on the phone. She slams the receiver down, glaring at me, a tempest of triumph.

"You've gone too far," she says. "I just turned you in."

—◈—

Events — horrible events, unlikely events — rush my way, drowning me in a storm of adversity that leaves me breathless, unmoored.

This time the Obersturmführer means business. As do the grim soldiers at his side. One of them cocks his weapon, leveling it at my head.

"Get in the car," he says.

"No sidecar?"

Silence. Then a vicious slap.

Goodbye serenity... hello Rhineland.

—◈—

...Which is only the beginning of a glorious itinerary down sentried roads, driving all night, stopping at checkpoints until I am delivered, far the worse for wear, to a mountaintop chalet.

Obersturmführer Klyster.

The last leg of the journey is accomplished in complete darkness, the obligatory balaclava once more in place. My thinking has slowed, I find I can substitute legitimate concerns for wild ones. I suppose the balaclava is a good thing: paradoxically, it offers *a ray of hope.* Perhaps they won't kill me. Perhaps I will survive and live to tell the tale.

Attempts at conversation have utterly failed. The few snatches of German I recognize, the banter that passes as chat between driver and guard, are banal, inane, devoid of the slightest clue.

Oberstürmführer Harald Klyster, the picture of conviviality, is there —just for me! — when we arrive.

"Call me Klyster," he says, pouring me a glass.

"*Liebfraumilch,*" he says. "The very best. In my view, equal to any of your Bordeaux."

Someone or something tells me to play along. This imposing officer, pomp and circumstance aside, needs to be toyed with. I press my luck.

"Where exactly are we?" I ask.

"Ah," he says, beaming like Helios resplendent at dawn. "That's for me to know...and for you to find out." His French is accomplished, almost flawless. Did I expect anything less?

The wine hits the spot. I don't care if it's doctored — I'm thirsty. I hold out my glass.

"Three guesses," he says, topping me off.

I swallow, I consider.

"I give up..."

"Welcome to Berghof," he says. "For the time being, your home away from home."

The information revives me. I look around. The place reminds me of Tiffauges, the chateau of the infamous Bluebeard, Gilles de Rais.

Berghof is High Command Headquarters. And aerie of the Leader. Perhaps I'll meet the Great Man.

"And to whom do I owe the honor?"

"Ach," he says, his pretend wistfulness oozing like a purulent sore. "Mostly you owe it to yourself! You made bad decisions —" here he inhales, " — decisions that landed you *here*. Bad for you and bad for the Reich."

Oberstürmie won't dismount. He is on a tear, gallivanting on his high horse.

"The forces of the Reich — in the person of a certain *Herr Wolf* — offered you a chance in a lifetime. With your talents, you could have brought an inevitable conclusion to an even more rapid close. But no. You could have transcended your miserable birthright, risen above your degeneracy, could have been a gleaming engine of the Wehrmacht. But no. You show your true colors, defy the inexorable. Henceforth it is my privilege to grind you into dust."

Whoa. Oberstürmie has issues.

"Herr Wolf?" I ask.

He glances quickly at a portrait of Hitler on the opposite wall. It's taken me this long to notice it. Hitler's mustache is a dead rat nestling on his upper lip. Oberstürmie darts his beady eyes back.

He clears his throat.

"Wolf is my employer," he says. "Let's leave it at that."

My captor is all business. He signals to the guard on the other side of the room. Together, they lead me down three flights of stone steps, finally unhanding me into the cold embrace of a cellar, a dungeon of sorts.

"Welcome to your final resting place, Maus," he says. Adjusting my eyes to the gloom, I see a windowless chamber of uncertain extent: bare damp walls, a small table, a chair, a bucket.

"Meet Berchtesgaden Bertha," he says, waxing triumphant, gleeful, downright mean. His service revolver is aimed at my heart.

The soldier, huffing and puffing, drags over a large iron ball. Events are dreamlike, barely sequential, uncanny. As in a trance.

"Hold still."

Looking down, as if from a great height, I see the younger man working at my pants leg.

In a moment everything — my glorious career, my life's work, *everything* — is utterly foreclosed. With satisfaction, he snaps the leg iron shut. Then they are gone.A short length of chain attaches me to the massive metal ball, my constant companion for the months and years to come.

If I survive.

The Perfect Dungeon.

The contours of the dungeon are almost perfect; the chamber matches in every detail the layout of my caged soul. My prison extends as far as my eyes can see. It is grey, murky, habitually crepuscular. The shadows are long; even though they are few and fleeting; these are the remnants of the fingers of available light. The grillwork looks out onto a bare corridor, patrolled irregularly by a wordless, expressionless Hun. I mark the passage of time by the arrival of food: thin porridges, gruel, a rind of cheese, served up in the same filthy basin day in, day out.

I relieve myself by squatting over a hole. The hole — the single point of egress from this nightmare of stupefaction — opens, as far as I can make out, to even greater depths of darkness. Far below this I hear the plangent roar of a cataract... or something far worse.

A wealth of time on my hands. Within days the elbows and knees of my garments are worn through. My captors, who have long ceased to identify themselves, provide occasional succor from the cold and damp: soggy clothing, a putrid pallet on the floor, a horsehair blanket.

Then there's the iron ball. Try as I might, I cannot wish it away. In desperation, I invoke every angel, every demon known to every grimoire written by man. I throw Akashic and yogic spells at it, hoping to paralyze the ball's confounded materiality — the sheer *is*-ness of it (it sits there, dumb, always the same) — with everything I've ever known, revamped and revised. Which of course does nothing but confirm my worst suspicions: all my efforts, schooling, the arcane studies and meritorious aspirations, were for nought. Nothing. *Nada.* Feelings — miserable but finally human — of universality, of concordance in suffering, sweep over me. Thousands, millions of souls out there are likewise in pain, caught up in the brush fires and adversity of mindless history...of historical event...driven by the madness of one man, his cowardly peons, and his nation, all united in rapacity and shame.

So what was the point? This accumulated wisdom, this concordat of schools and sorrow and learning — all this in the name of survival? Have I achieved this *summmum bonum,* this pinnacle of 'self-mastery', only in order to manage the hurricanes of self-doubt and suicidal thoughts now engulfing the lookout points of my mind?

Cast out self-doubt, Victor Rand: there is a hundred pound ball stapled to your leg.

The homilies and aphorisms are many, the take-home lessons are few and far between. Try as I might, in this state of mind, I cannot 'cook the books.' The ledger is written in deep, self-incriminating slashes of red ink. I've lost so very much...and speaking of the 'bottom line': What have I really gained?

Victor Makes Lemonade.

In a truly pluralistic society, those who do not wash
their clothes would freely rub elbows with those who do.

—Sol Deutsche, *Toward A*
Pluralistic Multiverse (undated)

Prison — a quaint notion for one such as me. The length and breadth of my present diocese is no larger than a gunny sack.

Educational and vocational opportunities seem to abound here. For a time, very briefly, I actually contemplate law school. I recall hearing that magazine subscriptions are free for felons. Perhaps I could appeal to the community of initiates in the Rhineland: *I am a convicted felon, and would like to take advantage of your penitentiary premium offer.*

My mind wanders, meandering to little known convolutions and byways. How much longer, this life of self-abuse, this search for meaning, for Djuna, for liberty?

Supernatural terror is a good thing: it means we believe something is really out there.

Would we feel quite as guilty if it was called *Riding Satan's Horse* (rather than 'jerking off')?

It occurs to me that the women of my dreams share one overriding feature: not only are they gorgeous and devious — they are also tomboys and who knows, perhaps even androgynes at heart?

It is in this exact frame of mind that I conceive a mad love for the American cowgirl Annie Oakley. (Annie is a way-ahead of her time roustabout known for her loose tongue: *"Hey sport, I'll wear your guts for garters!"*)

Annie Oakley

I spit upon the accomplishments of athletes everywhere, with the possible exception of the New York Yankees, professional wrestlers, and the Tour de France. I've always felt this way, lauding the achievements of the mind and excoriating the achievements of the physique.

Face it, Victor: you would have done better as a self-mortifying monk.

Did I say, *Go to hell?* Sorry. I meant, *Go to Herculaneum!*

Ever notice the dubious facial expression that all babies wear? What's with that, anyway? Do babies instinctively regret their arrival in such a haphazard world?

From where do our finer instincts — altruism, generosity, self-sacrifice

— derive? Bees, antelopes, humankind — all basically the same?

I must ask you, where's the honey? Does it arrive in the shape of municipal infrastructure we choose to name after Polish generals (such as *the Pulaski Skyway?*)

What benefits would I enjoy as the King's newfound friend? Discount vacations in the Sargasso Sea? Steerage aboard Davy Jones' locker? And what would Saint Mechthild of Magdeburg have to say about all this?

Why are Cartesian divers always so thirsty? Why do they keep coming back for more? Which puts on more weight — loaves and fishes, or Holy Wafers chased by Lourdes water?

Say the following to King: tell him that *the stench of death is my perfume.* He will be impressed.

Why Hast Thou Forsaken Me?

Lord, why hast Thou forsaken me? Why is every door closed?

Does this confirm my nagging suspicion...namely, that Le Seigneur simply doesn't exist? Or that he is having a good laugh at my expense? Or, worse yet, that he is lazy, a ragamuffin Sol Deutsche, who is simply stupid... or just doesn't care? The answer to these and related questions is far from obvious...but that doesn't keep me from clutching at straws, grasping at hints, at clues, discerned in the clear light of better days...

The iron ball. I am so lonely, so crazy with gloom and doom and the prospect of an interminable chain of tomorrows (I wouldn't even begin to know how to destroy myself, much as I might wish), that I stare at its rusted surface...actually praying that it would talk. Speak: reveal its 'nature', divulge and betray its essential Otherness, tell me *why it is in my life.*

Whatever happened to that old saw, about Cause and Effect? What became of merit, and virtue, and Right Thinking? Precious little! The ball and chain is a throwback, a cosmic curtain, a metaphor forged in ferrous and rust...A metaphor for everything barring the gates of Heaven: division, polarity, attachment, *ego.*

I wanted so much. I wanted the flame of a brilliant woman to heat the frigid runnels of my heart. I wanted the satisfactions of creative discourse, aimed on high and deep within, to make sense of my wanderings on this earth. I wanted a modicum of philosophic and career success, even hoping to enlighten and help evolve fellow travelers along the way.

I fell in love. I soared beyond myself, then found myself again in the memoirs of mystics and metaphysicians, whose divagations SEEMED to make sense. But did they? Look at me. I'm Icarus, tumbled from my phaeton just as it approaches the sun. I flew so high; achieved so much; now I grovel in the dust. What good is magic, what good are good intentions, when one's best efforts just staple them to an iron ball???

God Laughs.

One day runs insensibly into the next. My health and spirits are slipping; a man can only take so much. My thoughts — such as they are, scurrying and slipping away from me, like the vermin at my feet — are likewise time-worn. I have dismissed Djuna, and memories of a happier time, relegated them to precincts and districts forever lost to the past. Maybe they never happened. Or they happened to someone else.

Sleep is not sacrosanct — not in the least. My dreams buffet me between hope and despair, centered always on survival, escape, or its very opposite, doom.

One night — at least I think it's night —Sol Deutsche appears.

"Fancy meeting you here," the ragtag wraith says.

"Very funny, Sol. If I didn't know better, I'd thank you for getting me into this mess. But I'm not much in the mood for thanking these days — as you well know."

Deutsche fills a pipe, considers this.

"Thought you might go there," he says. "But there is a way out."

"Really."

"Where there's a will, there's a way."

"Spare me, Maestro," I say. (Jokes within dreams: *Impressive*, I think.)

"No, seriously. The Reich believed in you enough to bankroll you...

and to safeguard your folks. Who, incidentally by the way, are still out there, out of harm's way...I believe it's time to believe in yourself."

"Get serious, Deutsche. I've had it with dream weaving. I want peace. I want fulfillment."

He recites something from the *Goetia of Solomon.*

Suddenly I'm hooked.

Deutsche appears nightly and spells out the plans.

—⁓—

Sleepless nights...a ball and chain my constant and only companions.

What was the point of all this? I call out to my Lord and Master, yet seem to have been lost in the shuffle.

Host to morbid insight, to the shuffling past of dream- and semi-incarnate visions of this world and any others one might name. Among other specious insights, I finally recognize that the search for God...for order and meaning...is just that: a *search.* But the search is glorious. The search leaves in its wake a trail of art and beauty and confounded logic. The 'Grail' is Beauty — art and order, alchemy, the kabbalistic Tree of Life — not God. The alchemical work is a work of art. i.e., *Obscurantism* is the goal (the gaol) — in and of, for and by itself. There is no Oz. The spiritual journey itself is the goal.

—⁓—

Deutsche wants me to dig. As in, *literally.* Then dig some more. Whatever second sight he works on makes it perfectly clear: the recesses of the dungeon, hidden in darkness, provide ample cover for the mounds of pebble and mortar I chip at over the succeeding weeks and months.

I have a purpose in life. The grit beneath my nails, the raw and bloodied fingertips, remind me of the possibility of life. I know there is a world out there: I used to live in it.

Deutsche's sardonic mien hovers over me, a constant calendar in my dreams. He sings to me; he reads me news of the day; the long and short of it is that he buoys my flagging spirit, in the direction of home, family, and France. Together — I know this is a stretch for him — we resurrect the anthems of the Republic. The *Marseillaise* never sounded so sweet...

"Call me Sol," he says. "Think of me as light — your light of the sun."

The burrowing continues.

"Sol," I venture, after another barely distinct day of bending, hiding, and scraping grout. "How long has it been?"

"Coming on two years."

Crazy. Trapped like this, prisoner of a lunatic regime, three stories beneath the earth.

"Shouldn't I be digging *up*? As in up and out?"

"Thought you'd never ask," he says. "Relax. I've got it scoped out. The Resistance crosses borders, you see. There are certain...*sympathizers...*in important places. All you have to do is tunnel into the next room. From there I'll wager you can buy your way out."

Even the rats in the dark stare in disbelief.

The dream time parlay continues.

"A kind of Lend Lease?"

"If you like," Deutsche says. "Fact of the matter is, the paintings are stored here, right next door. They are your ticket to freedom."

"Not sure I follow, Sol. Please, tell me more. Or stop right now and grant me some dreamless sleep."

Turns out The Leader's been drawing...drawing and painting humorless landscapes ever since childhood. According to Deutsche, any of these will fetch unheard of prices in any venue, up to and including the black market. Any venue, including the greedy hands of the prison guard next door.

"Victor, you will ensorcell him. You will finally put your Third Eye to good use! In a heavy trance, astral curtains drawn, your guard will experience you as the most prestigious art dealer in Europe, bar none. Get your mitts on those paintings and the rest will be...gravy. You will leave this dungeon a *free man.* Back to work," he says. Then he disappears.

———

The Savior of the Reich an artist? Sketchy as it sounds, I proceed.

I claw, I scoop, I dig some more.

Finally I break through.

—*₥*—

The time weighs heavy. So do the ball and chain. Words cannot convey the horror of protracted — two years in all! — isolation. I come to know the intimate terrain of my skin, the convolutions, the wrinkles, the hills and dales where the dirt of many months congeals. Cleanliness and unstained drawers are quaint notions, things of the past. Whoever said *Hope springs eternal* was a besotted fool, not a prisoner in a God-forsaken dungeon in Bavaria...

Whatever hope, whichever remnants of the life force remain to me, I attempt to kindle, I hold dear. I exercise my aching limbs to the extent humanly possible, stretching my misaligned arms and legs toward the possibility of a tomorrow. I heave my sorry self to the work at hand, shoveling away with cupped fingers and the blunt edge of my grail, the tin cup they have given me for to drink.

Distractions are rare. One of the rats, a nimble fellow I name *Willi*, is more intelligent, more accommodating, than the others. His sleek body, tapering to a questing little snout, is the only sign of movement, of intelligent life, in this otherwise deserted realm. I train him, I keep him in tow: a spot of gruel at the top of the iron ball keeps Willi licking for hours.

Sol Deutsche not only suggests these veterinary maneuvers, he positively encourages them.

"You'll be a ring master yet!" he tells me. He promises me a top hat, a whip, freshly laundered jodhpurs. What more could I want?

"You'll want to lose that encumbrance," he tells me, referring to my grisly companion, the one hundred-pound sphere. Willi seems to agree, his whiskers testing the latest trail of slime on top of the ball.

"There's only one way out," Deutsche says. (Our conversations now efface the ambiguous boundaries of sleep. I hear him more or less constantly now.

My familiar (was it like this for Faust, too?) hovers on the margin of awareness, ready to intercede with suggestion, homily, unwelcome advice. His running commentary on my 'attitude' — usually critical, rarely positive — is another thorn in my aching side. Deutsche spells it out. He wants me to slather my ankle with food slops, repeatedly; Willi and his cohort will merrily chew me free.

He brooks no objection, reminding me of all I yet stand to lose: my life, my liberty, my dear parents.

He enlists bright-eyed Willi in the project.

—*m*—

Tentatively, at Sol Deutsche's suggestion, I have applied the remainder of a rotten Camembert to the arch of my left (cuffed) foot.

Willi, sniffing, making peremptory prods, looks me in the eye.

"Bear up, dear heart," he seems to say. (All this transpires in a haze, under the shroud of delirium.)

"Think yourself past this." He chews a bit. "It's all in your mind."

These are not love bites.

The pain is something fierce.

"No," I counter. "It's all in your rind."

The ordeal lasts for hours, I am transfigured, transfixed with the agony of each passing moment. Fellowship with Christ on the Cross would be a reasonable approximation. It takes every last bit of spiritual mettle to not cry out. *Tiphareth,* the solar plexus chakra, smolders as I stoke its loving presence with prayer, admonition, layer upon mental layer of vision and plea.

At last the rats are done.

The congeries of vermin have completed their grotesque meal. Human flesh! They scamper in every direction, in search no doubt of dessert...a flagon of spirits perhaps...maybe iced sorbets.

The resulting stump is horrible to behold, but right now there are more pressing concerns: either I stop the bleeding, or I exsanguinate, right then and there.

I apply strips of the filthy blanket to the uneven plateau of the wound.

I carry on, accepting my sorry portion without complaint. The guard, bless his thick neck and myopia, is blissfully unaware.

Business as usual.

A manhole, crafted from hundreds of hours of work, now awaits.

With Deutsche's blessing, I will somehow make it through.

—⁓—

What I find.

The spectacle on the other side of the wall is a delight and a surprise: a well-lit storehouse, interrupted every few feet by prodigious stacks of paintings, piled high atop one another from ceiling to floor.

"What did I tell you?" Deutsche says.

It's all here. Brushing cement and plaster from my hair (shoulder length by now), I limp forward, silent, cautious, taking the work in, trying to make sense of what I see.

—⁓—

Most of the canvases are unframed. The monotony is startling: hundreds of window-sized oil colors, dreary landscapes and cityscapes dully reflecting the niggardly light of some inferior (although technically adept) hand.

Hitler's art: soulless cartoons of vacuity and absence, without a single human face or figure in sight. Although this is hardly the time to flex my critical muscle. After all, forewarned is forearmed: a greater authority — in this case, Sol Deutsche — has passed judgment on these abominations of puce and sienna and muted greys, and declared them 'precious'. According to Deutsche, they are my passport to freedom. According to Deutsche, I can hand one over to the *kommandant* at the door and walk free. (Although walking is not what it used to be. 'Limping', grievously dragging the rat-amputated limb behind the good one, would be the more apt description.)

I choose a half dozen paintings at random, gather them up, and drag myself the best I can to the storeroom door.

It is open. Hardly daring to breathe, I lurch into the corridor, hoping for the best.

Sometimes the best is not good enough.

My further progress, and future plans, grind to a horrible halt.

Two guards waltz down the corridor and smirk.

*Deutsche, Deutsche, Deutsche...*where are you now?

Drawing upon some final reserve of strength, tenacity, absurd faith, I wave a painting at them: a lone castle on a hilltop, almost as bereft of warmth as this disastrous encounter in the subterranean couloirs of the Berghof.

Tuesdays (and every other day) with Deutsche have prepared me, at least in one sense, for this unhappy encounter with fate. My German is now more than adequate.

"Can I interest you in one of these?"

The guards chuckle – guffaw – then roar. Their mirth destroys what little faith I have in the moment, in myself, in my Guardian Nuisance, Sol Deutsche.

The guards walk up to me, examine the paintings one by one, then return them to me, clucking and sighing like hens...

"Hardly!"

His companion snickers.

"Surely you noticed the...wealth...the sheer *glut*...of these, in there?" He considers further, turns to his comrade in arms.

"Otto, how many of the Führer's...*masterworks*...(more belly laughs)... are stacked up in there? Four hundred? Five hundred?"

"Oh at least a thousand," the other man replies. "The entire lot of them – and a Deutschmark – might buy you a glass of beer."

Deutsch-mark. The word rankles, sears my violated soul, further topples my sense of things.

"Here," Otto says, relieving me of the worthless burden, "right this way."

I am beyond protesting. I collapse into their arms.

They carry me, limp and practically lifeless, off to another cell.

———

A soggy crumpled bleeding mess — that's me. At some point Deutsche makes an appearance, rousing me from my torpor.

"Things are looking grim," he says. "I'll grant you that."

My captors have been curiously silent about my attempted escape. Which has little to do with the recovery of the half dozen or so purloined paintings...that I know for sure.

"I have a back-up plan," he says. "If you're interested, that is."

"Not really," I moan.

"If you're interested in saving your country," he adds. "And your dignity. And your immortal soul."

"All right, go on," I say. "I'm all ears."

"This final stunt requires flexibility. Aerial talent, so to speak. Tell me: are you a high flyer?"

I have no idea what he's talking about. Rather than having him disappear in a puff of smoke, I put my best conversational foot forward.

"Actually Sol, I am. Once upon a time I trained in the circus."

"No! You're pulling my leg!"

"Actually — I'm not. One time, out of curiosity, and pique, I got shot out of a cannon. Somewhere in the Marais, as I recall."

"They really do that? It's not a trick?"

"*Pas du tout.* A giant puff of compressed air and *Wham!* you're aloft."

Deutsche is amazed: he wants to know how I came by the gymnastic skill to tumble through space and land not only alive but on my...feet.

"It's not rocket science. The net catches you wherever you land."

The conversational pause gives me just enough time to think. And to feel worse. What once had been a foot was now a searing anvil of pain. I toy with the blanket shard that serves to bandage the wound.

"Fantastic," Deutsche muses. "Simply fantastic. Listen up: you and I are about to do some high caliber sympathetic magic."

My erstwhile mentor has concocted a bizarre plan.

"Here's the drill..."

I lay aside any doubts I have about Deutsche's sources. The scheme he lays out is based on rock-solid intelligence — or is the pipe dream of a madman. (Or both.)

Crazy intelligence. The Nazis want to make it perfectly clear: they will brook no resistance. Their message to the French and their allies will be spelled out in the language of ultra-heavy ordnance. 'Big Bertha', an obscenely large cannon capable of lobbing massive shells over great distances, has been redeployed — in our very own Berghof backyard! According to Deutsche's sources, the Pantheon — the cradle, the very epicenter of civilization, the final resting place of Voltaire, Rousseau, and Victor Hugo — is the cannon's intended target.

This experiment in ballistics will be the first of many. The Nazis have been requisitioning all available iron — girders, andirons, car parts, *cannon balls.* The imperative is all-out cultural sabotage.

Deutsche thinks I can somehow tamper with the trajectory.

I'm willing to try.

This is a somber mission, a one-way ride to glory...and ultimate self-sacrifice. Immolation in the cause of freedom. An unintended change in the calculated weight of the projectile can cause a significant disruption of the flight path — and spare ground zero, our civilization's heritage, and the city of Paris.

I dwell on this zany scheme, playing it over and over in my mind..

It's not so zany. But there is much time to think.

What started Hitler down the evil path? Was it the magnet of power, the draw of the adoring crowd? Was it *Sieg Heil?*

No doubt. But something came before all that. The disconsolate paintings in the next room tell a different story. They speak of a stymied career, a young man turned down by an academy and public that dismissed his artistic bent. ''Ply your wares elsewhere,' they said. And he did — and made the rest of us pay in spades. Would I be locked in a dungeon, minus a foot, a wife, a life, if it weren't for the multiple rejections suffered by that morbidly sensitive young man?

I ponder Deutsche's strategy. I think about my magic, about all those who came before. What were the alchemists, the Lévis, the Tau Vincents of this world, really after? Whatever it was, they were willing to endure ignominy, desecration, *auto-da-fé* — in the name of what? In the name of religion, in the name of spirit, in pursuit of some abstract representation of God?

I think not. Rather, consider this: they were hot in pursuit of the most unholy Grail, the most precious and most forbidden treasure of all — the perfection of their *art*.

I sense great commotion outside these walls. According to Deutsche they are setting the monster, the mother of all cannons, up, nearby among the hills. Within walking distance, in fact.

A peculiar choice perhaps, but convenient nonetheless.

Soon enough I will see for myself.

POSTSCRIPT: NOT PACHELBEL'S CANON.

THE PRISONER TORE STRIPS from his blanket and trousers, fashioning 'uniforms' for his three vermin friends. The rats trusted him — he had been a steady companion, plying them with slops and leftovers from what little he had.

His black shoelaces, suitably sized, served as three belts; armbands; and halters. There were no tiny leather boots.

The rats accepted these ministrations — along with chow — without undue complaint.

The prisoner, an adept at magic, invoked the goddess of the moon. This was a propitious time, as the moon outside was full.

It was the dead of night; the guard was weary, open to suggestion. Imagine his surprise at the sight before him: three officers of the very High Command.

"Himmler...Goebbels...and der Führer!"

He could not believe his eyes.

"Who else?" the official on the right asked. "The Three Horsemen of the Apocalypse? The Three Mouseketeers?"

The men laughed among themselves.

"How can I be of service?" the guard asked.

"Glad you asked," the one known as *der Führer* said. "Be so kind as to release the prisoner. Then escort him outside, beyond the perimeter gate."

"*Ja wohl!*" The stupefied guard snapped to and unlocked the mighty cell door, then two others, leading the prisoner outside. The officials, still in high spirits, waved them on.

The yellow orb of moon hung low. The prisoner apologized for his limp but asked to continue alone.

He approached the big gun, noticing with great relief that he and the gun were alone. The cannon, the largest the world had ever known, was pointed at the sky.

How obscene, the prisoner thought.

He applied himself to the task at hand. The great maw was pleased to see him — it seemed to welcome him right in. With one great heave, he was in total darkness. He allowed himself to slide down the barrel until he came to rest against an iron globe.

My cannon ball, he thought.

Oddly enough, it felt like home.

At last he was doing the right thing.

Fomite

Writing a review on social media sites for readers will help the progress of independent publishing. To submit a review, go to the book page on any of the sites and follow the links for reviews. Books from independent presses rely on reader-to-reader communications.

For more information or to order any of our books, visit:
http://www.fomitepress.com/our-books.html

More novels and novellas from Fomite...

Joshua Amses — *During This, Our Nadir*
Joshua Amses — *Ghats*
Joshua Amses — *Raven or Crow*
Joshua Amses — *The Moment Before an Injury*
Charles Bell — *The Married Land*
Charles Bell — *The Half Gods*
Jaysinh Birjepatel — *Nothing Beside Remains*
Jaysinh Birjepatel — *The Good Muslim of Jackson Heights*
David Borofka — *The End of Good Intnetions*
David Brizer — *The Secret Doctrine of V. H. Rand*
David Brizer — *Victor Rand*
L. M Brown — *Hinterland*
Paula Closson Buck — *Summer on the Cold War Planet*
L.enny Cavallaro — *Paganini Agitato*
Dan Chodorkoff — *Loisaida*
Dan Chodorkoff — *Sugaring Down*
David Adams Cleveland — *Time's Betrayal*
Paul Cody — *Sphyxia*
Jaimee Wriston Colbert — *Vanishing Acts*
Roger Coleman — *Skywreck Afternoons*
Stephen Downes — *The Hands of Pianists*
Marc Estrin — *Hyde*
Marc Estrin — *Kafka's Roach*
Marc Estrin — *Proceedings of the Hebrew Free Burial Society*
Marc Estrin — *Speckled Vanities*
Marc Estrin — *The Annotated Nose*
Marc Estrin — *The Penseés of Alan Krieger*
Zdravka Evtimova — *Asylum for Men and Dogs*
Zdravka Evtimova — *In the Town of Joy and Peace*
Zdravka Evtimova — *Sinfonia Bulgarica*
Zdravka Evtimova — *You Can Smile on Wednesdays*
Daniel Forbes — *Derail This Train Wreck*
Peter Fortunato — *Carnevale*
Greg Guma — *Dons of Time*
Ramsey Hanhan – *Fugitive Dreams*

Fomite

Richard Hawley — *The Three Lives of Jonathan Force*
Lamar Herrin — *Father Figure*
Michael Horner — *Damage Control*
Ron Jacobs — *All the Sinners Saints*
Ron Jacobs — *Short Order Frame Up*
Ron Jacobs — *The Co-conspirator's Tale*
Scott Archer Jones — *A Rising Tide of People Swept Away*
Scott Archer Jones — *And Throw Away the Skins*
Julie Justicz — *Conch Pearl*
Julie Justicz — *Degrees of Difficulty*
Maggie Kast — *A Free Unsullied Land*
Darrell Kastin — *Shadowboxing with Bukowski*
Coleen Kearon — *#triggerwarning*
Coleen Kearon — *Feminist on Fire*
Jan English Leary — *Thicker Than Blood*
Jan English Leary — *Town and Gown*
Diane Lefer — *Confessions of a Carnivore*
Diane Lefer — *Out of Place*
Rob Lenihan — *Born Speaking Lies*
Cynthia Newberry Martin — *The Art of Her Life*
Colin McGinnis — *Roadman*
Douglas W. Milliken — *Our Shadows' Voice*
Ilan Mochari — *Zinsky the Obscure*
Peter Nash — *In the Place Where We Thought We Stood*
Peter Nash — *Parsimony*
Peter Nash — *The Least of It*
Peter Nash — *The Perfection of Things*
George Ovitt — *Stillpoint*
George Ovitt — *Tribunal*
Gregory Papadoyiannis — *The Baby Jazz*
Pelham — *The Walking Poor*
Christopher Peterson — *Madman*
Andy Potok — *My Father's Keeper*
Frederick Ramey — *Comes A Time*
Howard Rappaport — *Arnold and Igor*
Joseph Rathgeber — *Mixedbloods*
Kathryn Roberts — *Companion Plants*
Robert Rosenberg — *Isles of the Blind*
Fred Russell — *Rafi's World*
Ron Savage — *Voyeur in Tangier*
David Schein — *The Adoption*
Charles Simpson — *Uncertain Harvest*
Lynn Sloan — *Midstream*
Lynn Sloan — *Principles of Navigation*
L.E. Smith — *The Consequence of Gesture*

Fomite

L.E. Smith — *Travers' Inferno*
L.E. Smith — *Untimely RIPped*
Robert Sommer — *A Great Fullness*
Caitlin Hamilton Summie — *Geographies of the Heart*
Tom Walker — *A Day in the Life*
Susan V. Weiss —*My God, What Have We Done?*
Peter M. Wheelwright — *As It Is on Earth*
Peter M. Wheelwright — *The Door-Man*
Suzie Wizowaty — *The Return of Jason Green*